T0243998

Hungerheart

Hungerheart

THE STORY OF A SOUL

Christabel Marshall

A Sapphic Classic from
Sinister Wisdom

Hungerheart: The Story of a Soul
by Christabel Marshall / Christopher St. John
Public Domain.

Transcription by Sydney Schmidt

Sinister Wisdom, Inc.
2333 McIntosh Road
Dover, FL 33527
sinisterwisdom@gmail.com
www.sinisterwisdom.org

Designed by Nieves Guerra.

First edition, January 2025

ISBN-13: 978-1-944981-70-9
Simultaneously published as *Sinister Wisdom* 135
Printed in the U.S. on recycled paper

First Published in 1915

IN OMNES CARITATIS VICTIMAS
For all the victims of love

"Too late have I loved thee, O Beauty so ancient, O Beauty so new; too late have I loved thee! And behold thou wast within and I was abroad, and there I sought thee, and deformed as I was ran after those beauties which thou has made. ... Thou has called, thou hast cried out, and hast pierced my deafness. Thou has lightened, thou hast shone forth and dispelled my blindness...I am hungry after thee."

"Let the brotherly mind love in me whatever thou teachest ought to be loved; and again bewail in me whatever thou teachest ought to be bewailed. Let the brotherly mind do this, not that of the foreigner, but that of the brother, which, where it approves me, rejoices for me, and where it dislikes me is sorry for me, because in both cases it loves me."

[St. Augustine, *Confessions*]

HUNGERHEART
THE STORY OF A SOUL

**DEUX LIARDS COUVRIRAIENT FORT BIEN
TOUTES MES TERRES,
MAIS TOUT LE GRAND CIEL BLEU N'EMPLI-
RAIT PAS MON CŒUR.**

[Two farthings will cover all my earthly needs,
But all heaven will not fill my heart.
Victor Hugo, *The Legend of the Ages*]

Christabel Marshall / Christopher St. John

CONTENTS

INTRODUCTION:
HUNGERHEART
AND THE "LESBIAN NOVEL"

George Robb

Hungerheart (1915) is a pioneering work of lesbian fiction. Indeed, it may well be the first English-language lesbian novel—that is, a novel written by a woman who loved other women, which centers on same-sex desire. This forgotten novel does not fit easily into the conventions of a "homophile" novel. On the one hand, it appears to be a modern "New Woman" novel with its depiction of strong, active women living and loving independently from men. On the other hand, its use of religious language to mediate its love stories seems old-fashioned, even Victorian. The novel's fusion of self-reliance and submission creates a uniquely powerful voice for women loving women. In *Hungerheart*, same-sex love is naturally both physical and spiritual.

During the nineteenth century several European (mostly French) and American novels had included lesbian characters and situations, such as Théophile Gautier's *Mademoiselle de Maupin* (1835), Adolph Belot's *Mademoiselle Giraud, Ma Femme* (1870), and Henry James's *The Bostonians* (1885). Written by men, these books usually projected eroticized male fantasies of lesbians and depicted love between women as sinister and unnatural.

In the early twentieth century, for the first time, women who loved other women began writing novels about their own desires and experiences. The earliest such "lesbian novels" include Colette's *Claudine à l'ecole/Claudine at School* (1900), Liane de Pougy's *Idyllye saphique/Sapphic Romance* (1901), Renée Vivien's *Une Femme m'apparut/A Woman Appeared to Me* (1904), and Minna Wettstein-Adelt's *Sind es Frauen?/Are They Women?* (1901) These novels presented more sympathetic views of lesbians, but happy endings remained scarce. This might have been a strategy to circumvent censorship or to illustrate the effects of social intolerance. Novels by French women tended to invoke Classical history and literature to explain and justify same-sex desire. German lesbian novels were more indebted to the new ideas of "sexology," which came to dominate educated people's understanding of same-sex sexuality.

In the late nineteenth century, a number of male scientists and physicians—Karl Ulrichs, Richard von Krafft-Ebing, Henry Havelock Ellis—developed new medical theories to explain same-sex behavior. These sexologists introduced scientific terms such as "homosexual" and "invert" to label women and men who were attracted to their own sex. ("Lesbian" was seldom used by the sexologists and rarely appeared in English-language sources before the 1920s.) Scientific ideas about homosexuality centered on the concept of "sexual inversion." Inverts were seen as members of a "Third Sex," distinct from "normal" men and women. A female invert was thought to be a male soul in a woman's body, just as a male invert was a female soul in a man's body. Therefore sexologists usually described female inverts as mannish in appearance and behavior while male inverts were described as effeminate. This language of inversion, used to explain homosexuality, could also encompass what we now call a transexual or transgender identity.

Some homosexuals welcomed sexological discourse, since it offered them a scientific explanation for feelings that they had struggled to understand or had been told were sinful. Sexology naturalized homosexuality by positing that it was congenital and not a matter of choice. Sexological literature might also comfort homosexuals that they were not alone; there were other people like them in the world. However, sexologists also associated same-sex love with mental illness and degeneration. The inverts who appeared in their case studies were rarely attractive people.

Homosexuality may have been part of the natural world, but it was pathological and corrupt. Not surprisingly, lesbian novels that were indebted to scientific understandings of homosexuality, like Radclyffe Hall's *The Well of Loneliness* (1928), struggled to escape pathologizing lesbians or depicting them as freaks of nature doomed to lead lonely, unhappy lives.

In many ways *Hungerheart* is a more congenial lesbian ur-text than this better remembered successor. Christabel Marshall does not explicitly identify her protagonist Joanna/John Montolivet as a sexual invert. By avoiding sexological language and labels, she also avoids stigmatizing her characters and allows for a greater variety of interpretations. John can be read as lesbian, but also as transgender, or non-binary, or androgynous. Additionally, there is no dismal, tragic ending in *Hungerheart*, as in *The Well* and so many of the lesbian novels that followed it: isolation, suicide, heterosexual conversion.

Some contemporary readers may have missed the lesbian content of *Hungerheart* altogether, though it is hard to imagine anyone doing so today. For "sensitive" readers in 1915 the book is full of queer signifiers. When John went to Oxford (Oscar Wilde's alma mater), she lay awake at night thinking of Wilde "and wishing that I could serve a few days of his sentence in his stead." In other places, the novel quotes Walt Whitman or refers to the French novel *Mademoiselle de Maupin*, which featured an affair between two women, one of them cross-dressed as a man.

A highly autobiographical work, *Hungerheart* mirrors Christabel Marshall's own unhappy childhood and struggle to find a place for herself in a hostile, patriarchal world. Anticipating the narrative framework of *The Well of Loneliness*, *Hungerheart* includes a detailed account of John's childhood, describing how she, like Stephen Gordon in *The Well*, does not conform to the expected gender norms of a Victorian girlhood. Her birth parents named her John-Baptist though her adoptive parents called her Joanna, believing that it was "eccentric to give a girl a boy's name." She later reclaims John as truer to her nature. While there is some indication of John having masculine physical qualities (she was "more thickly and strongly built" than a girl), she is never depicted as a mannish lesbian, like Stephen in *The Well* or the butch case studies of the sexologists. Throughout the novel, men find John attractive; they kiss her, want to dance with her, propose marriage to her.

When John describes "mannish" qualities in herself and the women she loves, she is usually referring to tastes and temperament. As a girl she prefers toy soldiers to dolls and playing cricket with her brothers to playing house with her sisters. At school, where she learns to dance with other girls, she always took the role of "gentleman," and when she later danced with men, she tried to "pilot" them. John rejects the passive role assigned to the women of her era, desiring instead to lead an active and independent life.

Unlike Stephen in *The Well*, John never wants to be a boy. She wants a boy's freedoms and opportunities. When her brothers banned her from playing cricket because she was a girl, John reflects: "This was the first time that I understood that my sex might handicap me in life…Yet it provoked no desire in me to be a boy, at least not the kind of boy I knew." Later, when John's brothers go off to university and her sisters fret over finding husbands, she laments: "I was sorry to have been born a girl because for a girl apparently there was no human life, only a girl's life. I learned that man had his life as a human being, and his male life as well." When John wins a scholarship to Oxford, she hopes that college will "make a man of me" and "enable me to earn my living as a man."

In rejecting both the stereotypical roles of girl and boy, John aims for an androgynous ideal. She sought out friends and lovers like herself: "It has always been to men who are not ashamed to be womanly, and to women who are not afraid to be manly, that my heart has been attracted." She extolls her lover Sally as "a woman possessing many attributes that are generally praised as 'manly.'" When they set-up house together, "I used to wonder which was the husband and which the wife in the *ménage!*" Both women pursue their careers; neither is the domestic servant to the other. *Hungerheart* eschews the "butch-femme" dynamic found in other lesbian novels of the period.

Throughout the book, John makes it clear that she "had never cared" for the love of men. The first time a boy kisses her, she "wondered why it had not been great and white and shining... why he had suddenly seemed my enemy." Years later, when a man kisses her, she feels humiliated and fears that the kiss had left a mark on her "as disfiguring as a black eye." John has one, brief romantic friendship with a man, but could not reciprocate his sexual desire. "There was no hunger for maternity in me, any more than there was a desire to be loved as men love women." John believes that there are other women, like herself, "neither wives, nor mothers, nor mistresses, who are yet fulfilling themselves completely."

John's love and desire was only for women. Unlike many lesbian heroines, she had a roving eye. As a child she was devoted to a pretty servant girl. As an adolescent she became infatuated with a beautiful aristocrat, Lady Martha Ladde. She sent her love poems and gave her flowers. Heartbroken on learning of Martha's engagement, she declares: "I could love you more in a moment than he in a thousand years!" John later falls in love with a passionate Russian woman, Madame Pohlakoff, who wants to adopt John and carry her away from England. Madame calls

John "Ivan" and "my little boy." John forms a close partnership with Sally in which "they were as happy as a newly married pair, perhaps happier." Her love for Sally never wains, but she strays at times, first with a tempestuous Italian, Giovanna, and later with a capricious Pole, Marya. While on a trip to Rome with Marya, John experiences a religious awakening and converts to Roman Catholicism, a religion for which she had long felt an affinity.

In *Hungerheart*, unlike so many other lesbian novels of the time, women's love affairs are not seen as hopeless or unnatural or as brief stages before marriage and motherhood. Nonetheless, John believes that there is something missing in her life that her intimate friendships with women cannot entirely satisfy. Her "heart's hunger" is only fulfilled when she becomes a Roman Catholic and experiences a passionate love for God as well as for a cloistered nun. The novel ends with John proclaiming her love for the nun, which is bound up with her newfound love for God. John believes that it was in God's heart "that you and I have learned to love each other." Their "moments of union" might not be understood in the world, "but they are understood in heaven."

To end a lesbian novel with the protagonist's conversion to Roman Catholicism certainly seems odd today, when that church is a bastion of homophobia. And are we to assume that John has transcended her earthly passion for women with a higher (sexless) love? While not the tragic ending of so many lesbian novels written before the 1970s, it was probably not the "happy ending" envisioned by many lesbian readers then or now. Of course, *Hungerheart's* ending is open to multiple interpretations, and its religious sensibility transports us back to a world far different from our own.

That so many gay British literary figures, like Christabel Marshall and her fictional alter ego John-Baptist Montolivet, were drawn to Catholicism calls out for explanation. Other gay converts from the early 20th century include the writers and artists Oscar Wilde, Frederick Rolfe, Radclyffe Hall, Una Troubridge, Ronald Firbank, and Renée Vivien (born Pauline Mary Tarn). A century ago the Catholic Church was far less exercised over moral questions like abortion and homosexuality than they were by the threats of secularism and socialism. In Britain Catholicism was a minority religion whose adherents had long been persecuted and socially ostracized. For gay Britons conversion became another symbol of their marginal status.

For persons with strong aesthetic sensibilities, the Catholic Church's medieval ritualism, theatrical pageantry, and elaborately decorated sanctuaries were more satisfying than Protestantism's austere rites and minimalist style. Catholicism, with its cult of the Virgin Mary and panoply of female saints, was also less patriarchal than Protestantism. There was less pressure to marry in the Catholic Church, which extolled celibacy as a superior calling to marriage and which maintained same-sex communities of priests and nuns.

Hungerheart, which is subtitled "The Story of a Soul," is also part of an older tradition of using religious language to convey romantic desire. In some cases this might have been to mask or justify feelings otherwise considered sinful. In a culture far less secular than our own, religious language could also provide a more congenial way to discuss and understand same-sex attraction than the new, unpoetic and pathologizing language of sexology. In a 1911 "love journal," Christabel Marshall describes her feelings for her life partner, Edith Craig, as closely intertwined with her devotion to God: "It seems to me that when I think of Edy it is nearly always with a little prayer; not a conscious one, perhaps, but feeling as if I tried to turn my face to God for her." Four years later, Marshall similarly concludes *Hungerheart* with

John's declaration of love to the nun: "Very pleasant hast thou been unto me. Thy love for me is wonderful, passing the love of men." Here the novel invokes, and inverts, the Biblical verse (*2 Samuel* 1:26) that extolls David's love for Jonathan as "surpassing the love of women."

Even the most chaste interpretation of *Hungerheart's* ending cannot ignore the sexual language. John's love for the (cloistered) nun might preclude a physical expression of sex, but it is still infused with intimate, erotic desire. In other words, it is lesbian. John also expresses a desire to enter the cloister herself, and who knows where that might have led! Finally, is the reader really expected to imagine John returning to England to live a sexless life of prayer and good works? Earlier in the novel John had reminded readers that she and Sally would still be together at the end of her story. Given that *Hungerheart* has already detailed John's forty-year history of pursuing love with women, her love for the nun seems merely her latest, not her last, love affair.

Further Reading:

Claudia Breger, "Feminine Masculinities: Scientific and Literary Representations of 'Female Inversion' at the Turn of the Century," *Journal of the History of Sexuality* 14 (2005), 76-106.

Blanche Wiesen Cook, " 'Women Alone Stir My Imagination': Lesbianism and the Cultural Tradition," *Signs* 4 (1979), 718-39.

Lillian Faderman, *Surpassing the Love of Men: Romantic Friendship and Love between Women from the Renaissance to the Present*, William Morrow, 1981.

Lowell Gallagher, Frederick S. Roden, and Patricia Juliana Smith, eds., *Catholic Figures, Queer Narratives*, Palgrave MacMillan, 2007.

Joanne Glasgow, "What's a Nice Lesbian Like You Doing in the Church of Torquemada?: Radclyffe Hall and Other Catholic Converts," in Karla Jay and Joanne Glasgow, eds., *Lesbian Texts and Contexts: Radical Revisions*, New York University Press, 1990.

Martha Vicinus, " 'The Gift of Love': Nineteenth-Century Religion and Lesbian Passion," *Nineteenth-Century Contexts* 23 (2001), 241-64.

BIOGRAPHY
OF CHRISTABEL MARSHALL
/CHRISTOPHER ST. JOHN
(1871-1960)

Christopher St. John, the author of *Hungerheart*, was known to her friends and colleagues as Chris. She was born Christabel Marshall October 24, 1871 in Exeter, southwest England. She was the youngest of nine children of Emma Marshall, a children's book author, and Hugh Marshall, a banker. In 1874 the family moved to Gloucester, where Hugh worked as the manager of the West of England Bank. The bank failed in 1878, amid allegations of fraud, and Hugh narrowly escaped prosecution. Disgraced and impoverished, the Marshalls moved to Bristol, where Emma now supported the family by churning out historical romances for young readers. Chris experienced a lonely and unhappy childhood, bullied by her older siblings and ignored by her parents. Chris was so alienated from her family that in *Hungerheart*, her thinly disguised autobiographical novel, Joanna "John" Montolivet, the stand-in for Chris, is depicted as adopted. Her adoptive mother is a hack portrait painter and her adoptive father a white-collar criminal and sexual predator. Joanna sees herself as a social and sexual misfit. Her gender confusion, movingly depicted in the novel, probably mirrors Chris's actual childhood experience.

In 1894 Chris won a scholarship to Somerville College, Oxford (Manville College in the novel). Only founded in 1879, Somerville was one of two women's colleges at the prestigious Oxford University. Chris studied history and mixed with other bright, independent women. None of these women, however, were allowed to take degrees then, as the university believed that this would devalue the Oxford diploma for male graduates.

After university, Chris moved to London, where she worked as a secretary for Lady Randolph Churchill and her son Winston. During this time she also became romantically involved with the musician Violet Gwynne. When Violet rejected her to marry a man, Chris fell into a deep depression. Early in 1896 Chris nearly died from an overdose of pain pills, prescribed for a toothache. Almost certainly an attempted suicide, Chris's family claimed that it was an accident. Chris does not discuss this episode in *Hungerheart*, although the novel does detail a later suicide attempt under similar circumstances. For a while Chris returned to her family home, but after the death of both her parents in 1899, she embarked on a new life. She converted to Roman Catholicism, she began using the name Christopher St. John in place of Christabel Marshall, and she found work as a journalist in London.

When not writing, Chris was a constant theater goer. She became infatuated with the legendary actress Ellen Terry (called Louise Canning in *Hungerheart*), sending her gushing fan letters and love poems. In 1899 Terry invited Chris to visit her backstage, where she advised her young fan "not to wear your heart on your sleeve." That night Chris also met Terry's daughter, Edith "Edy" Craig (Sally in the novel). Edy was mending a costume when they shook hands, pricking Chris with her needle. "Cupid's dart," Chris insisted, "for I loved Edy from that moment." The two women began an intimate relationship that was to last almost fifty years, until Edy's death in 1947. Within weeks they had taken an apartment together in London. The bohemian theater world accepted them as a married couple. In 1900, when Ellen Terry bought Smallhythe Farm as a rural retreat in Kent, she gave Edy and Chris a cottage on the estate.

The women became lifelong collaborators in the theater. They managed Ellen Terry's career, sometimes accompanying her on tours of Britain and America. Edy also worked as an actress, costume designer, and producer. Chris served as Terry's "literary henchman," writing and translating plays for her and ghost-writing Terry's public lectures and memoirs. In 1900 Chris published her first novel, *The Crimson Weed*, the title referring to the red rose which had come to symbolize decadence. Much influenced by Oscar Wilde's *The Picture of Dorian Gray* (1895), Chris's novel had a gay subtext, though one involving male characters.

In 1903 Edy was briefly engaged to the composer Martin Shaw, to the surprise of her friends and family and to the serious distress of Chris, who attempted suicide through a drug overdose. This stormy episode is discussed in *Hungerheart*, though it remains mysterious. As Chris wrote in the novel, "how it ended I never knew…Her love affair fizzled out. She never spoke of it, she never explained."

Shortly afterwards, Chris and Edy became deeply involved with the women's suffrage movement. They joined several different suffrage organizations, including the Women Writers' Suffrage League and the Actresses' Franchise League (AFL). Under the auspices of the AFL Chris and Edy staged several pro-suffrage plays. In 1909 Chris co-wrote with Cecily Hamilton *How the Vote Was Won*, a much-performed comic play in which English women go on strike to compel their male relatives to support women's suffrage. Edy later directed Hamilton's *Pageant of Great Women*, which depicted 50 famous women from history. Edy appeared in the pageant as the lesbian painter Rosa Bonheur and Chris as a woman warrior. Chris does not include these theatrical ventures in *Hungerheart*, but she does discuss in detail her involvement with the militant WSPU (Women's Social and Political Union).

Under the charismatic leadership of Emmeline Pankhurst and her daughter Christabel, the WSPU called its members

Suffragettes, to distinguish them from the more moderate suffragists. In an attempt to radicalize a movement that most (male) politicians ignored, the WSPU began a campaign of violence in 1908, in which Suffragettes broke shop windows and destroyed public property. Initially Chris took part in the violence, and she was arrested in 1909 for setting fire to a mailbox. However, she soon became disenchanted with the autocratic leadership of the Pankhursts, who often made key policy decisions without consulting the rank and file. Chris left the WSPU, and, along with Edy, joined the Women's Freedom League, an organization run along more democratic principles.

The exciting women-centered plays that Chris and Edy staged for the suffrage movement left them disenchanted with the London stage. As Chris complained, "not a single play now takes account of women except on the level of housekeeping machines or bridge players." So instead of returning to this sexist environment, in 1911 Edy founded her own theater company, the Pioneer Players, to stage new and socially relevant plays, especially those by and about women. Chris wrote a number of plays for the Pioneers, including *The First Actress*. Chris would sometimes take small roles in the plays, often playing men, as when she portrayed King Herod in *An Early English Nativity Play*.

In 1911 Chris made a pilgrimage to Rome to affirm her Catholic faith. At this time she legally changed her name to Christopher St. John. In 1915 she anonymously published *Hungerheart*, a highly autobiographical novel which covers her life from childhood to the age of forty. It discusses frankly her ambiguous gender identity, her romantic relationships with several women, especially Edy, her involvement with the suffrage movement, and her religious conversion, which is strongly bound-up with her quest for love.

In 1916 the painter Clare "Tony" Atwood began living with Edy and Chris, forming a *ménage à trois* that was to last for thirty years. At first Edy warned Tony that "if Chris does not like your being here, and feels you are interfering with our friendship, out you go!" This did not happen, and as Chris later admitted, "the bond between Edy and me was strengthened, not weakened, by Tony's association with us." Tony brought stability to the relationship, acting as a peacemaker between the more volatile Edy and Chris. At the time, Tony was 50, Edy 47, and Chris 45. The three soon established a harmonious arrangement, working on their creative projects in separate studios and coming together for meals and fun. They frequently collaborated on plays, written by Chris, directed by Edy, and designed by Tony.

Their friends referred to the "throuple" as the "Smallhythe Trio," after the country house where they now spent much of their time, or "Edy and the boys." (Chris and Tony wore their hair cut short and usually dressed in trousers and jackets.) By all accounts, the trio transformed their Smallhythe cottage and garden into a magical place. One friend of the trio remembered it as "life enhancing—All three of them there, Edy, Chris, and Tony, made one feel that beauty was real, not a dream." The writer Vita Sackville-West believed "whenever you went there, you wondered whether you were living in the world you normally knew, or had walked through into a world more poetical, a world more romantic, a world where values were different."

In 1928 Ellen Terry died, and the trio dedicated the rest of their lives to preserving her legacy as an actress. They converted Terry's house at Smallhythe into a museum about her career in the theater (today managed by the National Trust). They converted the barn on the Smallhythe estate into a theater, and they hosted an annual Shakespeare festival in Terry's honor. Chris and Edy edited an updated edition of Terry's memoirs, and Chris edited a best-selling volume of Terry's voluminous correspondence with the playwright George Bernard Shaw. Christabel Marshall is better remembered today for her work about Ellen Terry than for her own feminist novels and plays.

During the 1930s, Smallhythe became a gathering place for an artistic circle of lesbians and bisexual women, including the composer Ethel Smyth, and the writers Clemence Dane, Radclyffe Hall, Vita Sackville West, and Virginia Woolf. Many of these women became acquainted with Edy and the boys through attending performances at the Barn Theater. Vita's estate, Sissinghurst, was nearby, as was the country house of Radclyffe Hall and her lover Una Troubridge. The trio made a strong impression on visitors, though many agreed that Chris was the strongest personality. Una described her as "brilliant and honest," but "violent too and incapable of compromise." Vita saw Chris as "a character made for Shakespeare" and imagined her as a warrior, "raging battle-axe in hand against false idols."

Chris fell passionately in love with Vita and they had a brief, but intense, love affair in 1932. Although married to the diplomat Harold Nicholson, Vita was more attracted to women and had previously had affairs with the socialite Violet Trefusis and the modernist writer Virginia Woolf. Vita was the inspiration for Woolf's 1928 novel *Orlando,* in which the protagonist moves across centuries, sometimes as a man, sometimes as a woman. Chris called Vita "my Lord Orlando," entranced by her gender fluidity. In one love letter to Vita, Chris wrote: "I know you must be a woman—evidence your husband and your sons. But I don't think of you as a woman, or as a man either. Perhaps as someone who is both, the complete human being who transcends both." Chris's passion for Vita led to violent arguments with Edy, with Tony and Radclyffe Hall acting as peacemakers. Ultimately, Vita was frightened by the intensity of Chris's devotion, and she pulled away. The two remained friends, but Vita avoided seeing Chris alone.

World War II, with its air raids and shortages, put an end to performances at the Barn Theater. Edy and the boys struggled to support the Ellen Terry Museum. Tony occasionally sold a painting, and Chris made some money as a music critic and calligrapher, but the trio were living primarily on money from a trust Ellen Terry had left Edy. When Edy died in 1947, she left Chris and Tony both emotionally devastated and financially strapped. Vita gave them money to live on, and the National Trust took over the Ellen Terry Museum, allowing Chris and Tony to live in their cottage rent free for the rest of their lives.

Christabel Marshall died in 1960 at almost 90, Tony Atwood in 1962 at 96. The two were buried next to each other in the village churchyard. Edy had been cremated in 1947, and she had asked that her ashes be buried with Chris and Tony "when the time comes." Unfortunately, by the 1960s her ashes could not be found. Sometime later Edy's cousin Olive, herself a lesbian, came across the ashes in a box of papers. She "popped across the road to the church and scattered them on the graves of the other two."

Further Reading:

Eleanor Adlard, ed., *Edy: Recollections of Edith Craig*, Frederick Muller, 1949.

Nina Auerbach, *Ellen Terry: Player in Her Time*, W.W. Norton, 1987.

Sally Cline, *Radclyffe Hall: A Woman Called John*, Overlook Press, 1997.

Katharine Cockin, *Edith Craig (1869-1947): Dramatic Lives*, Cassell, 1998.

Victoria Glendinning, *Vita: The Life of Vita Sackville-West*, I.B. Tauris, 1983.

Michael Holroyd, *A Strange Eventful History: The Dramatic Lives of Ellen Terry, Henry Irving, and Their Remarkable Families*, Picador, 2008.

Ann Rachlin, *Edy Was a Lady*, Matador, 2011.

HUNGERHEART

PART I

THE WORLD OF IGNORANCE

I
INFANCY

I

One night something extraordinary happened. I was dreaming of a wood in which bluebells grew. It must have been a fairy wood, for the bluebells made a tinkling sound, and were far brighter than any I had seen by day. They became so brilliant, it was past enduring. My eyes dazzled and ached, and I began to rub them with my fists. It was at that minute that I heard a voice. It was not a fairy's voice. It belonged to my nurse, Smarden.

"It's a sin and a shame to wake a child at this time of night for any one."

I agreed with Smarden and kept my eyes shut, pretending to be still asleep. I did not want to know that the light in which bluebells had looked really blue for the first time came from a candle held near my face.

"Come, Baby! Wake up, Baby!"

It was Mamma's voice now. I thrust out my fists to push her away, and scratched my right hand on the pin of a large brooch that she always wore. I can see it now. It had a green beetle in the centre and a gold rim with some marks on it. I believe that they were the signs of the Zodiac.

I was very fond of her, and yet I never missed her if she did not come and say good-night to me. Even in these days I think I had a longing to be loved separately, individually, not as one of "the children." Mamma was always occupied with our affairs in a lump. Another secret and unspoken disappointment was that she was not very young—more like a grandmother than a mother in my eyes. I used to wish that Nennie, the under-nurse, was my mother. I was singularly affected by her lovely curling fair hair, pink cheeks, and soft blue eyes with a dusky fringe of eyelashes. She was tall and walked very gracefully, like the Dream People, and if you were sleepy, she had a soft cushiony breast, the rise and fall of which under her blue print gown gave you a lovely contented feeling. And she never shook me roughly to wake me in the morning, as Smarden did. Smarden was very effectively ugly—not unlike Mrs. Noah in all essentials. She was rather grim, and yet not at all strict. I believe now she was a careless nurse, but in those days she was only Smarden, an institution in my life, the rock of it, the thing without which I could not imagine anything going forward.

On this particular night, Smarden was grumbling in her best style.

"Where's the child's dressing-gown?" said Mamma.

"Dressing gown! Did you ever hear the like! At this time of night!"

"Come now! Do be quick, Smarden! He has a train to catch, and he wants to see her, naturally."

"Not much nature about it," Smarden snorted. She began thrusting my arms into the sleeves of a diminutive red flannel garment, that had decreased in the wash as I had increased in size.

"She needs a new one," said Mamma.

"And not the only new thing she needs—not by no means," retorted Smarden. "She wants forty-'leven new things." She was always very short with Mamma. I had an impression that she didn't like her. Once a year at least, during my childhood, Smarden gave warning, and although she never went when her month was up, I could not grow hardened to her threats, and each time suffered torments, as I pictured the house empty of her kindness and her crossness.

Dragged into the dressing-gown, which was so tight in the armhole that I felt as helpless as a lobster on dry land, my bare feet covered by a pair of little red slippers, rather greasy about the soles, I was now lifted off the bed into Mamma's arms.

"Is it the middle of the night?" I inquired. The affair was now assuming the aspect of an exciting adventure. In the middle of the night one might see strange things.

"Yes," said Mamma, as she carried me along the corridor, Smarden preceding us with a candle. "But some one has come a long way to see you, and wants to hear you recite, 'There dwelt a man in a Country Town.'"

"I'd rather say about Percy and Douglas," I murmured.

"But you don't know that well enough."

"I know some of it. I know: 'And when his legs were smitten off, he fought upon his stumps.'"

There were tall elms outside, and they were talking in the wind. I began thinking about Mr. Wind, and wondering if I should ever see him, and find out why he cried so much. The elms looked taller than ever before. I think this must have been the first time I noticed the moon.

"Why don't people go out at night?" I asked. "I think the moon would make them nice and quiet."

"The moon's not good for people," said Mamma, as if that settled it.

The garden through the windows—big sash windows they were, with small panes and heavy wooden lattices—looked more beautiful and much more spacious than by day, though rather terrifying. The shadows on the grass were very black. I could not see any of the flowers except the white ones. How wonderful those white flowers looked, waving their wakeful silvern heads in the wind, swaying, swinging in such graceful motion!

I was plumped on to a chair in the drawing-room. One of my shoes fell off, and I tucked my bare foot under my nightgown. I can see that room very distinctly now with its bright blue rep curtains bordered with a strip of gaily-coloured flowers in woolwork; they were closely drawn. There were ottomans and chairs all over the room, like islands in the blue sea of Brussels carpet, which was faded, and worn, especially near the door. That door was a pale yellow, grained and varnished to imitate satinwood. Not for the first time, I was struck by the extraordinary number of chairs. The room always seemed to be prepared for a party.

To-night, lighted by one lamp, it looked desolate and mournful, and the many mirrors on the walls doubled in desolation. It was in a mirror that I first saw the mysterious man. At least I saw the back of his head, covered with thick light brown hair, worn longer than Papa or the boys wore theirs. The Dream People, too, had such hair. I gazed in the mirror, fascinated. Perhaps in the middle of the night lords and knights called on us.

"Here she is," said Mamma.

The mysterious man's head disappeared from the mirror, and as I no longer had any reason for staring at it, I removed my eyes to the room. I felt very small, and I was frightened.

The mysterious man had pulled up a chair to mine. He did not touch me, but looked at me hard. It seemed to me that he was laughing at me, yet his face was very serious.

"What a funny little beggar! Well, John, you and I have met before, though you don't remember it."

The word "John" stirred my baby mind and made me forget my shyness. "Yes, Smarden says my name is John."

"Well, of course it is. Weren't you baptized John?"

"We nearly all call her 'Baby' now," said Mamma. "And after all, Austin, when she grows up it will never do to call her John."

"It's her name all the same," said the mysterious man. "'John-Baptist'—that's your name."

"I can't think what made you give her a boy's name," said Mamma.

"Very simple," said the man. "St. John the Baptist is my favourite Saint."

"But why not Joan, or Jean, or Joanna, Austin? It's so eccentric to give a girl a boy's name."

"Well, it's done," said the man. "Perhaps the boy's name will protect the poor baby, and give her a man's strength to fight her way in this brutal world."

I remember this conversation by certain milestones. The actual words are necessarily coloured though not invented by maturity. The first milestone was the mysterious man in tears. Yes, he actually wept unreservedly, unashamedly, even as I, Baby, was accustomed to weep, and to be derided for weeping.

"Don't—please don't, Austin." It was Mamma's voice. Then she added, "Is there no chance of a reconciliation?"

"Reconciliation!" He got up and marched up and down the room. "Reconciliation!"

"How any woman can leave her child—"

"It's no good saying that sort of thing," said the mysterious man impatiently. "And she's not 'any woman.' John doesn't remember, I suppose?"

Mamma smiled. "Dear Austin! How could she? She is such a baby."

The mysterious man came over to me. I felt frightened of him, and his tears, and I put my fists in my eyes, as was my way when I was shy.

"Now don't be shy!" said Mamma reprovingly.

The mysterious man took my hands from my face, and looked at me again with that odd look which was like laughter and like crying too.

"She's not going to be pretty," he said. "That's one blessing. Does she know any prayers?"

"It's rather difficult. I was going to ask you what you intended to do about that."

"Say 'Hail Mary,' Baby," said the mysterious man.

"Hail Mary," I repeated.

"Say that every day, will you? Promise."

"She doesn't understand," said Mamma.

"Yes, I do," I said stoutly. This was not true: I said it to please him.

"Mary," said the mysterious man, as if he read my thoughts, "is God's Mother, and your mother, and she is going to take care of you until I come back."

I felt myself growing very red. Was it possible to have two mothers?

"And pray to Her for your father, your wretched father," he went on; and when he took me in his arms, and held me tight, I knew that he was talking of himself. And my mental terror was so great that I did not notice that he was hurting me.

What did it mean? Why had I been brought into the drawing-room at dead of night, to see a stranger who in a single moment had made the few familiar and solid realities of my life appear strange and unsubstantial?

"Have I two fathers as well as two mothers?" I inquired.

"No, darling, of course not!"

It was Mamma speaking. "Why, you silly little thing, of course not!"

My confusion was now so great that I burst into tears. Then Mamma took me away from the mysterious man, and comforted me and rocked me in her arms. I began to grow drowsy, and some very loud and angry words were my lullaby.

When I woke, the strange visitor was putting on a long overcoat.

"Well, there's nothing to do but to go, I suppose."

"When will you be here again?" said Mamma.

"Next year—some time—never perhaps," he answered.

I could not make out why the answer distressed me. It was partly because already I admired him and wanted to see him again when I was not so sleepy, and partly because I felt that he was unhappy. He did not look to me old, like most grown-up people, but like my heroes, who were handsome and young, heroes who were dressed like the Crusaders on their tombs in the Cathedral. I wanted to ask him not to go. I wanted to say: "I understand you—Mamma doesn't." I knew she could not, because she made him so impatient.

My return journey to the night-nursery must have been made when I was asleep, for I remember nothing between the vision of the visitor putting on that long brown coat, and Smarden shaking me with her usual, "Now, lazybones!" the next morning.

"Smarden," I said, "Mamma forgot about 'There dwelt a man in a country town.'"

To which I understood Smarden to answer that it did not matter, as it was a pack of lies. This was her usual criticism of anything outside the Bible, and the tracts of which she kept a store in her bedroom.

II

A child sees, hears, and understands far more than most people believe, but it has no powers of deduction.

I know now what a mature intellect would have deduced from the visit of the mysterious man. But at the time—I was, I think, three years old—it was to me a vision, startlingly clear, but limited, sending off no single ray of suggestion or possibility, and so it remained for years.

I never referred to it, though it often came back to me. For one thing, I was timid about asking questions. One of Smarden's favourite maxims was, "Ask no questions, and you'll hear no lies," and I came to regard it as a certainty that any question would be badly received.

In spite of the fact that my childhood was spent in the middle of a large family it seems to me, on looking back, to have been lonely.

There was a sharp division in the family. All above a certain age seemed absolutely venerable to me. There was Alice who acted as governess to the younger ones, and Winifred who never took her nose out of a book except to quarrel with Alice, and three brothers who were already out in the world, either at public schools or working.

The ones nearer my age came more into my life. From the first I see them—Milly and Edmund and Charlie. Charlie was very delicate, and Mamma was "anxious" about him. He was paid more attention than any of the others. He had special food, and a special chair, and a special tutor. He was always whining about something—or flying into a passion for which he was never punished because of his ill-health.

Edmund went at first to a day-school in our town, a cathedral town; and I always think of him as coming back from a football match in a jersey and very short flannel knickerbockers covered with mud. He was much the handsomest of the family. He had red cheeks, shining dark hair and eyes, and on Sundays, arrayed in a black coat and a stiff Eton collar, I though him beautiful, but I feared and dreaded him all the same. In spite of his bold-ness at football, he was a terrible coward; he led me into many scrapes, and then lied about them to escape punishment. He took it upon himself to "discipline" and harden me. I could not bear going high in the swing, and he would exert himself until he was purple in the face to swing me higher and higher, right up into the sky. The day came when I was pitched out, and a serious accident was averted only by my falling on the roof of the hen-house.... I gave a yell. Edmund fled. Nennie came from the servants' quarters and rescued me. My tears were stopped with a piece of bread spread with brown sugar.

It must have been soon after this that Nennie went away.... It is associated in my mind with a white world—everything in the old walled garden covered with sparkling snow—and with my lisping voice pleading persistently from breakfast-time, "Baby go out in the snow to-day." Smarden said that although the snow looked pretty it was very cold. "Deceitful stuff," she said vindictively, "like many things in this deceitful world." In the afternoon I tested the truth of this. I led a Dream army over the white plains...one of the De Courcys lost his life defending the colours.... It must have been while portraying his death, prostrate on a snow-covered flower-bed, that I suddenly felt my fingers and toes become very cold—they were so cold that they ached. It was a pain like toothache. The pretty snow became a fearful thing. I remembered one of Smarden's dismal stories of a woman who had become drowsy in the snow, and had lain down to sleep, and in the morning they had found her dead.... I began to cry, and ran indoors for comfort.

The short winter afternoon was closing in, and the sun looked like a flayed orange in the cold misty air. My goloshed feet made little sound as they pattered along the passage to the nursery. I remember that as I approached the closed door I was conscious that something strange, an unfamiliar thing, was taking place behind that door. As usual I had some difficulty in turning the handle.... Only by this do I know that I must have been very young.... A little child in a dark green frieze coat and white gaiters, with tiny hands and feet numb with cold.

Nennie was in the nursery, and Papa was with her—"the Guv." as the boys called him. It seemed to me that Nennie was trying to escape from him. He still had an arm round her waist. His face was very red and his mouth very wet. His ugly under-lip, which I always hated when it touched me, stuck out more than usual.... I can still see his face wearing a look that was silly and sheepish and greedy all at once, a look that made my cheeks burn.

"Leave me alone, you dirty old beast. Leave me alone! Aren't you ashamed of yourself? And the child here too!"

I had been paralysed with fright when I first saw them. They looked like people I had never known, like strangers in the street.... But at the sound of Nennie's voice I ran as fast as I could from the door to the hearth, crying out:

"You shan't hurt my Nennie—you shan't!" "The Guv." uttered an exclamation which sounded like "Damn," but it conveyed nothing to me. Besides, I was taken up with Nennie. Although I can hardly recall her features I see her always as my first love.

She gathered me up in her arms. I felt the comfort of her soft breast. The tears poured from my eyes, as they always did much later in life after an outburst of indignation.

"Don't cry, my Baby. Don't cry. Nennie isn't hurt."

"Oh, my Nennie, I love you so. I love you," I sobbed. "And my feet ache, and Baby go out in the snow no more."

She took off my soaking wool gaiters and hung them on the nursery guard to dry. Then she sat down in the rocking-chair, and soothed me into a delicious, drowsy calm.

"Papa isn't here now, is he?"

"No. He's not here now."

"Why was he here?" I persisted. For I could not remember his ever having come into the nursery to visit any of us.

"Better not ask," said Nennie. Then she said more, not so much to me as to the fire.

"Why, oh, why," she cried, "do we find it pleasant? Yes, I've found it pleasant though I have hated him, loathed him, wished him dead.... Not even young...with those horrible whiskers!"

I knew then of whom she was speaking.

"I don't like whiskers," I said sleepily. "None of the De Courcys have whiskers."

Smarden came in soon after with Milly—from a dancing-class I think. She scolded Nennie because my white gaiters were scorched. I can see them now dangling on the guard with a great brown mark on each leg.

I don't remember Nennie after that day. When she left, or why, or how, I cannot say. In after years I imagined that she just ran away. No one would answer my questions about her. One day, when Smarden and the parlour-maid were dusting the china in the drawing-room, Smarden missed an ornament. The parlour-maid said Ellen must have broken it. They then dropped their voices, and, although I was listening with all my ears for news of my darling, I caught only these words from Smarden:

"To think that a young girl like that should be so depraved!"

I guessed that this was not a compliment, and my young heart, still aching for Nennie, was hurt as if by a physical wound. I forgot that I was playing at being Denis, the noblest and handsomest of all the De Courcys. The illusion that I was starting for the Crusades with a cross on my breast and an immense sword at my side, vanished. I just had a hunger for Nennie's lap and her caressing hands and her delicious gay smile…. I wanted to go and pour out my misery to Mamma, but something stopped me…. Generally when I cried, she would tell me to try to be good like Milly. Nennie had never told me to try to be good. Yet I *felt* good with her. While she brushed my thick crop of hair, she used to say funny little things which made me laugh, and submit with a good grace to the hair-brushing, which naturally I detested.

She flits through my infant memories, a benign, gracious figure, one of the few people round me who was never disagreeable or quarrelsome, who never disappointed me. When I first saw one of those noble Greek statues of women with waved hair parted on straight, low brows, with dreamy blank eyeballs, and necks strong as marble columns; women tall and fine, with lovely draperies through whose transparent veil you see firm rounded breasts like pomegranates, spacious splendid waists, and long untired limbs, I thought of Nennie, and what to me meant maternity.

Yet I have no notion whether she was really like that. It would be strange if an under-nurse in an ordinary English household resembled those fair ideals of the antique world.

III

I have alluded to the De Courcys…. They were the chief family among the Dream People, and they had a splendid history…. I never needed any dolls or toys to play with; the De Courcys were inexhaustible. At the same time two dolls at different times filled a large place in my life. The first one, made of rag, and dressed in a sailor's kit, was my very own, my Jack, my more than a brother. He filled my head with all sorts of wild dreams of going to sea. The fact that I was a little girl and debarred from serving before the mast was by no means clear to me at this age. Later there came Dulcibella, a handsome wax doll, with blonde, curly hair, jointed limbs, eyes that opened and shut (often when you did not want them to do so), a squeaky voice in the region of the armpits, and carefully modelled fingers and toes. She was the joint property of Milly and myself, and I never had any real affection for her…. When she first came she spent most of her time in seclusion. "Too expensive a doll to be played with often," was the elders' verdict. Later, when her complexion had faded, and her clothes no longer interested Milly, she passed into my hands, and became

48

extremely useful. Once she figured in a poisoning case. I tried her, condemned to death, and hanged her.

Then there was Florrie, a wooden horse on wheels, big enough to ride. She—who decided her sex I cannot say—was the companion of many of my Montague wanderings. A bit of grey fur nailed on to her neck served her for a mane, and bright blue and red strips of paper pasted on her sides for housings. Her bit was securely fastened into her mouth with two brass-headed furniture nails. Her tail by no means matched her mane. It was black and bristling, of a substance that might really have been horsehair!

Now I was perfectly conscious of these incongruous component parts, and of the absurd wooden handle in front, with its base suggestion that Florrie could not move without being dragged along…. Yet, all the same, to me she was a sturdy roan of the purest breed, with flowing, ruddy mane and tail, capable of galloping miles without fatigue. I was always happy astride that magic mount…. On her I rode against the Saracens, streaming the ensign of the Christian cross!

By no natural means can I account for my Crusader obsession. I cannot remember who first told me of the Crusades. I do not know why the Cross from the first should have haunted me—haunted me as a thing for which people laid down their lives gladly. It seems to me that it came before any religious instruction of any kind, and was a reality long before I knew anything of the truth of which it was the symbol.

Once, in an ecstasy of love for it, I heated a skewer, which I stole from the kitchen for the purpose, and when it was red hot traced the cross on my left arm…. I had intended to do it on my breast, as all the De Courcys did when they vowed themselves to the Cross, but my courage failed…or was it that all my clothes fastened at the back, and I could not unfasten them without assistance? At any rate, the design was bolder than the execution. I did not produce a beautiful, shapely scarlet wound, as I had hoped, but a hesitating scrawl which quickly turned black, and festering, stuck to my sleeve.... When Smarden undressed me at nights, and tore the sleeve away from my arm—she was always a little rough—I suffered excruciating pain, but it seemed to me part of what I had done not to cry out.... After a few days, however, Milly noticed it, and told Smarden that I "had a bad place on my arm." There followed a humiliating bread poultice and other homely remedies, many inquiries as to how I came to have such an arm, and a whipping when, after a few mendacious and unsatisfactory replies, I told the truth. And I was left with a curious little white scar, which persists to this day, and a great wonder why I was whipped for doing what the De Courcys considered a glorious and high duty.

The contrast between my life as Denis De Courcy astride a roan charger, in the Holy Land, beloved and admired for my daring; as Denis De Courcy dreaming and reading in the great library of an ancient castle; as Denis De Courcy keeping vigil over my arms in the church, and my life as the youngest member of the Wingfield family, became heartrending as I grew older.

Was it a peculiar family life? I hope so. There was an entire absence of love in it. My dim memories are all confused by constant wrangling and quarrelling and bickering. I seem to see a menagerie of coarse little greedy animals. I cannot believe that all children are like that.

Prayers there were…family prayers, which meant nothing to me. I see a row of servants on their knees sprawling untidily over the dining-room chairs, and the dining-room table littered with breakfast. I hear either an indistinct mumble from Papa, or the clear, high-pitched personal voice of Mamma, and the voice of the eldest son, Stewart, outside the door: "It's beastly hard lines that I can't get my breakfast when I want it because of these confounded prayers."

My ideas of what it all meant were further complicated by Smarden, who took Milly and me down to the dining-room for the function, but never remained herself. Once I asked her why, and she replied in that decided way of hers: "Because it's stuff and nonsense." At a later time I knew that Smarden was not too irreligious, but too religious, to assist at family prayers…. She belonged to an exclusive sect, all converted souls, who worshipped in an upper room on Wednesdays and Sundays. Sometimes she would be betrayed into a discussion with Mamma or Alice or Winifred. All of them would grow very angry. "You're all lost," Smarden would say. "Every man Jack in this house is on the road to perdition." She would give a snorting laugh when they called her a narrow-minded old bigot. But she told me the story of Joseph most beautifully. Many a time I have gone to sleep on her knee, enraptured by the vision of a coat of many colours, and of a beautiful woman called Potiphar's wife.

IV

I learnt to read.

Years later I saw a little book entitled "Reading without Tears," and for the first time, the assumption in that title being that to learn to read was a difficult and painful task, I wondered why at a very tender age I had begun to read as easily as a puppy, thrown into water, begins to swim.

How I learnt, I haven't the slightest idea. I know I was self-taught, for I never had a lesson until the well-thumbed pages of "Little Arthur's History of England" had rendered up all their secrets to me.

This precocity was combined with the oddest ignorance. I was quite incapable of saying the alphabet, and for years I could not read the face of the clock.

Milly, older than I was, was still crying over a Child's Reader, and finding lessons from Alice an intolerable burden, when I was sitting in the nursery window-seat browsing on a large and heavy copy of "Paradise Lost," which was in the nursery because Smarden used it as a door-weight to keep the door open between the night-nursery and the day-nursery. What effect this Puritanical pasturage had on me, I don't know. I disliked very much all the parts about God…but the description of the fallen angels turning into serpents fascinated me while it left me terror-stricken…. And above all, I love the Seraph Abdiel. The sound of the lines,

"All night the seraph Abdiel unperceived
Through heaven's wide champaign took his dreadless way."

are in my ears now as often as summer returns; and "among the faithless, faithful only he," stirred in me the strangest hopes and ambitions, and ideals of loyalty—to whom, to what, who knows?

I have a strange maternal feeling for that small figure in the window-seat, doubled up over the large red book. I feel that I should like to clasp it to my breast, so young, so innocent, still so responsive to a gesture or look of love…. I should like to hide it in my heart from the evil to come. The funny little figure! Can it really be I—this baby in the holland pinafore and blue merino frock, with white socks not at all taut over the ankles, and well-worn strap shoes with wrinkled faces, the expression of which always reminded me of Smiles the bull-dog? Are those sturdy legs, scratched, and barked about the knees, really mine?—mine that crop of short yellow hair, like guineas, as some one once said…mine those wistful blue eyes, which so easily filled with tears…and so often left me defenceless to the rude jeer—"Cry-baby!"

The sun can no longer find that little me in the window-seat…cannot indeed find the window-seat, nor a panel of that pleasant room…. It was an old house, this home of my early childhood…ramshackle, ill cared for, a mixture of many styles. It stood in rather a poor quarter of Hercester ("a dirty slum," "the Guv'nor" called it), the sights and sounds of the town shut out by a spacious garden, in which grew some giant elms, where rooks and jackdaws lived a busy, quarrelsome, vocal life. There was a wide flagged path in the garden beneath the nursery windows…and odds and ends of pillars, bosses faintly carved, fragments of an earlier building, lay about on it unregarded…. I was told once that monks were buried beneath these flags, and that our part of the house was a bit of the monastery, which had been restored in Queen Anne's reign for a dwelling-house…. I hope it was true. It seems to me now that the magic of the place was monasticism…. It gave you such a strange feeling to go out into the world from that garden…to know, as you stood beneath the high, gateless stone wall at its far end, that just the other side was a sordid, narrow street, full of frowsy women and dirty half-clothed children—all as vocal as the rooks, but the cawing of the rooks did not frighten me as these human voices did…. "The Bull" was there too—"The Bull," my earliest conception of dark and nameless crime. It was for climbing over the wall one night to go and play billiards at "The Bull" that the second son, Giles, received a thrashing.

Giles was the "black sheep" of the family. When I first heard the name applied to him, I took it quite literally, and thought that he was covered with black wool under his clothes…. Once sent with a message to his bedroom, to tell him he would have no breakfast if he did not come down at once, I saw him half stripped, and his bare white back gave me one of the shocks of my life.

He was expelled from school, and the "Guv'nor" put him into the Bank with Stewart. Giles was short and fat, with a jolly round face and merry eyes.... He was musical, and could sit at the piano and play tunes picked up by ear by the hour, and sing rather nicely.... Winifred, who was learning music "properly," and practising Beethoven's sonatas, despised Giles's musical gifts, and said he "murdered" the piano. In a family where there was not much love lost between any of the members, Giles was particularly detested. He was "common," "vulgar," "low," "lazy." He got floggings from Papa, and tears from Mamma. As time went on, the merry eyes grew bleared...the jolly face coarsened, and acquired a cunning look in the perpetual effort to evade punishment.... In these days I chiefly regarded him as the "black sheep" who was cruel to cats and dogs, as some one who in the House of De Courcy would have been a scullion. Now I have a compassionate feeling that he was a spoiled comedian.

The boys did not like the garden because there was no stretch of grass in it big enough for cricket or tennis, but to me every corner of it had magic in it. A great vine grew against the garden side of the house...how much more beautiful than the late Georgian side which faced the street! I used to sit on the flagged path with my arm round the huge mastiff, and wonder if Smarden would make a grape tart again this year.... This year! What year was it?...What events marked it? I think it was the year I began to have lessons from Alice...and to nourish wicked feelings...feelings of hatred...of bitterness...of sullen rage.

What Alice taught me I don't remember.... I only remember *her*. She had a pale face, blue eyes and dark hair.... I think she was rather handsome, even though her nose had been broken in some accident. She had a sour, disagreeable expression, and was always complaining. She and Winifred quarrelled…they threw words at each other as if they were throwing stones…I used to turn very cold, and long for the nursery, where the world was warmer than here. It was in the schoolroom that these dreadful scenes took place—sordid, miserable scenes that seemed wholly purposeless, wholly meaningless.

I am sure I was a trying pupil. I can't produce any evidence, but I believe as an infant I was fairly good, obedient and sweet-tempered. With lessons began the period when I was what Smarden called "a young Turk."

I want to be honest, and that means being gentle to oneself as well as severe, and I should like to remember some definite crimes…. For what crime was it, I wonder, that Alice hit me in the face with her ringed hand? I only remember the cowardly back-handed blow, and the bloody nose, and the terrible rage which convulsed me. I rushed out of the schoolroom, along the long corridor to the blue rep drawing-room. There sat Mamma writing…and there sat Miss Canning, the mysterious Miss Canning who came to stay with us, and for some reason extended her visit from weeks to months and from months to years.

I burst open the door, and trembling with passion cast myself on Mamma.

"I won't be taught by her any more. I won't!" I yelled.

"Why, what's the matter?" said Mamma quite kindly. "Your nose is bleeding."

"She hit me," I gasped. "She dared to hit me!"

"Who hit you?" said Mamma, wiping my nose.

"Alice," I sobbed. "Oh, she is a brute!"

"Hush," said Mamma.

"You know she is," I cried. "She bullies you, she bullies us all…. We're all frightened of her…she makes us all miserable. Why should she?"

"How can you let the child speak like that?" said Miss Canning. "Her own sister! Too shocking!"

I looked round the room. In one of those lightning flashes which sometimes strike into every corner of memory and light up every object in it, giving one the feeling that one has gone out of a dark and narrow house on to a sunny upland, I remembered the mysterious man.

"Is she my sister?" I said in a loud, clear voice. "I don't believe it. I don't belong to this house. Some day he will come and fetch me."

Mamma looked at me anxiously. This is the first time I remember noticing her face.... It was very worn. The grey eyes were deep sunk in the sockets, the forehead was high, the mouth rather thin and meagre. It was a suffering face, the face of one prematurely aged, a face from which all mirth had fled. I think it was the face of a hero, yet in some ways Mamma was a coward.

She seemed cowardly to me at this moment. I knew we had a secret between us, yet she did not relieve my anxiety as to whether what I had said was the folly of dreams—an anxiety which was to torture me more or less all my life.

Then Alice came in, and Mamma hastily put me down from her lap. She did not escape abuse for "encouraging" me. Alice's anger with me was diverted. I was intolerable, but it was Mamma's fault. She had allowed me to grow up a little savage. She had allowed me to remain idle and ignorant so long that no one could teach me anything. The strife slipped away from me altogether. Alice said that if she taught the brats she ought to be paid a salary for it. "Why should I be your unpaid governess?" She had a fresh grievance because Winifred was to be sent to a finishing school at Brussels. "Why should she have all the advantages? I am the eldest. I was never sent abroad; I was never given a chance; I was never properly educated.... I am buried here in this dead-alive place…. You are always asking me why I don't marry…. Do you ever give me the chance of seeing any men?... You never call on any new people who come to Hercester…. You spend your time going to see the Dean."

On flowed the stream of petty recrimination…. Only once did Mamma show fight. This was when Miss Canning put in her oar.

"I will beg you not to interfere," said Mamma. "I wonder that *you* of all people have the face to teach me my duty to my daughter."

The scene ended, like many similar scenes, in Mamma's submission, and further concession to Alice, and tears.

I forgot my wounded face…. I had no choice, as every one else had forgotten it…and I tried to comfort Mamma. Her tears seemed to me dreadful, to remove the ideal which I coveted in the grown-up state—immunity from grief.

"What have I done that I should have such children?" Mamma moaned. "My children all seem to hate me."

"She often talked like this…. There were times, however, when she defended them from criticism with the ferocity of a wild-beast mother, and talked of their talents and their virtues with a pride, touching or irritating according to the point of view.

V

We left Hercester.

There was a financial crash. Strange men walked into the house and smoked pipes in the blue rep drawing-room. Edmund came and told me that he was afraid that they would seize his play-box before he went back to school.

"If I *do* go back to school," he added. "Mamma says she mayn't be able to afford it; it will be rotten if I don't. I was sure of my cap this half."

"I'll pay for you," I said impulsively. I saw him for the first time dashed, discouraged, sorrowful.

"You!" He laughed. "You are a silly! How much do you think a man's bills at Chappingham come to a term?"

"I've got some money in my money-box," I said. "You can have it."

"I expect the bailiffs will take that too, if you don't keep a sharp look-out, Baby," he answered. "It is a rotten shame.... There's poor old Laurie, who had set his heart on going to Oxford...they're going to send him packing off to China.... A clerk, you know.... Any fool can be a clerk, and Laurie's awfully clever."

"I shan't have enough money in my box for him too," I said. Laurie was the third brother. I disliked him. He was so cold, so sarcastic. I used to imagine that he must have a forked tongue. He had a way of hissing out cruel things between his thin lips.... I used to stare at them, thinking: "I know what your tongue is like, though you never show it." Yet in this hour I was sorry for him too...but not so sorry as I was for Edmund, who would perhaps never have that purple-and-gold football cap which appeared to be to him what a crown was to a De Courcy.

I went to Mamma with the money-box. She was sitting writing in her bedroom, and Papa was sitting there too. I noticed that his face was a queer colour. Once Edmund had looked like that when he had eaten too many sweets and was going to be sick.

They were so busy talking that they did not notice me, or if they did notice me, they were in the stage of an angry discussion when people cannot stop.

"I say the child has cost us twice over already," Papa was saying.

"Cost us £4,000!" cried Mamma. "What will you say next? You have squandered Austin's money, just as you have squandered mine. Poor fellow!"

"A worthless scamp…planting his child on us, then going off…. It's my opinion that he never intended to come back."

"That's not true! Something has happened to him. Austin could never do a mean action."

Mamma was told that she was infatuated with Austin. She said something bitter about Leonora Canning…. I listened, fascinated, afraid to stir…. I made a vow that I would never marry. As the conversation proceeded I saw that Papa wanted to get rid of me, while Mamma wanted to keep me….There was some talk of a cheap foreign school. Mamma said, "I will never do that until I am sure that he is dead." Every word left its mark on me, though I did not understand every word. I felt like one stuck all over with arrows, and all the joy that I had felt about offering the money-box was extinguished. I dropped it on the floor and burst into tears.

Mamma rushed at me.

"How long have you been here, Baby?"

I answered with another question.

"Won't he come and fetch me? Won't he ever come and fetch me?"

Mamma tried to comfort me with peppermint bullseyes, but did not answer…. And once again the vision of the mysterious man disappeared into the darkness. Or perhaps it would be truer to say that it was locked up in a cupboard; I knew where it could be seen, but I dared not ask for the key.

II
GROWTH

I

A great change came over my life when the Wingfields left Hercester. Up till then I had been surrounded by shabby great things. I had lived in spacious rooms, where the remnants of fine taste still lingered. The summers were often spent in an old stone farmhouse on the hills, and from there we drove sometimes to see neighbours who had houses of the same kind, only bigger and more stately....Such things I suppose influence a child, for I have noticed that those who have not been surrounded by them in youth never have quite the same feeling about them in maturity.

I have spoken of the blue rep curtains and the early Victorian ottomans at Hercester. But there were fine Chippendale chairs and tables as well. There were Downman drawings and Morland prints. There was a lot of nice old china.... On the day of the sale I made a raid on "Paradise Lost" and "Stumps," a little book about a little child who loved strawberry jam, but Smarden caught me, and told me I was *stealing*. I think she threatened me with a police-man, as on the day when I took a purple button out of a remnant basket on the counter in Mr. Lance's haberdashery shop.

I caught a glimpse of the auctioneer, as Smarden hurried us from the nursery to the street. Milly and I were going to the seaside with her until the new home was ready. He was holding up a water-colour drawing of a young man in naval uniform, the Wingfield who had been killed at Trafalgar. Then it was handed along the line of strange men who sat round the dining-room table.... "Five—five—going at five—Five pounds—I shan't dwell on it," said the auctioneer. It was to the sound of his voice that I left my first home.

Young as I was, I felt it very deeply.... The esplanade at West-sands, the yellow sands themselves, could not make up to me for my loss. The mastiff Nelly and the bull-dog Smiles had been left behind...with all the great shabby things. A little white dog called Fairy, with a curly coat and black eyes and a pink nose—a regular lap-dog—accompanied us to the sea.

It was just before I left Hercester that I had begun to realise the Cathedral and to love its lofty arches, its immense stained-glass window, and its massive stone pillars, faintly flushed with pink like a tea-rose. We went to the afternoon service on Sundays. The organ delighted me.... I had a hero in a yellow-haired chorister with a voice that sounded as easy and sweet as a bird's voice after a shower. I was ambitious to be a choir-boy like Geoffrey Brown.

And all this I knew had something to do with God, with the God whom Smarden represented as some one who would cast me into "the pit" (whatever that was) if I were not "saved." Saying "Our Father chart Heaven" (as I misheard it) and "God bless Papa and Mamma and everybody" also had something to do with God. "God sees you," said Smarden, and on a starlit night I found it easy to believe it, for there were God's eyes.

At Westsands the Dream people began to visit me less frequently...and when they came they were not so wonderful as they had been.... I date their decline from the day when I invited Milly to a De Courcy banquet.... A strange little element of coarseness began to creep in.... Milly's one idea was a baby. The De Courcys became domesticated.... My virgin knights left me for ever.

Milly was the constant companion of my youth.... We were dressed alike; we were given presents "between us"; we learned the same lessons; we had our hair cut the same way—short, with straight, thick fringes across the forehead, and clubbed ends just below the ears. It was the custom to say we were as alike as two peas, although my hair was a different colour, and I was much more thickly and strongly built. The colour of our hair did not differ more than the colour of our dispositions. I will say at once that Milly was a much better child than I was...very unselfish, very meek. But "aggravating," as Smarden said. She used to drive me to frenzy with "I don't think it would be right." I was guilty of the brutality of hitting her over the head when she made use of this formula to defeat all my plans. I remember once standing on a step above her on the stairs, and raining blows on her from the point of vantage. I remember, too, that I enjoyed it.

At Westsands we made the acquaintance of a little boy called Wegg—Orlando Wegg. He had a lovely complexion, large grey eyes—too large, I think now, for maturity has taught me that eyes should not be big any more than feet should be small—and a graceful figure.... Anything less like the rough, untidy Wingfields it would be difficult to imagine. His clothes were very spick-and-span; his tie and the hand-kerchief in his pocket always matched exactly. He seemed to have plenty of money, and was fond of treating Milly and me to curds and whey at the dairy. I observed that when he sat with us on the sands, he would put his arm round Milly, and if no one were about would kiss her ardently. I asked him once why he did not do these things to me.... I was not sure that I wanted him to do it—it seemed to me a little vulgar—but I was perplexed, and slightly mortified, by his preference for Milly. He answered that I was too like a boy.

At Westsands Alice had a love-affair.... While it lasted, our education was arrested. For propriety's sake, she would take Milly and me on the long excursions which Mr. Stanton arranged. He was tall and lanky, and I expect quite young, but he seemed venerable compared with Orlando Wegg.

When our boys came to Westsands for the holidays, Edmund said that Orlando was a little bounder who "wanted kicking." He also expressed surprise that I could play "gooseberry" to Stanton and Alice, I did not quite understand what he meant, but from that day I felt ashamed of going out with them, and preferred to play cricket with Charlie and Edmund.

I took the game very seriously, and it became the chief interest of my life. I made such progress that I was allowed to play in a match that Edmund got up.... At least I was to have played, but at the last minute a big Eton boy on the opposite side said he would not play if I did. It was beneath his dignity to play in the same match as a girl. That was a humiliating moment when I had to return home, arrayed in the lovely white flannel jumper and skirt that Smarden had made, and see my place taken by Alfred who cleaned our knives, and had no notion how to hold his bat, much less how to make a catch and throw in straight.

This was the first time that I understood that my sex might handicap me in life.... Yet it provoked in me no desire to be a boy, at least not the kind of boy I knew.... Edmund had been treacherous. He had not "stuck up" for my cricket; he had almost pretended that he did not know me.... No: I never had a blind admiration for boys.

II

Whether we were months or years at Westsands in furnished lodgings I don't know. A child has no sense of time. Think of the long, long day of childhood, and the short week, and the unrecognizable year! During this time we hardly saw the parents. We ran wild mentally, although good old Smarden looked after our bodies, so that we were always well. I read everything that I could lay hands on—Captain Marryat, Defoe, Sir Walter Scott, old plays, children's books, poetry. All were fish that came to my net. I did not select, but I did discriminate to a certain extent. There were days when I could read nothing but poetry, and before I was ten I loved "She dwelt among the untrodden ways," and "Go, lovely rose." I would recite to myself with great ardour "That which her slender waist confined," and "When love with unconfined wings." How beautiful it was to be a lover and to write such things to the beloved!

Another day I would be deep in "Tom Brown's Schooldays," or stories in "The Boy's Own Paper." I shivered over "The Duchess of Malfi," and was puzzled by "The Heart of Midlothian." Such strange ideas, such inexplicable emotions, seethed in my mind after some of this reading that I would have a reaction in favour of books that were easier to understand, and that did not provoke uncomfortable yet attractive thrills. In the sweet mystic atmosphere of Hans Andersen I found great peace. But there were times when I preferred the jolly, straightforward way fairy-stories were told by Grimm.

I remember all this reading far more clearly than my desultory lessons. Winifred, who returned from Brussels about this time, taught Milly the piano, but she gave me up as a bad job after three or four lessons. She said that I was hopelessly unmusical, yet of them all I think I missed the organ at Hercester the most, and later in life, when I loved music more, I grew to regard my neglected musical education as a tragedy. Winifred was more successful in teaching me French. I soon learnt to read it easily.

Strange, bitter, intellectual being—Winifred's life seemed to be wasted by hatred. She hated Alice; she hated Westsands; she hated England; she hated Smarden's religious opinions. She would talk with a venom that alienated me from her cause, even when her cause was just. She was never deliberately unkind to me, but she made me suffer all the same by her attitude towards others. All my life cynicism has distressed me, and Winifred distrusted every one and everything. She was never so happy as when her distrust was justified. "What did I say?" was her triumphant comment.

She would criticize Mamma in a most unfilial way for making favourites in the family. "The boys can drain her of every penny," she would say. "They can behave as badly as they like. She is infatuated with them. But with me—her one idea is to get me married, and off her hands."

"I'm not going to marry," I said.

"Perhaps you will never have the chance!" said Winifred, with that acid smile which was so disconcerting to me.

I remembered Orlando Wegg's preference for Milly.... But something stirred in me, lying far deeper than the possibility that no suitors would come my way, and I expressed it as well as I could.

"I've read things about marriage," I said. "It's a horrid thing. I would rather die."

Winifred shouted with laughter. "Come and listen to Baby's views on marriage," she said to Stewart, the eldest brother, who was at Westsands on a visit; and they both began to tease me, and teach me that if a girl said she did not want to be married, there was only one explanation—"sour grapes."

III

In describing my progress from infancy to childhood, and through childhood to maturity, I have aimed at keeping the knowledge of a later time out of it altogether—a difficult, perhaps an impossible aim. When you have learned a language, and can speak it easily, you find it hard to remember the days when you struggled in vain to express the simplest things. Who can make the child live again? Smarden is dead. I cannot ask her what I was like…if I could, could she tell me? Did she ever know? Did Milly ever know? She remembers some of my childish sayings: "Hold my hand, Nennie, and let me run faster than I can." But she does not remember that I loved Nennie, loved her as I never loved one of the family. Was it her beautiful face that caught my fancy? I know that in later years I was very sensitive to looks…and that "handsome is as handsome does" seemed to me a very unconvincing proverb. Yet the attraction that good-looking bodies had for me was complicated by some eager hope that they were the shadows of lovelier souls, not the fair clay houses in which something mean and disappointing dwelt. I believe that it was the soul for which I yearned, for which I always searched. Beautiful hands, beautiful lips, graceful movements, gracious ways—they were not things in themselves, but gates and windows through which I longed to enter, and penetrate to a beauty uncorporeal and mystical, a beauty not to be seen but felt.

IV

It was terrifying to become conscious of life.

I had lived on this earth eight or nine years and had never known that I was alive.

I do not know whether it is a common experience, this birth of consciousness that one is an individual, that one is isolated, that there is something inside one with which one must live always.

"I live…what am I? It seems to me that I am alone on this immense earth, and that I am moving towards a future still more immense! Oh how it frightens me! Let me go back to yesterday, when I went hither and thither like a puppy or a kitten…. I did not know then that I *lived*."

It came to me during an arithmetic lesson. Milly was wonderfully quick at arithmetic. I was wonderfully slow…but Alice pulled the slow pupil along with the quick one mercilessly, indifferent to the fact that the slow one didn't know whether she was on her head or her heels. There were confusing sums about cisterns: "If pipe A takes so long to fill cistern B…" I used to dream about an old lead cistern outside the Bank House at Hercester…. I was sure the cistern in the sum was ugly and had not crossed swords on it, and a Tudor Rose, and initials, and the date 1720 in charming figures. Meanwhile Milly had found out how long it took to fill the arithmetical cistern, and I would look over her shoulder and copy her answer. I cheated at arithmetic always. One day there was an exposure. Alice stormed at me. "Dishonest, dishonourable! Liar! Cheat!" I was shut up alone in my bedroom all that day, and given dry bread for dinner. Mamma came and spoke to me very seriously…but she supplemented the dry bread with some pudding.

This, however, was long after the revelation day.

Consciousness! I lived…I could not escape. I lived, and I must die. For the first time I began to reflect on this mystery of existence. How had I come into the world? And was it only that I might travel at last to that brink over which God was daily throwing people into a Pit, to burn "for ever and ever," as Smarden said.

On the smooth face of a rock at Westsands some one had painted in large letters "Where will you spend Eternity?"

It was a choice apparently between that pit and a place made of honeycomb…. I had pictured a honeycomb hillside down which rivulets of milk flowed when I first heard the hymn "Jerusalem the Golden," and the picture remained on the wall of my mind for years. Jerusalem lay on the top of this hill…a little town with turrets of pure gold. And in the streets of this little town people sang all day and all night…. They sang "for ever and ever."

The idea of "for ever and ever" appalled my young mind…. Long days going on for long years…processions of years, years, "without end, Amen," as they said in church.

To me it seemed of little consequence whether you burned or sang…. I could not contemplate joy without end with any less terror than pain without end.

Often at nights, after the day when I knew that I was alive, I distinct from Milly, I distinct from all persons round me, I alone with myself, I most terribly alone, I would hang, fascinated, over the abyss, and watch millions being thrown into it by invisible hands…. What had they done? They had been *born*. What was it to be born?… Hens laid eggs, cats had kittens, babies came to mothers…. They were "presents," brought by some one who came down the chimney (but why down the chimney?) like Father Christmas. I had my suspicions of this theory…but I had no other. In the course of my reading I often met the expression "delivered of a child"…How it puzzled me! Delivered? Surely this meant that the child had been taken away, yet apparently it meant that the child had come!

I looked up "Birth" in the dictionary…but a dictionary does not answer the riddle of life.

I had always been shy of asking questions. For a year or so before the revelation day I had not even wished to ask them… but now my head was buzzing with them. I wanted relief.

We had left Westsands, and were living on the outskirts of a West of England town. The house was an ordinary roomy villa, but outside stretched beautiful downs. A river flowed through a deep gorge. At the end of the little garden in front of the house grew a silver birch, a laburnum, and some lilac bushes. They had been planted to give privacy to 9, Downend Park; they had grown up to give me delight. The drooping gold plumes of the laburnum, the upright purple plumes of the lilac, toss over my memories of the period. I loved them. I remember hearing the birds twittering excitedly, quickly, gaily in the bushes one May morning…and thinking how nice it would be if there were some one whom I could take round the neck, and ask and ask, and tell and tell.

Mamma came in at the garden gate. She went for a walk before breakfast every morning…. It was part of her admirable energy.

"Mamma…please tell me something. How did I come?"

The effect of the question was very astonishing.

"Come! What do you mean, child?…" she said sharply. "Has any one been talking to you?…"

"No." Why was she so angry? And why did I without rhyme or reason recall at that moment the blue drawing-room at Hercester?

"I don't mean what you mean," I said, with an instinct that we were at cross-purposes. "How does it all happen? That's what I want to know. How are people born? Why are they born?"

Mamma looked relieved. "Who's been putting such ideas into your head, Baby?"

"Please tell me," I insisted. In spite of the loveliness of the morning, the terror of life was on me.

"You know the angels bring the babies…and then they grow up…and the angels bring *them* babies."

"Alice is grown up, and they haven't brought *her* a baby."

"Of course not…she isn't married."

"Why do angels only bring babies when you're married?" I was getting disheartened. I saw that Mamma was laughing.

"You're too young to understand that," she said, "When you are older you'll know all about it."

The old, old answer! I felt as indignant as though Mamma had talked to me in baby language. And why one moment did she say "You're too old to do that," and the next, "A little girl like you can't understand."

That afternoon Milly and I played cricket with Ernest on the downs. Ernest had discovered that I bowled well enough to give him practice, and that Milly was quite capable of running and picking up the balls he hit. He was a handsome youth of about fifteen, with curly brown hair and hazel eyes. He was at a tutor's in Downend Park, and he and I struck up a friendship, the first friendship of my life. We had a sort of "understanding." He never snubbed me, never teased me as the Wingfield boys did, though he would make me bowl for him for an hour on end... and would order me about like a slave.

We stood at the gate. Milly had gone in.

"Ernest."

"Yes, Johnnie." That was his name for me. Others, if they did not call me "Baby," called me "Joanna."

"Have you ever thought how we came into this...why we are here, you and I?"

He looked at me curiously.

"Don't say 'You are a rum little beggar,' please, don't, Ernest!" I pleaded.

"I wasn't going to."

"Well, have you ever thought about it?"

"I know...I've known for years."

"Tell me, then, Ernest.... I want to know. I keep on thinking.... It vexes me."

"You should ask your mother, or old Smarden."

"They tell me such silly things...Ernest, or else they say, 'You'll know when you're older.'"

"Well, you will."

"I think it's a shame to be here...to have to be here, and not to know why."

"Great Scott, Johnnie! You're never going to blub about it."

"I'm frightened!" I cried out. I flung my arms round his neck. He did not attempt to shake me off.

"Why?" he said quite kindly.

"There's something I can't remember," I sobbed. "Something I knew once...I don't really love them in there." I waved one arm at the house. "Perhaps the angels brought me to the wrong place."

"Stop blubbing, and I'll tell you what I can.... You're such a kid... No! I can't talk to a girl about these things!"

"Oh, yes, you can, Ernest.... You've always said I'm not like a girl. Why, I can shy a cricket-ball straight, Ernest...you know I can."

Ernest took my arms from his neck and held my hands.

"They love each other."

"Who love each other, Ernest?"

"The woman...the man...they love tremendously. The child is made by their love."

"It's made, not brought, then," I said. I noticed that Ernest's cheeks were very red, and that his eyes shone.

"I think it's all rot that one should be ashamed to speak of it," he said. I didn't know what he meant by this...and his explanation was to me no explanation. Yet it satisfied me; I felt that he was telling the truth as he knew it—that he believed in this strange love...as Mamma had not believed in the angels. I was glad that the day had not ended without my putting my arms round some one's neck...and telling, telling—not what was in my heart, perhaps, but at least *something*.

V

I don't know what impression emerges from my confused memories...nor to what end the little scenes that I have excavated from the buried years contribute.

In the eighteenth century I am told that the Palatine looked nothing more than a mound of earth, all overgrown with trees and shrubs and grass and wild flowers, surmounted by the Villa Mills. Even now, years of patient excavation have revealed little of the glory of the dwelling-places of the Cæsars. Yet these shapeless heaps of stones, these mutilated pillars, these shreds of mosaic, these damp underground passages give a better idea of the splendour that was imperial Rome, than the complete pasteboard reconstruction of the Palatine in the museum below. It is with this in my mind that I refrain from completing or restoring any broken incident that I remember. Let me deduce from it, but let me not use the deduction to construct a whole life in pasteboard. It is only with a mature mind that I recognize how valiant a woman Mamma was.

She took the whole burden on herself—a penniless husband, to whose name after the failure of the Hercester Bank some disgrace attached, a growing family clamouring to be fed and educated and launched in the world. Her own income (she had brought a very substantial dowry with her from her Quaker family) not being large enough to meet the clamour, she began to sell her pictures.

At Hercester she had painted portraits and copies of old masters for love and for amusement. She had extraordinary facility, and could turn out a large picture so rapidly that it seemed a miracle that the canvas could be covered with paint in so short a time, whatever the quality of the work. She did not have a proper studio at Downend Park, but painted at one end of the dining-room, where she had a platform and screen for her sitters. Sometimes, when commissions for portraits were scarce she would go to London or Florence or Antwerp and paint some copies of famous pictures, for which she seemed always to have a sale.

Although the whole family were maintained by her labour and by her Quaker father's caution in having locked up her income in Chancery, they did nothing but complain of their lot. Never can a benefactor have had less encouragement, less gratitude.

Morning after morning the industrious if common-place brush addressed itself to its task. Mamma must have covered miles of canvas before she died…. She was a brave woman, not an artist…. A picture finished represented to her a school-bill paid. She was not troubled by an artistic conscience. Her taste was for the "pretty," and I first heard of Whistler as some one whom Mamma disliked intensely. She seemed angry that he made money and achieved fame.

Once or twice her steady career of noble pot-boiling (for it was noble in its self-abnegation) was interrupted by such an artistic success as a picture being hung at the Academy. Then her ingenuous pride was wonderful to see.

"Mamma baiting" was a favourite Wingfield sport. It strikes me now as incredible…. She had saved her husband from trial and imprisonment, and was now supporting him and his children, yet he hardly ever gave her a kind word. Instead he, to whom she had been so merciful, attacked her incessantly for being over-indulgent to her sons. He complained of his food, and flirted in his weak middle-aged way with every woman that he came across.

This grievance of Mamma's indulgence to the boys was perpetually in Alice's mouth too. During the time we lived at Downend Park I never remember a meal when Mamma was not bullied.

But she pursued her devoted, unwise way. She hid those filial letters asking for money. She crept down at dawn to open the front door to her dissolute Giles. She was for ever giving him "a chance," "a fresh start," and paying for it.

Winifred was not so cruel as Alice on the subject of the boys. But she mocked at Mamma's pictures, and at her sentimentality. If Mamma used a French word Winifred derided her accent.

I have always remembered all this. Now for the first time I can define it. Constantly I saw Mamma silently crying behind the teapot at the breakfast-table. This hurt me horribly, much more than when she retaliated...though that was bad enough. To this day a quarrel, and the exchange of hard, angry, ugly words make me feel as if the blood had rushed from my head and left me very pale.

Never was there such a family for quarrelling. For dinner on Sundays as a special treat there was cream.... Some one was accused of taking too much. That was enough to set the table in a roar of recrimination.

Milly would intervene to protect the one whom she considered most shamefully abused. She won the sobriquet of "little peacemaker." For some reason or other her peace-making irritated me.... She was, as our German housemaid said, too "self-right."

At Hercester Mamma had gone to the Cathedral regularly, and had taken us children to the afternoon service. At Downend Park the church was a long way off, and we only went if the weather was very fine. I hated the church as much as I had loved the Cathedral. Since my friendship with Ernest I had "grown up" a little. The first sign of my development was an inability to take things as a matter of course—such things as going to church on Sunday.

I much preferred the Sundays when we read a chapter of the Bible to Mamma as a substitute for church-going. I am afraid I had the dimmest idea of what it was all about, but I loved the sound of the words, and the pictures that they conjured up. "I am the true Vine; my Father is the husbandman." That reminded me of the vine at Hercester. So interesting did I find the Bible that I began in secret to read it from cover to cover.... I read it as later on I read "The Three Musketeers" and "Les Misérables."

But I was speaking of Mamma—of lion-hearted Mamma. I wish now that I had loved her more…and had understood better the brave struggle which she carried on day by day, a struggle unsweetened by any sympathy, unalleviated by any reward. Surely now I should be incapable of the mercilessly critical attitude from which most days I regarded her. I was even impatient of her tears.

VI

I make excavations in my twelfth year and a spring day comes to light, a day on which I was in a sense born again.

It was a shining April day—how April can shine! We were at breakfast, at least those of us who were punctual. Mamma saw the postman coming up the path and rushed to meet him. It was her custom. She dearly loved her post! A letter—no matter from whom—could always cheer her up.

She came in again with the bundle of letters. There was one for me from old Smarden, who had left us. It began "My darling Baby," and out of it fell a tract called "Repent Now." Smarden had given notice so often that no one thought she would go when the month was up. It was only when her mustard-coloured tin box was hoisted on to the cab, and she, encumbered with parcels of illuminated Scripture texts, stepped into it, that we had to believe that her dear, ugly old face would be seen no more in the house of Wingfield. For nights after her departure I lay awake weeping. For some time I wrote to her every day, and promised her that when she was old I would bring her tea and coffee and cocoa…. When she wrote to Mamma, rather tentatively asking to be taken back, I was indignant that Mamma did not run to meet her half way, but answered frigidly that what Smarden had done "could not be rectified all at once." I looked over Mamma's shoulder as she was writing, and when I saw those words my heart seemed to be beating itself to death in an empty hollow. To this day the word "rectified" gives me an unpleasant feeling.

Where was all that grief now? As I read old Smarden's confused, affectionate lines, I was ashamed that my wound had healed…. In a few short months I had grown accustomed to being without her.

Mamma's voice rang out across the table.

"Henry!"

Papa did not look up from his paper.

"Henry! Poor Austin is dead!"

Papa said: "I knew this would happen. I knew he would never come back…. What has he left? What arrangements has he made?"

Mamma did not answer, but went on reading her letter.

"He died at sea…oh, what a tragedy!... The purser says he was alone…but for the ship's doctor, and a priest…. There was a priest among the passengers…. They are sending back his effects here."

"And why here?" Papa growled. "I call it great impertinence."

"Our address was among his papers…the only address…Oh, poor fellow!"

I was quite self-possessed…and was clear, very clear…. My perceptions were clear and fresh. I left my chair and my breakfast and went round to Mamma. She threw her arms round me and gave me a rare hug.

" I know who's dead, Mamma."

"Oh, child!" Mamma's tears poured on my head. They rolled down my cheeks, tasted salt in my mouth.

"I remember the night he came," I said.

"You can't remember! You can't!" Mamma sobbed. "You were too young—such a little thing…no higher than that."

Alice came up. "Let me read the letter." By fair means or foul she read all Mamma's letters.

"No, no!" Mamma cried. She got up and went out of the room, taking her letters with her.

"There's no need to get into such a state!" Alice called after her.

"I always thought your mother was sweet on that fellow," said Papa.

I found Mamma in her bedroom, sponging her tear-stained face. This familiar sight helped to steady me. I caught hold of the bed-post, striving to stop the burning stream of wonder rushing through my head with a question. But I could not find my voice. Besides, I did not know what to ask. I twisted my thumb in and out of my fingers, and remained silent.

I remembered how seldom Mamma had ever answered my questions. It would be useless to ask her! And how difficult it would be to make her believe that I really remembered, although "Austin," my dreamfather De Courcy in Crusader's mail, and the mysterious midnight visitor made a composite picture in my mind. To-day the picture seemed to speak, to say over and over again, "Pray to Her for your father, your wretched father."

I was ashamed to think that I had never prayed for him— never once. It was a long time since I had prayed at all…. A remark of old Smarden's flitted through my head: "Says everything but her prayers, and them she whistles."

Mamma dried her face, and went to the dressing-table. I could see her anxious, harassed face in the glass.

"Your cap's crooked," I said; and instantly I remembered another day when her cap had been crooked after a scene in her bedroom at Hercester. I heard Papa saying cruel things…things that had stuck in my baby soul. I heard the money-box drop on the floor. I heard again the name "Austin." On the crest of that recollection I struck out into the unknown.

"Is my mother dead too?"

Mamma turned round as if some one had hit her. Her lips moved…. She held out her right hand…as if she hoped that some one would put into it a word that she could not find.

"Why, Baby!" she gasped…. "I'm your mother…Why—oh, why do you think—"

"Don't cry…please don't cry, dear Mummy." I stood on tiptoe—and put my arms round her neck. "It would be such a pity…you've just washed your face. Your eyes aren't so red now. Don't cry. I know you're my mother, as Papa's my father…. I was asking about the other one…the real one who goes with my father Austin…. I know you're my mamma, my dear mamma… but where is she…the one who made me."

"Made you!"

"Yes. Ernest says two people love each other…love each other tremendously…and then they make their baby…. Where is my mother who loved my father Austin like that?...Have I ever seen her?...Shall I ever see her?"

I began to tremble all over. I felt if Mamma did not answer at once, I should die. All my life seemed to have swept on great wings of desire to far-off horizons, leaving me empty, fainting to death.

Mamma said: "That Ernest is not a fit person for you to know. I shall write to Mr. Sharpe and tell him what sort of a pupil he has! Any boy who could talk in that way to a little girl like you must be bad to the core!"

VII

Soon after this, Ernest went away.

Mamma had forbidden us to speak to him, but when I heard him whistle in the road outside I forgot all about that. Milly had gone out to tea. I had been left behind because I had been naughty, and Papa, after giving me a caning, had put me to weeding the front lawn. I ran out into the road just as I was, hatless, and dressed, I remember, in a red twill frock and a holland pinafore.

"Come for a walk," said Ernest.

"I've promised I won't."

"I call it beastly unkind of you," he said. "I'm going away to-morrow."

"For always?"

"Yes. Well, I don't ask you twice." He began to move off. I ran after him.

"Don't, Ernest. I want to come...but I'm afraid to go in and get my hat. Alice is at home."

Ernest swallowed his objections to the unusual. It was before the days of the "no hat" craze.

"Come along...what does the hat matter? I love your hair, John."

Somehow this pleased me.

"I like dark hair best," I said.

"Do you? I think brassy hair like yours is ripping. Will you give me a bit to take away with me?"

"Rather!"

"That's so like you!" he said, laughing. "You'll never know how to flirt—never. Let me show you how you ought to have answered."

He began to put on absurd airs and walk with mincing steps as if he had on a skirt. Then he burlesqued a high soprano. "Why should I? What do you want with my hair? I never heard of such a thing!"

"Would you like me to go on like that?" I inquired solemnly. "I'd give you all my hair if you wanted it...my head too. It's splendid to give things."

He stopped his parody.

"You are a dear!" he said. "Girls go on like that to make men keener…they pretend they're offended to make us run after them."

"Not all girls."

"It's in their nature."

"It isn't! It isn't…. Have you ever read 'Romeo and Juliet'?"

"No."

"You just read about them!"

"I only read Shakespeare when I've got to." This seemed to separate me miles from Ernest, although we were walking arm in arm.

"She isn't offended…. She loves him after one look of his. She wishes she were like the sea, to give him things for ever."

"Very silly of her."

"Don't, don't, Ernest," I cried. "Don't call Juliet silly…. I love her."

"What's the use of loving some one in a book?"

I did not know how to answer him. Our difference of opinion had made me feel as if I were going to cry.

We began talking about cricket, and a discussion about the batting averages, and the different cricketers' chances of being at the top that year took a long time.

Later on when we were in the wood he cut off a bit of my hair with his knife.

"I shall keep that until you are Lady Lackden," he said, methodically putting it away in his pocketbook.

"Until I am what, Ernest?"

"Perhaps you don't know…. I shall be Lord Lackden some day."

I stared at him amazed.

"And I'm going to marry you. I hate your family…but we needn't have anything to do with them…. As for you…you're the jolliest little thing I have ever met. You are—you are—well, you are just what I want.... I want a man!"

"But I'm not going to marry," I said.

"Not yet, of course....How old are you, John?"

"Eleven, I think.... No one seems to know."

"Well, then...in six or seven years, when I am twenty-one, and you are seventeen—"

"But I don't want to!"

"You will, though! That will be all right. You're going to be Lady Lackden. I wish I could get my beastly old grandfather to ask you to Lackden now! You'd love it. There's a moat with great pike and carp in it...and a huge park where one can lose oneself, and lots of pheasants. I'll teach you how to shoot. We shall be jolly rich...and jolly happy.... I shan't care if they say I've married beneath me—"

"Beneath you!" My pride blazed up.

"Don't lose your hair! I only meant that—"

"You're a little cad," I said. Then my anger dissolved in tears. He put his arms round me and kissed my eyes and hair.... He covered me with kisses.

"Don't...don't, Ernest.... People love each other when they kiss like that.... Don't."

"I can hear your jolly little heart beating."

I shook him off. There was something about him now that I hated.

"Let's go home."

"All right." He got up from the grass...and took my arm in the old Ernest way. We walked very fast, and we were very silent. When we reached the gate it was nearly dark. We had been together for hours and hours.

"Good-bye, little John," said Ernest.

"I should like to kiss you good-bye."

I put my arms round his neck and fondled him, but I felt that he was sad and dispirited.

I watched him swinging down the road in the dusk, a tall graceful figure…. I thought of the splendid dark head that the straw hat concealed. I thought of the young Alexander. And I wondered why it had not all been great and white and shining… why he had suddenly seemed my enemy. To marry an enemy! To marry a stranger! To marry at all!

I never saw him again.

III
JUVENESCENCE

I

I was more of a woman—or of a man—than most girls of my age, and more of a child…. I continued to sulk and cry at times like a very small child. I was as ignorant of many things as a very small child. Yet I dreamed—long dreams—not at all childishly.

It was of my father and mother that I dreamed.

As the facts were quite colourless, I put colouring touches. There was a puzzle in my head, and a hunger in my heart. But I kept my thoughts to myself.

My life glowed with a beamy reflection of my father's image. He was handsome, gallant; he spoke foreign languages perfectly, he travelled through foreign countries because the noble English family to which he belonged had disapproved of my mother.

I painted the mystery surrounding her in tender colours. She was beautiful. Love streamed from her. She was young. She was like the human fruit of spring.

Days came when I hugged reality and the Wingfields, when I said, "What's the use of fancying things?" Yet "fancying things" was always the chief consolation of my life.

"Tell me anything you are thinking about; ask me anything you want to know," Mamma would say at times. But I, remembering her excessive trembling when I had asked her if my mother were dead, dared not put questions to her.

I was much younger than Milly, yet I knew more about the facts of life than she did. Her ignorance annoyed me. "I can't help laughing!" I would say when she betrayed it in speech. But

I did not laugh. What was to happen to children who could not learn these things without being told?

I began to think about what I should do if I had children. "They shall always be told everything, but they shall be told beautifully...and by some one who loves them enough."

I spoke to Mamma on the subject, and felt my cheeks aflame. She said I must not be "morbid," must not think of such things at all until I was older.

Vaguely I resisted her prohibition. The thoughts were there. They could be made beautiful or ugly; they could inspire and strengthen, or they could degrade and weaken. But they could not be destroyed.

Morbid! How the word rankled. Was it fair? I had no morbid curiosity about sex. I reached a certain age without feelings of any kind. The first real passion that was born in me was a passion to be accounted a human soul—to have my humanity recognized before my sex.

I groped after this truth. "There is no sex in souls." Years afterwards I found it confirmed by St. Paul, the supposed champion of the male against the female.

It was the impossibility of finding in my surroundings any response to this passion that turned me for a time into a girl-hater. I was sorry to have been born a girl because for a girl apparently there was no human life, only a girl's life. I learned that man had his life as a human being, and his male life as well. I looked round me, and thought that women had been driven out of their inheritance of a common humanity, and had become merely females. Their minds had been cramped by this, as their bodies had been deformed by tight-lacing. They were chained to the rock of womanhood and were pleased with their chains. Made arrogant by the sensation of a wide and deep humanity at its dawn, I dreamed my destiny to be that of Perseus.

II

The days of my juvenescence seem much farther off than those of my infancy. I remember with difficulty, I remember with bitterness.

Mamma moved house again. This time the villa was less villaish. It lay on the fringe of a great wooded estate, and was near that river gorge which looked like a Turner picture, that beautiful gorge which at Downend Park had seemed as far off as the Promised Land. We had a rose garden, and a servants' entrance. We had "bettered ourselves." The cloud which had hung over the family since the failure of the Hercester Bank seemed to have lifted. Once again Mamma went into "society," but it had not the same solidity as Hercester society. She gave no dinner-parties here, only afternoon "at homes." I heard much talk about people "calling" and not calling. To live in the houses which had been built on the Gorges estate, of which ours was one, implied a concern about the precise social standing of your neighbours.... It was an atmosphere of pretentiousness. There were poor county immigrants who gave themselves airs because they were well connected, and rich town natives who perpetually strove to convince this diluted aristocracy that if blood will tell, money will shout.

It vexed me to the soul to see Mamma's servility to both parties. I could not understand her pleasure at being invited to one of those rich tradesmen's heavy dinners. I was keenly alive to the patronising airs of the demi-aristocrats. At this stage I had a profound belief in aristocracy. I had plunged early into the waters of chivalry, and fondly dreamed, after a course of Malory, that sensitive hearts and noble minds were more likely to be found in people who were "well-born" than in those whose ancestry was undistinguished.

It was not until much later in life that I realized that to be proud of anything that you possess is to be a snob secretly, and that to honour others for what they possess is to be a snob openly.

Only when I began to love people for what they were, not for what they had, did I purge myself of the last humours of my youthful snobbishness.

In these Gorges Woods days I nourished a good deal of "class feeling." I thought much of blue blood and long descent, and swelled with the certainty that I belonged to an ancient race. I looked in the glass, and my features seemed to bear witness to it. This was some consolation to me for not being pretty. I turned over the pages of Debrett, and wondered which coat of arms was mine, and what high-sounding motto.

"Let the strong and the mighty laugh at me." I will confess all the same.

It troubled me to find no mention on any page of that fat red book of a "John-Baptist" having been born. It seems to me now foolish, incredible, that I could not ask my father's name; the question was never silenced in my heart. But then I dared not risk the ruin of the palace that my imagination had reared. Always I could pass out of the world that I hated through its stately doors. I had a shrewd instinct that no one outside this palace would utter the flattering words that I longed to hear.

Want of hard work and of the society of children of my own age may have been responsible for my continual dreaming. Up to the time I was about twelve my lessons were intermittent, and when Milly went to a boarding-school I had no companion.

I had a famine in my heart, and did not know for what food I longed. I had a perpetual thirst, yet no desire to drink at any but the purest flood.

III

Across this grey indistinct time, there floats a gold thread never woven into the piece, light and unsubstantial and detached.

Scarlet fever broke out at home and I was sent away hastily. For the first time in my life I was completely separated from the house of Wingfield. A weekly letter from Mamma was the only thing that reminded me that there were Wingfields. There was so much to enchant me, and to scare me, in my new surroundings, that I had no time to think of them.

I was to stay with "the Gosboroughs." That was all I knew. My scanty wardrobe was packed and off I started. From the moment when I arrived at the station, and a tall footman picked me out of the crowd and put me into a roomy landau in which two enormous horses were fidgeting and champing, I felt exhilarated rather than shy. The tall footman, who treated me with a deference that seemed to me absurd considering our relative sizes, left me in the shadowy interior of the landau, and disappeared into the station again. I longed to put my head out of the window and ask the coachman when we were going to start, but there was something about that imposing drab back which discouraged me.

It was possible that at the Gosboroughs I should find some one who would tell me of my father…and of my mother…. The Gosboroughs would divine my thoughts…my proud thoughts, which were not for the people who lived at Gorges Woods.

The footman reappeared conducting two ladies. I liked the look of the younger one at once. She was tall and dark-haired. She wore a rose-coloured felt hat and rough tweed clothes of a masculine cut, the kind of clothes that the demi-aristocrats of Gorges Woods never wore. She had a sort of insolent, off-hand manner, which struck me as very splendid. I found myself envying the maid who hung about this magnificent creature, receiving her instructions about the luggage with many a submissive "Yes, my lady."

In the course of her arrangements she turned to me and said bluntly: "Have you brought a maid?"

I blushed, and stumbled over my answer…. Suddenly I felt very insignificant, and wished that I had not been thrust into an alien world where a maid was expected of me.

"I really beg your pardon," said my dark lady, as the carriage startled, and the light from the street lamps enabled her to see me more clearly: "I didn't see what a bit of a thing you are…. I should have said 'nurse'!"

"I haven't had a nurse for years," I answered, and a great wave of longing for old Smarden swept over me.

The dark lady laughed.

"And how old are you now?"

"Thirteen, I think."

"You *think*!" She laughed again. It was such a fine, jolly laugh, and her teeth were so beautiful that I wasn't offended.

"And what's your name?"

My usual answer to this question was "Joan Wingfield." But now I answered "John-Baptist," and thought as I uttered the words that perhaps it was in a carriage like this that my gallant father and my lovely mother had driven away after their wedding; to such music of swift hoofs they had kissed…and I forgot the existence of everything but my passionate dreams, and they had no shape…they were here and there like the wind.

I think my dark lady said, "What a weird name!" Then she heeded me no more…. It was a moonlight night, but misty. I could see clearly only for a stone's-throw round me. Now and again the light from the carriage lamps would fall on blots of copse; cottages appeared and vanished; I saw silver-grey meadows and smoking purple ploughland. Fir-trees started up to meet us, and sank down again instantly. Church steeples were strangely magnified. The bare branches of the birches looked like rigging. On we went clattering past cross-roads, up ridges, never slackening our pace. And all the time my dark lady and her companion talked about London and people there in a language which I did not understand, a curious, brief, allusive tongue. They never seemed to explain anything. Both had a basis of mutual knowledge of persons and things which made it possible for them to convey a history in a sentence, a tragedy in a word, a scandal in a meaning smile. To my raw little mind it was most puzzling how they understood each other. When my dark lady said "Poor young Rangemouth!" the elder lady replied, "I know!" and the next remark, "Can you understand her fascinations?" was at once taken up with, "A man's woman, I suppose." It was like a game of chess, with no waits between the moves.... "Have you been to Crupples before?" asked my dark lady of me. It was a relief to hear something that I could understand.

"No."

She told me then what a beautiful old house it was, praised the trees in the park, said there was a moat and a drawbridge.

"But this is dollish country after Scotland," she concluded.

IV

Both my companions were asleep when the carriage turned into a straight avenue lined with a double row of elms. They woke up as the horses' hoofs thudded over the wooden draw-bridge and clattered into the cobbled courtyard. The great door flew open. The light flashed on the footmen's silver buttons, as they hovered round the carriage, taking wraps and handing out its occupants.

I stood dazed in the big hall. A young man, a girl and a boy came in from an adjoining room, and welcomed the dark lady enthusiastically. They called her Martha, and the elder lady "Aunt Eagletower." I stood unnoticed, and crying inside because I felt so lonely. After what seemed to me an age, the little boy came up to me.

"Are you Joanna?"

"Yes," I said, happy at being assured that my presence at Crupples was not some terrible mistake.

"Mother said you were coming. She said you were thirteen, though. You can't be. You're not any bigger than I am, and I'm only eleven."

"I don't really know how old I am," I said hastily, mortified that I looked so young.

"That's funny," he said. "I thought every one knew by their birthdays."

I changed the subject.

"Who's the dark lady who came out with me from the station?"

"Mutty…. You know. Lady Martha Ladde. She's my cousin. I say! how long are you going to stay?"

"I don't know."

"I heard Mother say that if you were a good child and gave no trouble she'd keep you all the summer."

I was affronted.

"Perhaps I shan't want to stay."

"Why not? Is it nicer where you live? Crupples is a very decent place. There are lots of fish in the moat. Can you fish? I'll teach you, if you like."

A solemn butler approached the other group and said to the young girl: "Her ladyship would like to see Miss Wingfield in her room."

The girl said, "How stupid of me! I forgot all about her!" Then she came over to me and asked me if I would come upstairs and "see Mamma." I followed her upstairs, slipping now and then, to my confusion, on the polished oak steps. All the way up, the walls were hung with full-length portraits of men and women in the costume of every period from the Tudors onwards—stiff, lifeless portraits, taken individually, yet forming in the mass a complete pictorial chronicle of a great English family.

It was always winter or summer with me in these days. It had been summer in the carriage, swinging along on the easy springs, with my knees touching the knees of glorious Lady Martha, for whom already I thought of laying down my life.... It was winter now, as I watched how easily the Gosborough girl walked up those slippery stairs, as I noticed her silk stockings and well-made shoes, and detected condescension in the poise of her head. I had thought in the carriage that I was being conveyed to the sphere to which I belonged.... Now, shy and sullen and shamefaced, I recognized that I had no place there.... The shabbiness and scantiness of my little wardrobe troubled me for the first time in my life...I felt both timid and savage in my new surroundings.

Lady Gosborough was in bed. I remembered that Mamma had said she was paralyzed.... Her face had the pallor which comes from inactivity; it looked the more white and waxen because her hair was very dark, except on the temples where it was turning gray. There was something very remarkable in the expression of her eyes.... In the eyes all the activity that had been exiled from the poor limp body seemed to have taken refuge. I felt that they sprang up to meet me as I approached the bed, that they gave me the welcome that I had missed. She spoke to me very kindly, very sweetly. My heart, hardened and dried by the careless indifference of the others, sucked up the sweet tones, the dear, gentle manner, as thirsty land drinks drops of rain. The instinctive and cruel repulsion to her helplessness that had filled me when I first realized her state, a repulsion to ugliness and sickness that I have never been able to conquer wholly, was transformed into confidence. Her chestnut velvet eyes seemed to say: "I know you are a little bird wounded by life." Her intuition into my suffering gave me a sensation of happiness.

The girl left us together, after having asked me for "my keys for the housemaid." I explained with reddening cheeks that my box was not locked.

"I expect you wonder why you are here," said Lady Gosborough. "It's all very strange, isn't it? but in a few days you won't feel strange."

"I don't feel strange with you."

"That's right…. The worst of it is I can't be downstairs much. They carry me down to meals—sometimes. Which of them have you seen? That was my daughter Lettice who brought you up. Arthur is the only one near your age. He is my baby."

"Yes, I've seen him, and a boy who's grown up, and Lady Martha."

"The grown-up boy is Oliver, my eldest son. Then there is Claud, who is away, and Violet. She is grown up too."

She began to ask me questions about myself and my life. I did not try to hide myself from her; I answered willingly, but I could not always express myself. Patiently she helped me to unswaddle my obscure and stammering soul. She told me how just before her illness she had seen me for the first time, "a tiny mite," with such a sad little face.

"If I had not fallen ill—if it had not pleased God to take away the use of my limbs, I should have had you at Crupples then."

"To live?"

"Yes. Would you have liked that?"

"Yes, very much, if I could not have lived with *them*."

She stretched out a hand to me, but said nothing.

"Won't you tell me about them?" I asked. "Why does no one tell me? Do they think I don't *know*!"

My heart and brain began to tremble before the coming of the light.

"Little one, what do you know?"

"Nothing," I said, "except that my name isn't really Wingfield. Do you know, I hate the name…I hate it."

"You mustn't hate it. Mrs. Wingfield has been very kind to you."

"I don't want people to be kind to me." There was a passion in my heart if not in my voice. "I want love, even if it is unkind…. At nights I dream of such a different world—where I love every one and every one loves me. No one looks at me curiously…no one says, 'Hush!' when I come near…. My father and mother don't quarrel every minute about money!"

Lady Gosborough caressed my burning face with cool fingers. "Can you trust me?"

"Yes," I said doubtfully, for somehow I knew that she was not going to tell me what I wanted to hear.

Yet she told me beautiful things, noble things…. She adapted them to the thought of a child, and I understood well enough. I understood that I was sheltered by the name I bore; it stood between me and sorrow. She explained that my father himself had wished that his memory should be blotted out…. I was to go through life as one of the family to which I had been handed over.

"And they have been kind?" she asked anxiously.

"Yes." I longed to say that I had been starved and beaten and bullied—treated like a step-child in a fairy tale. The lie appealed to my romantic sense—a sense which has often led me far from truth—but at that moment such a romance seemed paltry by the side of what I had actually endured. I had been kept clean, I had

had good clothes to wear, and sufficient food to nourish me. My straight, agile body, clear skin and shiny hair testified that my life had been healthy. It was only my mind that had been starved, only my sensitive heart that had been beaten, only my soul that had been neglected.

Lady Gosborough kindled a new light in the obscurity of that soul…. She begged me to remember that nothing mattered except what I was…I myself…. If I were unhappy I must not be ungrateful. It might be that I should have to suffer because some other little ones were incapable of suffering.

"It would be nice, all the same, to have a little happiness for myself," I said, for I had a great horror of pain.

"I hope you will have a great deal," she answered.

That night I stood upright for hours at my bedroom window gazing into the star-strewn moat below. It seemed to me that I was changed, that I should never be the same again. A spark had darted from Lady Gosborough's soul, and transfigured mine with fire. For the first time some one had spoken to me of the dignity of existence, of the necessity for gratitude for life. The impression made on me was the more vivid because she who had said these things was the wreck of a woman…. It was from the lips of a paralytic that I first heard the gospel of joy.

I looked out over the wide park wrapped in a moonlit mist. I could hear the clash of the red deer's horns, and the long melancholy screech of the night owl. Huge oaks and elms threw gigantic, grotesque shadows on the tufted grass…. The air through the casement was soft. All this exterior world suddenly impressed itself on me like a kiss.

V

I soon discovered that Crupples was not a happy household, in spite of the many things there that should have been productive of happiness. But the sorrows of the Gosboroughs interested me, and drew out my sympathy, whereas the sorrows of the Wingfields had alienated and irritated me. If coarseness and grossness in vice have always increased my horror of it, sordidness in misery has always increased my shame and suffering at witnessing it…. At Crupples I was to see much misery, but it had an element of grandeur…. It was never common or mean. I felt it developed me instead of thwarting and stunting me.

The tragedy of Lady Gosborough was in itself grandiose, heroic, romantic…. She had been a great beauty, I learned, and a wilful one. Her father, a bookish peer of scientific attainments, had strongly objected to her engagement to Oliver Gosborough, because it was well known that the Gosboroughs were an eccentric family, whose eccentricity had too often turned to insanity. Lady Constance Lynne, however, was not to be dissuaded by her scientific Papa. She had many commonplace suitors. Oliver delighted her with his whimsical humour, his old-fashioned sporting top-hats, high stocks, his passionate love for birds and beasts and wild flowers. The English character at its best. So he seemed to Constance Lynne. Then she saw Crupples! Crupples settled it. She would often say to her children: "I married Crupples."

The queer poetic twist in Oliver Gosborough's nature turned to something less attractive when he succeeded to the title and settled down to manage Crupples. His old father had been notoriously miserly; and in middle age Oliver began to develop this unamiable weakness, which had been undiscoverable in his youth. He was much affected by the news that his younger brother's reason had given way. After this he seemed to become more and more eccentric himself. Lettice told me that as long as her mother was about all was well. She fought the idea that there was a Gosborough curse.

"Shall I tell you why so many Gosboroughs go mad?" she said one day to Lettice in my hearing. "It is simply because they are always thinking it is 'the Gosborough way.' It's a form of family pride. If they would employ their minds, would fill their idle hours with work, the spectre would fly from them."

I used to feel that spectre stalking along the passages at Crupples. I saw it behind Lord Gosborough's chair at dinner. Its derisive laughter was in Claude's fits of wild merriment. I watched Lettice coquetting with it.... It made Violet wonderful and annoying in the same moment.

I saw more of Arthur and Lettice than of Violet, yet I always felt more at ease with Violet. Lettice was so disconcerting. She would take me long rambles in the park; her air of freezing disdain when I broke the silence which weighed on my spirits made me desperately self-conscious. I was sure I had said something stupid or commonplace, something that had the Wingfield touch; and to Lettice Gosborough more than to any one else I owe the fact that for years I was afraid to be myself.

She had an inordinate pride of race, and the highest praise that she could give to any one was, "he is such a gentleman," or "she is a lady." While I absorbed these views greedily, and strove to make them mine—I was at an imitative and impressionable age—the soul of the rebel stirred in me. I thought sometimes of the squalid lane at the back of our Hercester garden, of the dirty children, prematurely aged mothers, the drunken husbands. I wondered why the monstrous difference between them and Lettice should exist, why she had too much and they too little.

VI

Arthur had a tutor, and I shared his lessons. I learned a little Latin, some French grammar, and a great deal of history and literature. I showed no great aptitude. Mr. Cranley always wrote "Very good" at the foot of my essays, but he was pained by the carelessness with which I did my preparation. I had no difficulty in getting through it, after a fashion, in a very short time. This was the temptation to which I yielded night after night. I never really applied myself to my tasks, and if Violet happened to be playing or singing in the library where Arthur and I did our "prep," I let it go till the next morning, when in the five minutes between breakfast and Mr. Cranley's arrival I managed to study enough to pass muster.

I can see Violet now at the piano, her fine well-cut features illuminated by her wild soul. She sat very still on the music-stool, with a very straight back, her head slightly upraised, and her rather large well-formed hands bringing such sounds from the keys as made me wonder if this could possibly be the same detestable instrument that Winifred Wingfield played.

Sometimes she would sing too. Her singing voice was not in the least like her rather petulant, high-pitched speaking voice, with its excess of emphasis and abrupt cadences. She could poise her voice without the slightest trouble. She gave to each phrase a separate greatness; sometimes the passion in her voice moved me so much that the tears fell on my Latin primer. I dared not to wipe them away, for fear that Arthur should see me and tease me.

During these moments I felt as if the doors of my nature had been flung open. There poured of them a crowd of bright spirits. They danced on the threshold, singing "We are free! We are free! Music has made us free!" In a moment I dreamed a hundred tumultuous dreams—heroic, erotic, infantine, splendid, all at once. In imagination I was calling, "Oh, come to me! My beautiful one, come to me!" To whom did I speak? For whom this passion, untrammelled by conceptions of good and evil? I dared not give the being a name, but I knew very well that in this ecstasy I could always feel Lady Martha, could always see her insolent face, and the long eyes out of the corners of which fire crept and flew back again....

VII

When Arthur went to school, Mr. Cranley left, and I had no more regular lessons for a time.

A French governess came to rub up Lettice's French before she "came out"—the great event of her debut in society was near—and I attended the *causeries*, but Mademoiselle and Lettice seldom noticed that I was there...I picked up what I could by listening.

My real education was carried on in the library, where for hours I read undisturbed. Lady Gosborough was undergoing treatment from a Swedish doctor that autumn, and I saw her seldom. As I grew out of my clothes, some of Lettice's old ones were altered for me. I liked them, but they formed a taste for a quiet, expensive style of dress which was disastrous to me in later years.

I learned to ride, too, under Violet's direction. She was an accomplished horsewoman, and found it hard to be patient with my deficiencies.

"Your seat's good enough, but your hands!" she would exclaim. "The horse has as much sense as you have. Don't treat the poor fellow as if he were a wooden horse on a merry-go-round!"

I loved horses, but I could never get on terms with them, and could not decide whether this was due to temperament or to want of experience. Violet admitted that I had plenty of pluck, and could "stick on." There her commendation ceased.

Lord Gosborough's "queerness" and Lady Gosborough's invalid state kept visitors away from Crupples. Once or twice while I was there Oliver had a few friends to shoot. Violet and I, in thick nailed boots, followed the guns. I grew used to seeing the slaughtered pheasants piled up in a shining heap, and caught the infection of pride in a good bag.

To one of these "shoots" came Lady Martha Ladde. I heard of her coming with a beating heart, and creeping into her bedroom on the afternoon of her arrival put a red rose on her pillow, accompanied by four lines of verse which owed more than was right to Shelley. She came by the same train that had brought me to Crupples for the first time, a year earlier. I wondered if she would know me again…. To myself I seemed entirely changed. Crupples had been the first test of my adaptability, and I could not help knowing that I had passed the test with an ease which surprised me. All the little tricks of manner and conversation in which no one can ever be instructed, but which Gosboroughs and others of their class appear to absorb with their mother's milk, had not escaped my notice. I was no longer "farouche" externally, though I had not lost an atom of my shyness of soul. I knew as much about the history of Crupples and the Gosboroughs as any member of the family, and there was, I believe, little to suggest that my early years had been spent in very different surroundings. When Lord Gosborough "tipped" Arthur, he tipped me too, and the possession of money completed my transformation.

It was rarely that I thought of the Wingfields. Once a fortnight I was reminded by Lady Gosborough to write, and I wrote, either to Milly or Mamma. I wrote the kind of letter that says nothing. Their letters to me I would often keep in my pocket for days, unread. Sometimes I had twinges of conscience about my increasing scorn for the whole family, and my desire to forget them, but the banality of the letters, the complacency with which I could see Mamma forming the words, "care of the Right Honble. Lord Gosborough" underneath my name on her envelopes, quickly dried up the stream of remorseful affection which rose when my conscience was active.

VIII

Lady Martha came down to dinner with the rose tucked into her dress. Her neck looked dazzlingly white above her black velvet gown.

She was radiant, gay, and most entertaining. The Gosboroughs went little into society, but Lady Martha was in the thick of its diversions, full of its latest stories, able to poke fun at its notabilities, to tell us what people were reading and eating, whom they were marrying, and what was their newest religion. "Mutty" had an appreciative audience. Oliver and his regimental friends rocked with laughter; Lord Gosborough was less gloomy and irritable than usual; Violet and Lettice said frequently, "Isn't she wonderful!"

Only Claude and I sat silent at the table, Claude because he took no interest in anything except music, and I because any "smart" talk of this kind even in these days roused my antagonism, and brought before me that vision of the inhabitants of Bull Lane, Hercester, who stood to me for "the poor," for those who had too little of everything except dirt and misery.

I was utterly ignorant that revolutionary ideas were in the air, that thousands of people in England at this time were beginning to question the sacredness of the rights of property, to deny that there was no connection between the purple and fine linen of Lady Martha Ladde and the rags of Martha Jones, to cherish immense illusions as to the approach of a day of reckoning. My attitude was wholly instinctive. I never heard the expression "lower classes" without a shudder. If they were "lower," what had made them so? Sometimes—though I had a terror of crowds and to this day have never been in a vast assembly of people without feeling physical repulsion to the contiguity of the huge, sweating mob body—a voice inside me would cry out with the people's voice against the untroubled assurance of the Gosboroughs and their kind that they had a right to their "too much." "We are as good as you!" this unheard voice hurled at Lady Martha. "Some of us are worth all of you put together." By "we" I think I understood all who are outcasts, all who are oppressed, but nothing was very clear. Another side of my nature was hypnotized by beauty and luxury. I admired those who were on terms of familiarity with them. I admired and envied what I felt could never be acquired. What education, what advantages, what freedom that wealth confers, could turn a Bull Lane child into a Lady Martha? Generations had gone to make her. I studied her. Was she a high type of humanity after all? Or only a lovely animal, a thoroughbred, whose flesh was firm and white, whose hands were fine and delicate, whose walk was like a procession? Was she so witty? She never said a really witty thing, but her conversation danced along on light feet.

It was she who first taught me that hate, and love which has no spiritual fraternity, are much the same thing. I hated and loved Lady "Mutty."

IX

I was with her alone at last. It was autumn, I remember. The grass in the park was damp and strewn with decaying leaves. A north-east wind had brought a soft mist with it that deadened all noise.

There was I, overjoyed to be walking by her side, but she was discontented because she had strained a muscle in her back and could not hunt that day. Her entire obliviousness to the fact that she was conferring joy, quickly affected my own triumphant gladness. I recognized for the first time the imaginative quality in my attraction to her. In absence my devotion flourished and flowered profusely. Actual intercourse was a disillusionment. I fought this recognition, for it was bitter to me…. Had I but seen as clearly that autumn day as I do now, that I was born not to rest in any human affection, I should surely have been content to dream of it, and should have shunned beating my wings in vain against realities. But I could not believe that the "in vain" was permanent. Some day, some day, I urged, the closed gates will open, and the interior will be more glorious than the fairest dream.

I walked by her side in silence, thinking that it would be sweeter to be indoors, where we could sit by the fire and hold each other's hands. The thought that when we did go in I should not be able to linger about her, overclouded the bright present. Tears came to my eyes as she talked of the world where she was sure of admiration and distinction, and of delights which I should never know. Everything that she said hurt me, because it was all bound up with complete separation. She spoke of her approaching departure.

"I can't stand Crupples for long," she said. "The hunting's fair, … but everything else gives me the hump. There's a blight over the place."

"But you'll come back next year?" And as I put the question, I implored her dumbly not to hurt me. I felt so defenceless, clothed only in my sensitiveness, that was so easy to wound, so easy to destroy, and to sacrifice.

"That depends. I may be married by then. I don't think Edward would like Crupples."

"Edward!"

I felt as if I had lost the sensation of all my other limbs in the terrible beating of my heart.

"You saw him the other day. He came over to luncheon from the Winberrys'."

"You mean that Lord Edward Pomfret?" To me my voice sounded violent and unfamiliar, but Lady Martha was insensible to the change.

"Yes. He's my young man. We're not exactly engaged yet; but we are 'walking out'." She laughed merrily; her words and her laughter smote me in the face. I staggered as if, indeed, she had given me a physical blow. "And that would not have been so vulgar," I thought with a spasm of rage.

"You mustn't do it…. You shan't marry him!" My spirit contracted to remember the bald-headed soldier with the rather prominent pale eyes, the tall weedy figure, the large moustache, the tired, bored manner.

"Not him!" I cried, poisoned by the remembrance. "Oh, my angel, not him!"

It was the first time I had ever called her by an endearing name. As it passed my lips, I seemed to lose all consciousness that I was a raw child, a child of her own sex, and to become master of the secrets of love.

"You funny little thing!" she said. "What's wrong with Edward?"

"I could love you more in a moment than he in a thousand years!"

She laughed. Then perhaps she felt that she was wounding me, for she became serious suddenly.

"When you are older you will know that there is a wonderful mystery in a man's love for a woman." This struck me as commonplace, and I stuck out my underlip in scorn. "It is as mysterious as life itself." Her voice had become impetuous. Her eyes shone. "I have been a tyrant all my life. I have never thought of obeying any one, or doing anything except what I wanted to do. I love my liberty…yet now he dominates me…I humiliate myself

to please him…I don't even know whether I love him or not….
I just feel that it has to be, that we can't help ourselves. I can't
escape."

I was silent, because I could not express the vague tumult of
condemnation within me.

"Not that I want to escape!" Her light, mocking tone returned.
"One must marry, you know. I don't want to be an old maid.
I had always intended to have my fling until I was thirty…. I
counted without my Edward! It won't be a very brilliant match,
but we shall be quite comfortable. What's the matter, John? Are
you cold?"

"No," I said, but it was not true. A dreadful chill had seized
me, and my teeth were chattering. I felt an almost physical bitterness in my mouth; her words were poison to me. I looked at her
from that day with different eyes, and across a depth of separation
that my dreams could not bridge.

Later, when she had left Crupples, I heard them all talking
of her engagement, and was surprised to find that they viewed
it with approval.

Why I suffered from it I could not tell. The very thought of
her beautiful manly brow, of her whole noble, graceful person in
proximity to "Edward," filled me with horror. I hoped I should
not be told when the wedding was to take place, for I dreaded
that day as a day that was going to inflict on me unheard-of
tortures.

I was not told, because by the time it came round I was far
away from Crupples.

X

Lady Gosborough assured me, when, suffocated by sobs, I went
to her room to say good-bye, that I was going back to the Wingfields

106

only for a visit. She said it was right and kind, and that I must be brave. The time would soon pass; I was to look on Crupples as my home, my room looking out on the moat would always be called mine. But all her dear consoling words could not remove a presentiment from my ill-divining soul. I clung to her and entreated her not to send me away, although the carriage was at the door, and my luggage had been sent to the station some hours earlier.

"Oh, dearest," I sobbed in anguish, "let me stay. If you send me away, I shall never see you again. I know I shall never see you again!"

She wiped away my tears tenderly with her living hand. The dead one lay inert and heavy outside the white velvet bed-quilt; to-day it filled me with terror.

"We are in God's hands."

This was the first time I had heard her speak of God. It made a great impression on me, for Violet, when I had once asked her why Lady Gosborough did not make me go to church on Sundays, had told me that her mother thought it "all nonsense."

"We are in God's hands." That steadied me. Violet came in to say I should miss the train if I did not come at once, and scolded me for upsetting her mother. She pulled me away from the bed, but there was really no need, for my grief and rebellion had left me; I was very sure at that moment that there was a God. For the first time the possibility of divine compensation for suffering flashed on me.

"I'll feed your rabbit till you come back," said Arthur as I got into the carriage.

I smiled at him, knowing that he loved me, and that this was his way of expressing his love.

One of the Crupples housemaids travelled with me as far as the junction where I had to change for Ripton. She seemed surprised when I kissed her at parting.

"I hope we shall soon see you back, Miss," she said with her well-trained domestic manner.

"Oh yes, I shall soon be back," I answered, trying not to break down. When the train moved out of the junction, and I had waved my hand to her for the last time, Crupples receded into infinite distance. It seemed a great while ago since I had felt with my whole soul Lady Gosborough's last kiss, her tender tears, and caressing right arm. At the thought of the Wingfields and Gorges Woods every trace of goodness and gentleness disappeared from my young heart. I arrived possessed by some malignant demon, a demon who urged me to scorn everything in the Wingfield household, to be irritated by every question, angered by every slovenly habit, distressed by every error in taste. I noticed that Mamma, who had written so touchingly to Lady Gosborough that her heart ached to see me again, was apparently anxious to hide her affection when she had gained her object and got me back.

I think I must have been away two years, but it may have been longer. The family seemed to have changed greatly, or was it I that had changed? I could not settle down. Violet and Lettice wrote to me constantly at first, and so did Arthur. Their letters had a blessed touch of originality which warmed my heart, chilled by an atmosphere in which every one thought other people's thoughts, and took their ideas from books and newspapers.

Arthur's letters were love-letters! Most of them began "My darling Sweetheart," and contained calculations as to the number of days and months and years that must be lived through somehow before we could be married. In one he wrote: "Do forgive me, darling, for not writing before, but I am sending you mushrooms to make up for it.... A heron has been seen here by the moat several times lately: oh, darling, if you could see him! Oh, sweet-heart, when we are married, what fun it will be! Do write to me, and let me know at least if you are all right." In another: "My wig! how I do miss you. I am quite dull in every way since you went." Another assured me that "I have made up my mind to marry you, bar *jocking*.... My love for you compared with my love for any one else is as an ellefant to a flea."

But no extracts do justice to Arthur's letters. Here is one entire:

"DEAREST DARLING,—My love for you is at the highest point. When you come to see me at school, bring me a few bits of butter-scotch if you don't mind. If it is any trouble to you at all, don't trouble about it by any means. If I were asked to sell your letters, if I sold them at all—which would be an impossibility for me to do—I should at least charge £100,000 for a quarter of one. It is frightfully cold in the mornings now. I want to know in your next letter whether you have another fiancé besides me; if you have, his name. I wonder if any one else would be cruel enough to try and take you from me; if so, whether you would be cruel enough to marry the villain. You would break my heart if you did. Darling, anyhow I hope and pray and believe that you would never be so wicked. Think of what I would do for you, how I love you, how madly in love I am with you. Write and promise me soon that you will never be so wicked, so *mercyless*.

"You are the dearest of the dear.
"From your affectionate lover,
"ARTHUR"

Dear little letters, written in a large boyish scrawl, what slight value I put on them then! Now they give me the same joy that all young simple things give me. If men could keep the *cor pueri*! When I see the sticky little leaves open in the spring, I think of

Arthur Gosborough and of his young heart opening as simply and naturally, and I am steeped in an emotion which wipes out the intervening twenty years.

XI

Lady Gosborough was dead. The news did not come as a shock to me. I had known when I had said good-bye to her that it was a last good-bye. Violet wrote and told me that she had died of heart failure during the night, and that she could not have suffered at all. "Only last Wednesday she spoke of you, and said: 'I wonder if Mrs. Wingfield would let Johnnie come back now. I miss the child.' She said, too, that she was afraid you would always have to suffer a great deal, but that you would be all right because you were made of fine stuff.... My father is terribly upset, and not at all well. We shall all go abroad for a year, I think. None of us can bear Crupples now she is gone. Where has she gone? I ask myself.... Now I would like to believe in God.... I would like to believe that her suffering will be made up for.... I forget that I am writing to a child. Sometimes you talked so wisely, I forgot you were a child. But this reminds me. Be careful about Arthur. I believe it's more than a childish fantasy. I stand to him now in his mother's place, and I would rather you didn't go and see him at school, even if you were able to do so, which isn't likely."

As I read this letter, I felt my soul turn pale within me. For the first time I realized how slight was the tie that bound me to the Gosboroughs. Violet never even suggested that I should go abroad with them. She said nothing about my going to Lady Gosborough's funeral, which was a relief and yet a wound. When I had been at Crupples I had been treated like one of the family, but now I knew that I was very much outside it, and I wished, as rebellion corroded my heart, that I had never left the house of bondage. I was ashamed that I could not mourn Lady Gosborough's death unselfishly. Where grief at her loss ended, and bitterness at being thrust back by it into a milieu that I loathed began, I could not tell. They were confused within me as good and bad were hopelessly confused.

Mamma, chiefly because Alice flatly refused to resume my education, sent me to Ripton High School with Milly. Milly, as a result of the entrance examination, was placed in a high form, I in a low one with children younger than I was. I could not understand this, for I felt that I knew more than Milly. I was a complete failure at this school, both morally and intellectually, and I have a less lucid impression of the time I spent there than of any period of my life. I have forgotten all my school-fellows and all my school-mistresses, except one. This was the prettiest mistress, who taught drawing; I formed an ardent attachment to her, but intercourse with her was more of a disillusionment than intercourse with Lady Martha had been. She was, to tell the truth, common and uninteresting, but I exerted imagination heroically, and wrote her letters which embarrassed her greatly. I soon grew weary of Miss Lamb, and transferred my affections to a barmaid who sat in front of us in the village church near Gorges Woods, which the Wingfields attended on Sunday afternoons. My acquaintance with Miss Brown was confined entirely to an exchange of smiles. But her smile meant so much to me that I went to church merely to get it. A starving man may not find much sustenance in a lollipop, but he will probably take it in preference to nothing at all.

The hunger I had to find some one to love burnt me more with every inch that was added to my stature. It was *to love* I yearned more than to *be loved*, and I was entirely free from sexual instincts. When Mamma pointed out to me what a miserable existence an unmarried woman led, holding up Alice and Winifred as object-lessons, asserting that they were bitter and morose merely because they had not married, I listened coldly. "The love of a good man," was Mamma's ideal.

"Have you been so very happy?" I asked her once, with the cruelty of youth. She burst into tears, but protested that her children had made up to her for everything. I wondered how they had done it, since they had inflicted cruel disappointments on her.

IV
EDUCATION

"When I read the book, the biography famous,
And is this then (said I) what the author calls a man's life?
(As if any man really knew ought of my life,
And so will some one when I am dead and gone write my life?
Why, even I myself, I often think, know little or nothing of my real life,
Only a few hints, a few diffused faint clues and indirections
I seek for my own use to trace out here.)"

[Walt Whitman, *Leaves of Grass*]

I

"A few diffused faint clues and indirections." That is the most that I have achieved in the survey of my childhood and youth.

What has been my object? Has it been worth while?

It is not my life that I have sought to trace out here, so much as my progress towards the great day when I knew for the first time why I was created, and for what I had been chastised and reproved, and prohibited a resting-place in love or work or pleasure.

I call unto me souls like me, and beg them to listen. It is for "the brotherly mind" I write, not for that of the foreigner.

"Is this, then, what they call a woman's life?" I have often asked myself, when I have read works of fiction, or autobiography or biography, which had for their aim the dissection of a woman's heart. She is the heroine of a happy love-affair, or the victim of a tragic passion. She plays with men, as with fire, and the fire burns her; or she tempts them, and they fall. Her childhood is but a preparation for this great game where she is either to triumph or to fail, this great rite where she is to be priestess or victim. She exists for certain episodes in man's life. Her glory is to bring him into the world. It is maternity that crowns her existence, and the life of a barren woman is always represented as miserable and incomplete. The history of women, as chronicled not by male historians only, but by themselves, is the history of their devotion to men, or of the passions that they have inspired in men. Sexual love, beautiful and hideous, noble and base, is the promised land for every girl born into the world, and those who see it only, and never enter in, are the despised and rejected ones, the loveless ones whose heart-hunger excites pity or contempt.

The idea that there may be women, neither wives nor mothers, nor mistresses, who are yet fulfilling themselves completely, who are not poor or starved in their singleness, but rich and fed with angels' food, is one which the natural man rejects as incredible, and the natural woman entertains perhaps for a moment in a lifetime, and dismisses for ever as the folly of dreams.

Yet in the very ancient ceremony of the Consecration of Virgins, it is written: "Without diminishing in any degree the honour with which Thou hast clothed the married state, nay, even in confirming and enlarging the blessing which from the beginning Thou hast pronounced upon that union, it hath pleased Thee that some souls of *nobler stamp* should decline the marriage bond, and thus being called to realize the lofty mystery which that bond represents, should abstain from earthly espousals, and aspire with all their hearts' whole love to that divine union of which earthly espousals are but the type and symbol."

When I became acquainted with those sublime words with which the Catholic Church exhorts the nun on the day of her profession, my turbulent life had almost reached its meridian. Yet they brought back to me all the finest aspirations of my youth, aspirations that soared far beyond the fruition of earthly love. And I was touched with a profound pity for those who, through their birth and upbringing, are wholly ignorant of the existence of that mystical union, the definite goal for aspirations which beat their luminous wings in vain in the atmosphere of this world.

In my struggles towards the light of love, on which the nurse-maid Nennie, my unknown father and mother, Lady Martha, the drawing-mistress at school, yes, even the barmaid, all had an influence, I never dreamed of a fairy prince who should deliver me from the anguish of unfulfilled desire. I had a wild fanatical hatred of the idea of marriage. For years I could not see a wedding without a pang, a pang caused not by jealousy, but by terror. The lamb in the embraces of the wolf—this was my conception of the honeymoon.

The mind of the "foreigner" will not understand this, but the brotherly mind will run to me.

Brotherly minds of mine, neglected in the study of woman-hood, this was written for you! You remember your dazzlingly white youth, when your hearts were ardent, when they dilated with passion, yet were free from all definite desires, because each desire dissolved into beauty itself! For you the symbol always rose from the object, like the fragrant cloud from burning incense. What were the material grains to you? You could not touch and handle the smoke, but it was yours to see it, to follow it heavenwards with wistful eyes.

II

I cannot remember when I first began to cherish a great ambition to write. I know I wrote very little before I left Crupples. At no time could I write easily, and at first I shrank from expressing any personal feeling, still less any personal experience. The pleasure that I got out of writing was from the first mingled with pain and humiliation. It seemed to me that if I could but learn to express things beautifully, the famine in my heart would vanish. The trouble was that I could never cherish any illusion that what I wrote was of any value. My first efforts were ballads, for I believed myself to be a poet, and considered poetry the only form of literature worth considering. These ballads were ballads of failure and defeat. My heroes all failed. They were betrayed and forsaken.

I had a liking for the grandiose, and while attending a day-school where I was always at the bottom of the class except in history and literature, I wrote of Vikings seeking death alone in burning ships when defeat was near, of dethroned kings, of prisoners eating out their hearts in dungeons, of exiles returning to find their loves married to other men. In imagination I lived in a world where suffering and death were the common lot. Distrustful of my gift for verse, which was indeed very slight, though not always ignoble, I turned to what seemed to me the easier medium of prose, and wrote one or two short stories which were as gloomy as the plays of Cyril Tourneur or John Ford, whom at this period I preferred to Shakespeare. A dreadful attraction for the abnormal and perverse things in life began to have power over me, and the sweet purity of my instinctive antagonism to the ordinary dreams and ambitions of girlhood was obscured by clouds rising from a mysterious abyss into which my youth and innocence gazed without fathoming its darkness.

III

Who is the artist? Any one, I suppose, with the desire for expression, that torturing desire which is sometimes, as in my case, so far greater than the skill which interprets it, whether in music or paint or bronze or the black word on the white paper.

At fifteen I was steeped in great literature, yet I could not rest in its beauty. I hungered to produce, yet what I did produce turned me sick with its ineffectualness, and barrenness of invention.

I had not discovered that the secret of learning to do a thing is to do it, to do it constantly, perseveringly, bravely, to shun despondency as Satan, and exaltation as Beelzebub. My swelling pride ignored this humble course. I dreamed of glorious future achievements and tore up present mean ones. There is this to be said for my dreaming: it consoled me for all that I missed in life.

Mamma found my "Ballad of the Viking Thorwald." An old lady, rather deaf, came to luncheon. She was a novelist, but I did not know that. After luncheon Mamma said to the old lady: "I want to read you something that this child has written. I think it wonderful."

I felt myself blushing to the roots of my short, thick hair, but Milly told me afterwards that I was deathly pale.

"No, no!" I cried in anguish.

"I should like to hear it," said the old lady with condescension.

At the first line, delivered in Mamma's high-pitched, over-emphatic voice, I saw a sneering smile on Alice's face, and I rushed out of the room.

Once outside, I was rather sorry I had not stayed. I began wondering if my favourite lines—

"His flaming heart returns to fire,
No cold corruption can it know—
The mighty sea his dirge shall quire,
He is not mocked by human woe"

would be appreciated. I sat on the stairs, tingling with expectation.

Presently the old lady and Mamma came out of the dining-room. They were smiling, which I thought a bad sign. Mamma, detecting me bundled up at the foot of the stairs, called out that Miss Ould wanted to speak to me.

I slouched over, self-conscious and miserable.

Miss Ould looked at me kindly.

"Little girl, I want to give you this for your modesty in going out of the room just now."

She put half a crown in my hand. I had a vague idea that she was all wrong, and that it was pride or hatred of Alice which had led to my flight, but I was silent.

"Say 'thank you,'" said Mamma. As I did not obey, partly because I was choking with disappointment that it was my modesty and not my genius which was being recognized, she added: "Are these the manners you learned at Lady Gosborough's?"

At the mention of that dear name, the tears came to my eyes. Miss Ould intervened.

"She's shy. I like children to be shy. Well, Joanna, I think you will write something of mark some day."

"Do you?" I cried. "Thank you! Oh, thank you!"

I hugged that encouragement to my heart for years. It was the first compliment, and the last, that I received from a comrade in letters!

IV

What I called vaguely "the impersonal life" was not my aim. I would live entirely in an imaginary world, and fly the pleasures and the pains of the real one. I schooled myself to love solitude, and believed honestly that I was never so happy as when alone poring over some book. I read in Aristotle—a translation of the "Ethics" was at this time my Bible—that the man who loves solitude is either a beast or a god, and I was anxious to prove myself the god.

There were times when I relaxed my mental and emotional austerity. At such periods of relaxation I wanted to be like other girls. I demanded new clothes, and took great trouble, if Mamma conceded them, that they should be nice clothes. I had an eye for colour, and was distressed if my clothes were badly made, but I don't think I was vain in the ordinary sense of the word. I imagined that I looked plain but interesting, weighed down by the cruel conviction that it would have been better for me if I had never been born; and the glass reflecting a pink, wistful baby-face with an incongruously powerful nose, and a pair of bright blue eyes, "glass eyes," as Smarden had called them, always irritated me. I never looked in the glass if I could help it. Once when I was fielding in a school cricket-match—my early prowess at cricket was easily maintained now that the competitors were girls—I made a wonderful catch, and heard some one among the spectators say, "What a pretty child!" This mortified me exceedingly, for it had no relation to my secret ambitions and hopes.

A very different sensation was roused in me when Madame Pohlakoff, who was sitting to Mamma for her portrait, said in my hearing: "Your youngest daughter has a very noble forehead." The horrible glass, when, just afterwards, I went up to brush my hair for luncheon, did not confirm the Russian princess's words, but they pleased me all the same, perhaps because I myself when looking at any one always focussed the brow first, and if it were too round, or too narrow, or vexed with little cares, withheld my admiration of the face beneath.

Why Madame Pohlakoff was in England, and how she came to be painted by Mamma I cannot say. I fancy, from what I knew of her later, that the commission for her portrait was an act of generosity on her part, for when it was finished she never sent for it, but told Mamma to regard it as hers, and to sell it if she could.

She was staying in the neighbourhood of Gorges Woods with Lady Rackersham, but on the days she came for her sittings she would lunch with us, keeping on the Russian court-dress in which she was being painted. In her national head-dress encrusted with pearl and turquoise, with rubies and diamonds shooting fire here and there in the dense blue-and-white, her white brocade dress cut very low and in a straight line across her marble-white bosom and shoulders, which bore the scrutiny of daylight bravely, she looked as much out of place as one of the famous Crupples stone chimneypieces would have done had it been set up in the Wingfields' trifling dining-room, with its furniture on the hire system, and its insipid family portraits, and interiors of foreign cathedrals from Mamma's facile brush.

I used to gaze at her transfixed with admiration, watching with profound enjoyment the lips that said such delicate and witty things. She recognized my absorption with an easy smile, the smile of a beautiful woman who accepts such admiration formally as a sovereign accepts the cheers of a crowd. She had spoken to all the others, but to me not a word. In this silence I found something exquisite, as if what we had to say to each other could not be spoken until the right moment came. Her voice was lower than most English voices, suffused with a slight opaque quality. Alice called it "gruff." Her dark hair was swept back in a powerful fold under the gorgeous head-dress. I noticed that tears often came into her beautiful eyes without any reason that was obvious. Once when there was a family row at the luncheon table, and Alice addressed Mamma in the bitter, scornful way to which we had grown so sadly accustomed, she rose to her feet, and remained standing for a moment, her whole attitude expressing a noble and severe indignation. The strange action made a great impression on me, and I knew she was not speaking the truth when, with a laugh, she sat down again and said with her charming foreign intonation:

"You will excuse! I had thought we had finished."

That was a half-holiday, and, the meal over, I went into the schoolroom to read. I had no room of my own. I shared a bedroom with Milly, and I learned concentration from being compelled to read and study where people talked, and even walked over you occasionally.

This day, however, the room was empty. I had an essay to write for the next day on "Perseverance," or some such vague banality; but the only words that formed themselves in my brain were: "She ought to have died untouched, for only a god could have loved her without being ashamed."

Madame Pohlakoff sailed into the dusty, ink-stained schoolroom, for which she looked too large and radiant, as a racing yacht might on a muddy pond.

"Your Mamma says something must dry. I find them tedious. Moreover your excellent Papa has just re-entered from his office, and I find his manner—*comme il me regarde* [how he looks at me]—offensive."

"He is not my father," I said, reddening.

"No! that surprises me nothing. And what is going on behind this little boy forehead?" She stroked my brow caressingly.

"I was thinking of your husband," I said bluntly.

"Which one?" She laughed merrily. "I have had two husbands."

I gazed at her helplessly.

"Does it so surprise you?"

My answer was tears.

Why they did not seem utterly foolish to her I don't know. She sat down by my side, and with an impulsive tender movement put her arm round my neck and drew my head on to her bosom. What bliss I felt at the touch of that cool, beautiful flesh. "Oh, if this were my mother, my own mother!" I thought.

"Poor little soul, so easy to slay!" she said. "I understand *parfaitement* [perfectly]. You do not like to think of me married too...to a Mr. Wingfield."

I was seized with a wonderful joy that she had come so near the truth.

"Nor to any one," I said, half to myself. But she was quick, and heard.

"Ah well.... That is life. We are born, we marry, we die.... I think I could not have married an Englishman, however.... You, too, will marry, little one."

"No," I said. "Do you know what Keats says? That is how I feel."

"What does he say, you dear little thing?"

I quoted solemnly: "Notwithstanding your advice I shall never marry, though the most beautiful creature in the world were waiting for me at the end of a journey.... The roaring of the wind outside is my wife, and the stars through the window-panes are my children."

"Alas, he was a man!"

"He was a poet," I said.

"And you are a poet?"

I felt suddenly small and humbled.

"No. I wish I were...but I know what poets feel."

"You have the poet's heart?"

I was silent.

"That will bring you great suffering without the poet's gift to comfort you."

I felt the inexorable truth of this, but put up a fight.

"I may be able to write something."

"Yes, ...but believe me, your heart will always be the greatest thing about you...your little human heart. I felt it the first day.... I saw it shining in this milieu, like a pearl in a rubbish-heap."

She moved my head from her breast. Any movement that threatened to take her away, and with her the depth of monstrous wealth that her tenderness had opened, was intolerable.

"Oh, don't go!"

"There spoke the heart! I am sorry when you shall love.... You will be *déchirée* [torn up], consumed. What a temperament! *Ecrivain* [writer]? Oh no... Why, your thoughts will be burnt before you can get them on to this!" She tapped my exercise-book.

Her words were like shafts of light...discovering strange things in the darkness. I contrasted her expressiveness with the awkward dumbness of English-women, if their souls found themselves for a moment in contemplation of the interior life.

"Was the father, I wonder, a Russian? This hair is not like the English fair hair.... Often in Russia I sit down and talk like this to one I have not met before, and may not meet again for forty years...perhaps never again in this world. Yes, we Russians talk easily about eternal questions. It may be a stupid way of passing the time, but if you are used to it, it seems strange to be with people who clown, or are silent. We all have a little playful spirit...a butterfly soul playing over the real one. It carries us away...and persuades us that all intercourse should be light...and all pleasures silly. It is quite right to let it deceive others, but in England they let it deceive themselves, until they have no more the power to go below the surface. What are we? In what do we believe? For what do we hope? It is good to speak of these sometimes, but in England they are flippant or phlegmatic when one turns such questions inside out. Yet their butterfly selves flitting on the surface are heavier and less radiant than ours. Remember it is a good thing not to mind being stupid. To talk cleverly about stupid things, as the English will—that is truly *embêtant* [annoying]! How the child listens. That is truly Slav!"

Alice came in, but Madame Pohlakoff continued to hold me in her arms.

"My mother is quite ready for you now," said Alice, in that bitter-sweet voice which always roused the devil in me.

"I come." She rose to her feet and gathered up her long train over her arm. "Courage, little friend, and *au revoir.*"

Innate curiosity triumphed over superficial good manners. "I supposed she's been complaining to you," said Alice. "I must tell you that she never speaks the truth. My mother spoils her…she has her own way in everything…yet she is never grateful. If you knew what my mother has done for her you would be surprised that she can behave so badly."

Madam Pohlakoff looked at Alice with a lofty coldness, a disdain which affected me more than it did Alice. She took out her cigarette case, and slowly lighted a cigarette.

"And you, Mademoiselle…. Do you behave well to your mother? But you make entire, complete mistake. Those tears are not, as you think, the tears of one who complains. So holy they are, so touching, so wise, so great a credit to this little one, that… But I waste my time. You could not understand if you had a thousand years in which to think over it!"

She smoked her cigarette insolently at each pause she made, and she paused often, to find the right English words. I expected to see Alice crumple up, but she seemed unaffected by Madame Pohlakoff's indictment.

"I expect you think she is much younger than she is. She is nearly grown up, nearly sixteen! I never cried at her age."

"No, Mademoiselle? But perhaps you forget. It is long time ago."

With that she walked out of the room, with a look that was bright with the gleam of battle. Her last remark did affect Alice, who was very sensitive about her age. She vented her wounded vanity on me.

"Little beast!" she said. "You have been putting her against us."

"I never even mentioned you."

"I daresay not, but you cried, and got pity."

For once I refused to be drawn into a vain, miserable wordy quarrel. My preoccupation with some secluded life, some profoundly secret thought, had grown immensely during those minutes when my head had lain on that beautiful bosom. I was absorbed in such sweet concentration that Alice's venom spluttered harmlessly over me. To be angry with the passing irritations of reality seemed impossible at that moment.

V

Such were the joys of my young life. In events, however eagerly anticipated, I found disillusion and weariness. Moments when a soul came near, moments of communion, I stored in my heart and sealed with an inviolable seal.

The next thing that happened was that Lady Rackersham invited me to luncheon at Gorges Court. This caused a commotion at Fernleigh, Gorges Woods. Lady Rachersham had never "called" on Mamma, nor on any of the tenants of the houses which had been built on her husband's property. At first Mamma was inclined to be flattered by the distinction conferred on me, but Alice soon talked her round. Lady Rackersham had recently given evidence in a notorious divorce case, she was tarred with the same brush as the principals in the affair. She was not a "nice" woman, said Alice.

"You who take boarders for the High School"—this was one of the ways in which Mamma tried to augment her inadequate income—"how can you think of letting any one in this house visit that woman? What would the council say? It's not to be thought of."

Mamma said that Madame Pohlakoff came to Fernleigh from Gorges Court. Why should I not go to Gorges from Fernleigh? Alice retorted that Madame Pohlakoff's visits were a matter of business, and even so she regretted them.

"I believe she is just as bad as Lady Rackersham; but of course any one can take you in. You ask Papa what he thinks of your Madame Pohlakoff!"

The discussion raged at the breakfast table.

"Oh, she's been a gay lady in her time," said Mr. Wingfield with a knowing smile.

"That's a lie!" I shouted out. "How dare you even mention her name!"

"Don't, Baby, don't!" whispered Milly, the peacemaker.

"I won't have her insulted! You say these things because she won't have anything to do with you. She thinks you all dirt except Mamma…so you abuse her."

"You ought to be whipped," said Mr. Wingfield.

"Yes, that is your one idea!" I was in such a passion that nothing could have stopped me. "That, and kissing, and doctoring used stamps so that they can be used again!"

I think it was the allusion to this very petty form of swindling in which I had watched him indulge from my infancy that maddened him. At any rate he threw his plate of porridge at me. Most of the porridge went on the cloth, but the plate hit me, and my lip began to pour blood.

"Take that, you little bastard!"

The blow and the word stung my memory into activity.

"Yes, you have called me that before…that day in the nursery at Hercester when you seduced Nennie."

I expected another blow, but he seemed to collapse, and his fat red cheeks turned a pale green.

"What do you think of a young girl using such language!" said Alice.

Milly and our two boarders looked terror-stricken, as if a tiger had suddenly been let loose in the dining-room.

Mamma rose quickly from behind the tea-urn, and bundled me out of the room. I was crying now and quite submissive. I was struck by the fact that her horror was all for the word I had used. She kept on telling me that I must never, never use that word.

"It comes of reading books you ought not to read," she said. "If you knew what it meant, you would not have said it, of course."

I went to school with a swelled lip, and an aching heart. The heart-ache was more because what I had said seemed to me humiliatingly absurd than because I resented my injury. In the evening I was easily persuaded to say I was sorry, and I received one of the slobbering kisses that I loathed. This, I thought, would win consent to my going to Gorges Court, but I was wrong. Mamma had found another excuse. She ought to have been asked too…. This excuse did not seem to be on all fours with the other one—that one must not be contaminated by the hospitality of a woman who had been mixed up in a divorce case—but I saw it was useless to argue the point.

VI

I saw Madame Pohlakoff again, splendid in a cruel little hat made of kingfishers' wings, and an austerely plain blue serge coat and skirt. She had called to say good-bye before leaving for Russia. Mamma was not at home, and she was just stepping back into the carriage when I rushed out into the drive and seized her hand. The notorious Lady Rackersham was in the carriage, not looking at all wicked, I thought!

"This is the child, Muriel," and Madame Pohlakoff added something in French to which Lady Rackersham smiled a good-humoured assent.

"I will come back for you in half an hour, Marie."

"No, don't do that. I will walk. And you will walk some of the road with me, will you not, *chérie?*"

"Rather!"

"It is a very little young child to-day," she said as the Rackersham carriage drove off. Her warm caressing smile inundated me with happiness, but I resisted the accusation of youth, as the very young always do.

"I am fifteen," I said, "and I feel years older." What had struck me most about her the other day was that she had treated me as an equal, had talked to me as if I were quite "grown-up." I was afraid that now she might begin to say, "You are too young to understand."

We went first to look at the portrait. She asked me what I thought of it.

"It makes you look too pretty," I said. "Isn't it funny that Mamma should paint? She's not an artist at all. You can see that, because she paints and paints and never learns anything."

Madame Pohlakoff laughed. I misunderstood the laughter. "Perhaps I am talking nonsense. I know I often do."

"Not at all…. You mustn't be afraid of seeming ridiculous. Everybody is, but you mustn't be like everybody else."

She looked at the portrait again.

"I admire Madame Wingfield. She is heroic. What industry! What self-sacrifice! She tells me that for ten years she has maintained you all by her brush. But courage and virtue do not make people paint well. What enigma! I know an artist, a dirty little Frenchman…oh, so mean, *un ramasseur de sous* [a penny collector]! Quarrelsome, vain, impossible…but on canvas, *mon Dieu!* What sublimity, what mastery of technique. He paint me. You would wonder. He saw into the depths of my soul. There in that portrait is the woman married at sixteen to one of her own rank…

perfectly fit alliance. He was in the Cossack Guard…handsome in the way I care not about. Kind, but a sensual beast! An animal, I say…and I a child. I knew nothing, nothing. Believe me, without tremendous spiritual love marriage is a *Schweinerei*. But I must not talk to my little poet like this."

"Yes, yes, you must," I cried in a voice full of spontaneous feeling. "I want to learn of you!" I pressed her hand, and added bashfully, "I can learn of you, because I love you."

And indeed our whole conversation that day seems to me to have been like a declaration of love. It was autumn, then and always my favourite season. We walked in the woods at random. The wind was cold and the blue sky wintry, but the trees were resplendent like burning things, and the dry beech-leaves like a path of animated gold under our feet. I know I walked along with my mouth open in a child-like stupor. Incomparable moments, in which my soul went wandering to the further limits of life!

She told me of Andrei's death by assassination, a week after he had given the order for the Cossack Guard to fire on the crowd who had come to petition the Emperor. She told me she felt his death to be just, for a thousand innocent peasants, trusting in the mercy of their Little Father, had been slaughtered that day. But his family and her family had been outraged by her abstention from sentimental grief. To them the dead man became by the manner of his death a martyred saint. "Saint Andrei! Ah no! I tell you he was an insect who stung my body and soul with his lust." Yet immediately after these words, which seemed to me terrible, she added, "God knows I forgive him…. It would be indecent if I did not…seeing that I too am an animal. My two children should have been enough to fill my life after his death…. But when they grew big and clumsy and could not sit on my knee any more, I wanted something else…. This is something you can't understand yet…. It's a kind of madness, I think.

People thought me 'folle' to commit a mésalliance…a sin against my noble blood to marry one of the bourgeoisie…a sin against my children to give them such a stepfather. But what were those sins compared with my sin against myself!… I think I fell in love with Nikolai's shoulders! Contempt for his humble origin, for his want of refinement, did not help me…. Pushkin, our great poet, says a man will fall in love with some beauty, with a woman's body, even with a part of a woman's body, and he'll abandon his children for her, sell his father and mother, and his country. He will become cruel, even though he is normally kind—a liar, however truthful, just because a woman has pretty feet, and he wants them. Pushkin writes often about women's feet…. La la! In my case, shoulders…. The line from the ear to the shoulder, so perfect…. My Nikolai! Now he grows fat…. He will not work, because I have money…. He becomes a *malade imaginaire* [imaginary invalid]! And my children despise me…. I am—what do you say?—'cut,' isn't it?—by my own class. Princess Andrei Rashatinsky…that is one thing, and Madame Pohlakoff! *c'est tout autre chose* [it's quite another thing]!"

As I listened, an anxious longing possessed me to question her endlessly, to discover every aspect of her—why she was great rather than good, to understand why the temple of her body was still so pure and fair, and why she could laugh in the midst of so much accumulated sorrow. But the time had come for our farewell.

"I have paid Madame Wingfield just twice too great sum for that picture, *chérie*…do you know why? She mentioned that you wish to study at Oxford, but that even if you won the scholarship she could not afford to give you the little extra allowance necessary…. She promise me to devote £200 of my £400 I have paid to that. So work for your scholarship, little poet."

"Oh, how can I thank you!"

Oxford had been my dream ever since we had gone there for the day to see Charlie Wingfield, for whose college expenses Mamma had had to work harder than ever. I had a fond idea that college life would be quite different from the narrow school life, with its girlish curriculum, and flat-chested, uninspiring school-mistresses. I looked to it to make a man of me and to enable me to earn my living like a man. I dreamed of walking round Addison's Walk with the oblique sun falling across my book—open at "The Scholar Gypsy." Lectures, tutors, spires and ancient grey buildings, college gardens, the river, and the tall young men in white flannel "shorts" walking down the Long Walk to row in one of those slender needle-like boats, had all gripped my imagination. I was never so selfish, however, in all my life as not to know when my exhilaration was not shared by another, and I saw a shadow on Madame Pohlakoff's face as I poured out my gratitude. Immediately I began to pretend that I was not so over-poweringly glad.

"I had another plan, *chérie*," she said. We had come to the great wrought-iron gates of Gorges Court, and both of us were melancholy at the approaching farewell. "I wished to adopt you…to take you back to Russia; but Madame Wingfield would not consent."

And adventurous wish to go and a feeling of relief that I was not to go were equally strong in me.

"Why won't she let me go?" I asked.

"She say, 'As long as I live I will protect the child from bad influence. I owe it to her dead father!' You see, *chérie*, I am a bad influence."

"No, you are not," I protested. And again the thought of anything evil existing in that noble, beautiful nature hurt me. Was she not a thousand times better than Alice, who had never done anything really wrong in her life—or even than Mamma, who had been so uncharitable about Lady Rackersham?

"Well, it is good-bye.... Take care of your complexion. It is exquisite, *vraiment!* [truly]. Like a rose. Let us keep our hearts on high! Do not lose your little-boy look, that is so original. When your hair grows longer, and you must turn it up, you must have a simple coiffure. Do not let any one persuade you to endeavour to look like other people. You will never doubt that I know better than these Englishwomen what is distinction.... I know you will not."

I asserted with tears that I would always remember what she had said.

"No tears," she said tenderly, putting her arm round my neck. "Let us keep our hearts on high. You have a tendency to sadness, little one. Well, be sad in your own room. Do not inflict it on others. That is bad manners. I want you to have exquisite manners. The first thing I loved in you was your dear little bow of courtesy. We shall write to each other, shall we not?...and you shall spend a vacation with me, when you are at Oxford. Now I am going to kiss you.... Never kiss, *chérie*, except with your soul...not man nor woman. A kiss is foolish if it is not sacred."

Her left arm joined her right round my neck, and hugging me to her, she kissed me again and again. Her white teeth seemed to glitter like stars, her face in the dying autumn light was beautiful like a pearl. Each kiss was a seal on what she had taught me... and I felt that was more than all I had learned at school or out of books. Of me indeed she might have said, "I holp to frame thee."

V

INDEPENDENCE

I

The surprise of my schoolmistresses and the Wingfields when the news came that I had won the Open Exhibition in History and Literature at Marville College, Oxford, was natural, as I had never shown any marked ability at school, and even while I was cramming for the examination could not resist turning aside from the imposed books to read poetry and philosophy in which I was not going to be examined. Then I was younger than the other competitors—not yet seventeen—and when I started for Oxford for the examination the headmistress said: "You must look upon it as a trial trip for next year."

That I should have won £75 a year by answering questions about Chaucer and Shakespeare and Milton on the one hand, and about the growth of Parliament on the other, seemed to me very strange, and it seems stranger still now, when it is as much as I can do to remember the dates of the Kings of England.

My success was announced at school during "break." There were loud cheers, or to be accurate, shrill cheers; many girls to whom I had never spoken, suddenly took an interest in me. I was slapped on the back—which I disliked, for the touch of any one with whom I am not intimate has always given me a feeling of physical repulsion. The cricket eleven, of which I was a member, were particularly effusive.

I rushed back to Gorges Woods at midday red-hot with the excitement of victory. My experiences in lessons and games and gymnastics had taught me that I should never really excel in anything, because I could never *sustain*, although I could be brilliant intellectually and athletically, in spurts. Yet here I was, labelled cleverer than those big young women of eighteen and nineteen with whom I had competed a month earlier in the library at Marville! Exultation was natural.

I felt I must tell every one. I began with the man at the toll-gate. A privately owned bridge crossed the river between Ripton and Gorges Woods. He said: I'm sure that's very clever of you, miss, but what do womenfolk want with so much learning?" Then, breathless from my run over the bridge, I whirled through the hall at Fernleigh into the dining-room, and seized hold of the parlour-maid Anne, who was laying the table for luncheon.

"I've got it! I've got it!" I shouted.

"Got what?" she said crossly. "Mind my cap, Miss. It's clean on to-day."

"I've won the scholarship at Oxford."

"That'll mean more expense for your Mamma," said Anne sourly.

"No, it won't. It's £75 a year!"

"Well, you needn't put the forks crooked, if it is!" said Anne.

Her refusal to be impressed did not upset me at all. My only idea was to find some one else to tell. Alice was playing the piano in the drawing-room, and playing it in that aimless unmusical way in which most people play it—the way which gave me a lifelong prejudice against the instrument.

"Alice!" I must have been drunk with excitement to imagine that she would respond, but I had a vague notion that every one must be pleased at my achievement. "Alice. I've got the scholar-ship!"

She stopped playing for a minute, and looked at me coldly.

"It doesn't interest me." She went on playing again. To this day that Melody of Rubinstein's gives me a bitter taste in my mouth. My childish rapture was reduced to dust in a moment.

For a long time I had not thought much about the Dream father and mother. Crushed and humiliated, I turned to them, and begged them to pick me up and comfort me; I hungered for their pride in me. The incident was so small, and so huge. For days I was affected by it. "Can all this grief and disturbance be merely because Alice has snubbed me?" I asked myself.

II

I had been at Oxford a year when Milly sent me a telegram to say that Mamma was very ill.

I sat in my room considering it, and smoking one cigarette after another without noticing that I was smoking.

It seemed a long time indeed since my first term at Marville. How timid and shy and young I had felt at Didcot Junction that day I had come "up," and had watched the undergraduates in their untidy tweed Norfolk jackets crowding into the Oxford train! There were some Marville students on the platform too. There was no particular mark on them. Some were well dressed, others wore hard, unbecoming straw hats like the High School girls. Some wore coats and skirts, and other "jibbehs" of green serge. Some carried golf-clubs, and others flowers. It seemed to me that they looked at me as if I had no business to be going to Oxford. I, feeling miserably strange to myself, for my hair had not long been "done up," found my cherished dream of independence becoming a horrible nightmare.

All this timidity, this unwelcome sense of being "out of it," had soon passed, but disappointment and disillusionment remained.

Life at Marville was a perpetual reminder of women's disabilities. We women students did not live in a college of crumbling grey stone, hallowed by venerated memories and traditions, but in a hideous red-brick building that might have been a reformatory. It stood outside the charmed circle where the men's colleges were bunched together, and from it stretched northward the residential quarter of the town—regular, neat, depressingly villaish. Our exterior was not more different from Magdalen and Christ Church and Trinity, whose very names filled me with longing to be one of their sons, than our interior. Instead of two rooms, a "bedder" and "sitter," often in the old colleges dark, poky, and shabby, but at their worst indefinably romantic, we had one room allotted to us, and were expected to conceal during the day the fact that our beds were beds. Instead of slouching to lectures in cap and gown, as independent units, we, fully dressed in outdoor garments, even to gloves, had to go in pairs or groups chaperoned by one of our own tutors. When we arrived at the lecture we were given seats at the high table near the lecturer, an invidious distinction which I felt to be a humiliation. In those days (I do not know if the position has improved) we women students were made to feel that the University was conferring a great condescension in admitting us to mutilated privileges.

From the first I had fallen among the set of students who appeared to have come to Marville to enjoy themselves rather than to work. They were richer, pleasanter, jollier than the studious, hard-working ones. They were less pedantic and less plain. I made no friend, but I was on good terms with these girls, and strove to emulate them in their frivolities. It was usual for those who could afford it to supplement the bare and mean furnishing of their rooms by bringing pictures and ornaments from home. I soon transformed my room, through the obliging readiness of the Oxford tradesmen in letting me run up large bills, into a kind of museum.

Whether my taste for fine fabrics, beautiful colours, and mezzotints was an instinct, or whether it had been planted in me at

Crupples, I am unable to say. At Oxford it ran riot, yet I was never satisfied. Often I longed to pull down my room and rebuild it, because nothing could disguise the ugliness of its proportions. There were days when I could have thrown everything that I possessed out of the window, moved partly by a passion of remorse for having spent so much money, and partly by weariness of the ill-gotten possessions.

Even to-day, with the alarming telegram in front of me, I was wishing that my apricot velvet curtains were yellow. It seemed to me that a true daffodil-yellow would have gone better with the grey walls. But then I could not have had coppery tea-roses in the room. I had bought them that morning at an expensive florist's on the way back from my Constitutional History Lecture at Merton. They certainly looked exquisite against the apricot velvet.

My conscience began to reproach me for thinking of this when Mamma was dying. I felt sure that she was dying, although Milly's telegram was worded non-conditionally, so that, as I thought bitterly, it should not cost more than sixpence. I had been back to Ripton only once since I had gone up to Oxford, for invitations to spend my vacations at the homes of some of my college friends had not been wanting, and I was glad to accept them. I was living in a fool's paradise, spending money as if I were rich and independent, playing the part of a young exquisite, so far as the limitations of Marville allowed, and I dreaded the shock that the Wingfields would be to my pose.

Nor was this all. I had an increasing dread of being told anything about my origin. The time had gone by for that. Several times, when I had spent a fortnight at Ripton at Christmas, Mamma had tried to open the subject; and I, who had once been so anxious *to know*, now preferred ignorance. She took me to my first ball—a *bal poudré* [powdered wig ball] it was, I remember—and on seeing me with the white hair which made my features look more clearly cut and my eyes deeper in colour, she exclaimed.

"You are just like his grandmother. He showed me a miniature of her once. You are very aristocratic-looking, Joanna."

This pleased me, but my experiences at my first ball soon depressed my crest. I hardly danced at all except with Charlie, the only one of the Wingfields who went to dances. I felt miserable, sitting down by Mamma, who knew no one to whom she could introduce me, and dancing with Charlie to escape the ignomity of not dancing at all. This was the evening I "came out." It had struck me, before we started, that I looked rather wonderful in spite of my big nose. My thick hair, with a suggestion of undulation in it, took the powder well. The Ripton hairdresser was enchanted by my eighteenth-century appearance, which my white chiffon dress with a high-waisted blue ribbon increased. I darkened my eyebrows and eyelashes slightly, but the natural rose-colour in my cheeks made rouge unnecessary. Anne, who helped me to dress, said: "I never knew you had such a chest, Miss. It reminds me of that foreign lady your Mamma painted." This remark recalled to me what Madame Pohlakoff had said of distinction, and cheered me up wonderfully for not being pretty.

Yet at the ball I created no sensation. Girls with red arms, girls with thin necks, girls with dun complexions which looked more dun beneath their powdered hair, weather-beaten girls, pretty girls floated past, encircled by partners in hunt-coats and uniforms, but for the best part of the evening I sat by Mamma in her ugly old red velvet evening gown, and her best lace cap, which she had put on for such occasions ever since I could remember, and longed for the earth to swallow me up.

At last a young man in ordinary evening dress approached me, and asked me to dance. Mamma was looking the other way when he came up, and I went off with him gladly, although the consciousness that it was rather odd of him to ask me to be his partner without an introduction vaguely disturbed me.

We waltzed well together, although, as all my dancing had been learned at Marville, where I danced "gentleman," I showed too great an anxiety to pilot him.

"I know you quite well by sight," he said. "I see you at lectures."

We immediately began talking Oxford. He told me he liked the three-cornered hat I had worn last term, and my button-holes.

"The men at the 'House' who go to Dickenson's lectures call you 'L'Insolente,'" he confided.

"But why?" I asked. "I don't think I am very insolent."

"Well, you look at us as if we were dirt!"

"Only when you stare," I said, remembering glances at the high table which I had though an impertinence.

"By Jove! I wish they could see 'L'Insolente' to-night. They would be more frightened than ever."

"I did not frighten *you*," I said, irritated by this intimation that I was formidable, like Miss Bence, and Miss Carr, and other plain bespectacled Marvillians. "You seemed quite sure that I would dance with you."

"I thought it was a pity the best-looking girl in the room shouldn't be dancing."

"Don't pay compliments—I hate it!" I said shortly.

"You look far the best in powder, anyhow," he said.

"I don't mind your saying that, because I think it's true," I answered, mollified.

"Did you think it very forward of me to ask you for a dance?"

"Did you think it very forward of me to say 'yes'?"

"Of course not!" He smiled pleasantly. "I'm not a bit conventional. If I had tried to find our hostess, she would have introduced me to lots of other girls, too. That wouldn't have suited me. One dance, one partner, is my idea of enjoying myself."

"But I saw you dancing just now!" I exclaimed.

"I was trying her. She was weighed in the balance, and found wanting, or rather found too heavy, in every sense of the word." I looked at him. His cheerful conceit amused me. He was rather an emasculate young man, with dark hair brushed back from his forehead—not such a common fashion then as now. His hands were white and long-fingered, his whole appearance rather weary and delicate. There was something refined about him, yet something common too. The rhythm of the dance tunes had got into my blood, and I wanted to dance, but after one or two waltzes he insisted on "sitting out."

Late in the evening Charlie tracked us, and said Mamma was tired and wanted to go home.

"It's really very selfish of you," he said in the true Wingfield up-braiding tone. "You ought to have thought she might be tired."

"Well, go and get her then," I said. "She takes ages to say good-bye."

I began to follow Charlie, but my partner took hold of my arm. "Wait a minute," he said. "I want to thank you."

I was utterly unprepared for the kiss he gave me. I did not cry out "You brute," or rub my lips. I was not thrilled with any wonderful sensations. It was humiliating to me all the same that this rather common young man's mouth had touched mine. I felt that I could not have given such a kiss unless my soul had been in it, and I felt instinctively that he gave such kisses often, and meant very little by them.

"You're not angry, are you?"

And I wondered how often he had used just these very words in just these very circumstances.

"Angry is not the word," I said seriously.

He looked at me curiously, trying to fathom my thoughts.

"And you'll come to tea with me next term?"

"I don't even know your name." My voice sounded far away from me. I did not care whether he told me his name or not.

"Roderick Cave, Christ Church—generally known as Roddy."

The band had stopped playing. I saw Mamma and Charlie in the emptying ball-room, saying goodbye to our opulent hostess. I could even hear the words, "I hope your young people have enjoyed themselves." Some of the dancers came to sit out in the conservatory where we were standing. It seemed to me that they looked at me meaningly, as they had not looked at me before. I had a strange fancy that the kiss was visible on my lips, as visible and as disfiguring as a black eye. I thought, too, of a closed garden into which some one had trespassed, and had been quite insensible of the fact that it had never before been trodden by human footsteps. I longed to see in the intruder something noble and precious, a traveller who did not frequent the common ways, but had come from far, from very far, impregnated with beautiful things. A terrible heartsickness seized me. There struggled with it generosity, and a sense of fair play. Resentment would have deepened my humiliation, by making me a mean shifter of responsibility, a complainant, pleading the weakness which had invited insult. In that moment was born a lifelong determination to blame no one except myself if anything were taken from me. For what could be taken, if I did not give?

III

My thoughts revolved round Roddy and my first dance. I did not move to go and ask the Warden for permission to go home, as I ought to have done.... We were driving home from that dance in the Ripton fly, and Mamma and Charlie were pretending that we had all enjoyed ourselves, and that it was a great thing to have gone. I could not, even with my lips, join in their complacency. I had a great envy of the ball at which Juliet had first seen Romeo,...and was tortured by the thought of the ball at which I had seen instead—Roderick Cave! There kept sounding in my head, like bells, those heart-rending immortal words:

"Oh you too early seen unknown and known too late!"

I saw Juliet moving in the stately dance, a bow ready to be drawn by an unseen hand, a joy intense to gravity, a flame hot to whiteness, a youth full of deep things.

"Ah, she doth teach the torches to burn bright!"

I remembered that as I had entered my ballroom I had felt a burning radiance stream from me. Had some one apprehended it, how willingly I too would have descended into the tomb!

Milly unfastened my dress. She was looking very plain in her blue flannel dressing-gown, her eyes heavy with sleep, her hair screwed up in curling-pins.

"Tell me all about it," she said, more as a matter of form than because she wanted to know. "I am sure you were the belle of the ball."

"I should have enjoyed it very much, if there had been no-body there."

"Where *do* you mean?"

"Oh, never mind!" I said crossly.

"Powdered hair makes you look much older," went on Milly, as she went back to bed, "but awfully distinguished."

I could have hit her. That word again! Madame Pohlakoff came to me at once; her beautiful serene face reproached me. Her voice like metal wrapped in velvet, said: "A kiss is foolish when it is not sacred."

IV

A second telegram came from Milly. "Much worse. Come at once."

142

This roused me. Yes, I must go. I must go—there was no doubt about that. There was no escape. Yet with what reluctance I prepared for the journey! What object was there in going to see some one die?

In the cupboard in my room was some champagne which I had bought recently for a supper-party. Very early in my college career I had substituted wine and "cup" for the mild cocoa which most Marvillians were content to offer their friends at the "ten-o'clocks" which were a Marville institution. I had just lunched, but I wanted to blunt the edge of my repugnance to being brought close to sickness and death. I drank a whole bottle, and fished a black dress out of my wardrobe.

My neighbour in A corridor saw me off. She was the niece of a rich cotton-spinner in the North of England, and I had spent part of the last vacation with her.

"I hope your mother isn't so bad as you think," she said at the station. "I have never got over losing mine."

"I lost mine before I knew her," I answered.

"I don't understand." She stared at me, as well she might.

"It's all too complicated to tell now, Sunny. Besides, would it make such a difference if it were she? I don't know."

"That champagne's got into your head. I wish you hadn't taken it."

"I wish, on the contrary, that I had another bottle for the journey."

"I can't bear to hear you talk like that. It seems so—so—"

"Indecent? I suppose it is. If you knew what I would give to not go! There's such horror waiting for me at the end of the journey."

"You may be of use," said Sunny.

"I hope so." I was glad at that moment to think that I had been nice to Mamma on my last visit. I had done my best to shield her from Alice's bullying. I had sat and read Tennyson to her; I had cleaned all her paint-brushes, which she was never to use again; and had insisted on her having nourishing food. As I approached Ripton, a great tenderness for the dying woman conquered my repulsion to being summoned to her death-bed. I was touched as I contemplated that heroic life which had been spent as freely for me as for any of her own children. All my life I had thought that she did not understand me, and had been impatient of her mediocrity, her excessive respect for social position, her servile endurance of Alice's petty tyranny. I had disliked her dowdy clothes, her paltry taste in furniture, her Puritanical hardness on immorality, which she regarded as the only real sin. Her love for her children had seemed to my harsh young judgment all sentiment, and lacking in warm depths. Never had I known her clasp one of them in her arms with that tenderness, that overwhelming emotion with which Madame Pohlakoff had clasped me that day in the schoolroom—a clasp which my whole soul feels once more after the passage of twenty years. Her very abnegation had not won my respect because she talked so much about it, and was so often moved to tears because she could not afford luxuries which seemed to me not worth any one's ambition. When she had failed me, I remembered, it had always been through fear. The incident of the minever came back to me. She had a whole set of this lovely fur which some one had given her in exchange for a picture. I had put it on—cap, stole, and enormous muff. She decided that I must have it, because it became my complexion. Immediately there was an outcry from Alice. Immediately the gift was withdrawn—"for the sake of peace," Mamma said. I used to argue with her that such peace was dishonourable, and led only to worse war, but she said no good came of fighting. For this reason it was useless to fight for her. She would go over to the enemy in the middle of the action, and leave her champion to look very foolish.

But I seemed to see the virtues in all these weaknesses as I approached Fernleigh. In Mamma the desire to spare others pain was almost a disease. I could not doubt that it was to spare me pain that she had kept me in ignorance of everything that I ought to have known. She had not allowed for the persistence of a memory. Such memories may persist even from two years old. Although I had never spoken of it, the memory of my father, oppressed by grief, walking up and down the drawing-room at Hercester, had stood out through my life like a spot of light in darkness. I could feel him squeezing me close till it hurt, and saying almost hysterically: "Pray to her for your father, your wretched father." That frenzied beautiful face! I often recalled it most vividly. And now my adopted mother was passing into the silence of death.... I must arrest her passing; I must demand why and how I had been left at that old house in Hercester, and where she was who had given me life. Had she deserted me? Well, I could understand that.... I had seen infants, little lumps of red flesh, differing little from one another. I had known mothers who handed them back to wet-nurses with a sigh of relief, and had felt that the sublime image of maternal love was not created by the original instinct of an entire sex, but by the instinct of a few blessed and chosen ones. All who give birth to children are not mothers, just as all who couple are not lovers.

We went into the sick-room, Milly and I. The presence of two nurses showed me how grave the illness was. The night-nurse had foregone her day's sleep, because soon she would be able to sleep her fill. I felt the shaking of my heart. I dared not look at the bed for a moment, for fear of reading there my sentence of death as well as the sick woman's, for fear of seeing that thing dissolve which was not the hope of all being made clear, and yet was similar to it.

How distant from life, how secluded was the room! One of the nurses lit the gas.

"Surely she ought not to have that light in her eyes!" I said, impatient of the woman's noisy movement, impatient of everything.

"She does not see anything now," the nurse said, in the hard, practical tones of one in whom mortal sickness roused no imagination, and to whom it brought no terror.

It was then I looked at Mamma.... She had still been rather stout when I had last seen her. Now she had shrunk to the dimensions of a child. Her grey eyes were wide open, but I saw that "their sense was shut." Nothing about her moved except her hands, which twitched ceaselessly at the sheet, poor little hands on which the veins stood up in great purple knots.

All my impetuous anxiety to question her, which had been flaming higher and higher during the journey from Oxford, went out suddenly like a torch in a cold blast of wind. I knew that I had come too late.

"Why didn't you send for me before?" I asked this of Milly with indignation, although I knew it was unjust, seeing that I had spent five hours in wilful inactivity after the first telegram.

"No one thought she was really bad until yesterday," Milly answered meekly. She was always ostentatiously meek. "Even now Dr. Billing says—"

I interrupted her fiercely.

"She's dying!"

"Oh, don't speak so loud! She might hear."

I was amazed at this.

"Have you all been trying to bluff her into thinking she isn't going to die! Isn't it possible she might like to know?"

"Dr. Billing said we weren't to depress her while there is hope."

"Dr. Billing's an ass!"

One of the nurses smiled at this. "He hasn't been, either, since she had a rigor at two o'clock."

"And you haven't sent for him! Why not get another opinion? Why not do *something*?"

"I think it's very unkind to talk like this," said Milly, breaking down. "I've hardly been in bed for a week, have I, nurse?"

"You've been very good, I'm sure," said the nurse to whom Milly appealed. She was the day-nurse, and looked more humane and gentle than the other one. "There's very little to be done in these cases," she added. "It's septic pneumonia.... Old people can't rally."

"Mamma's not so old," I argued.

"No, but she's had a hard life of it, I should think. She's worn out."

The other nurse had just shovelled some meat extract into the sick woman's mouth. She did not resist at all, but I noticed that most of it trickled out again. I shuddered, and longed to run out of the room.... It was just as the longing had shaped itself that the vacant grey eyes seemed to fix me, and one of the twitching hands was stretched towards me. At least I thought that this was so. I went close to her, and took her hand. It closed over mine at once.

"What is it, dear? What would you like me to do?"

"Read." The word was very faint, but quite distinct. I remembered that the last time I had been with her I had read her Tennyson's "The Two Voices."

"Get me a Tennyson, quick, Milly."

"But she can't hear—"

"Oh, do get it!"

I was immensely encouraged by feeling the hand moving up and down my arm.

"That's what she wants," I thought. "A hand to clutch."

I moved to the foot of the bed, however, to read, anxious not to rob her of air.... She gazed at me seriously, uncomprehendingly, as I hurried through the stanzas of the poem that she had loved:

> "I cannot gift that some have striven,
> Achieving calm, to whom was given
> The joy that mixes man with Heaven:

> "Who, rowing hard against the stream,
> Saw distant gates of Eden gleam,
> And did not dream it was a dream."

"Could anything be more absurd!" It was Alice's voice. "The idea of reading poetry, when she is so ill!"

I shut up the book, and without resentment. Perhaps it was absurd. But that "rowing hard against the stream" moved me to the first tears that I shed at this bed of death. It seemed an epitome of the life that was ending, and I began to wonder whether the heroic rower, whose heroism had been shown in such shabby, mean, repellent circumstances, with never a touch of glory to redeem it from the commonplace, was now going to find some rest and some reward.

During my year at Oxford I had endeavoured to crush my inquiring soul with a crude materialism. The fool had said in her heart "There is no God." Eternity there was, but in a moment, in a flower, not in a fabulous heaven or hell. We had nothing to complain of. We had come out of nothing, and were going back to nothing. There were only two facts in life—birth and death. How tragic that we should worry so much about the manner in which we travelled from one fact to the other! Great were the achievements of men, but the achievements of ants were as great in their proportion, yet no one claimed that ants had souls. What was the earth but an ant-heap in the millions of worlds with which the firmament was studded? Perhaps the ant, too, had illusions of immortality, that enabled it to perform its duties towards its community with a secret hope that there was another world where the lazy ant would be punished and the industrious one rewarded. I hardly got so far as formulating this theory; I was ignorant, more ignorant than is common, of religious principles, and I never scoffed at them. Faith seemed to me most beautiful.

When we discussed such things at Marville, some one would ask me whether it did not seem to me very terrible, if death were annihilation, that millions of saints throughout the centuries had sacrificed all joy in this world for the sake of a seat in the great white rose of Paradise, and that martyrs had bled for a pious lie? I said it seemed to me nobler to die for a dream than for a reality. Were not people always sacrificing themselves for the sake of something quite unworthy? Were they not daily offering themselves as victims to their own imagination? Imagination appeared to me the secret of every passion, every joy, every pain that blessed or afflicted man. For unimaginative people very few things existed. Without imagination there was no beauty in the universe, there was no such thing as love.

And then a voice within me would whisper: "But who endowed man with this imagination which illumines all animate and inanimate things? How can he, formed of mortal dust, and returning to it, imagine the infinite and the immortal?" I was troubled by that faint inner voice…for it was my destiny as a little ant, born in the course of nature to die in the course of nature, that enabled me to bear with some stubbornness the mystery that surrounded my life. Between those two facts, what did it matter whether I was Mrs. Wingfield's child, or the child of another? On days when my imagination was inactive, I had no curiosity about the past. I could say to my imaginative part, in the manner of Iago: "You have no father, no mother…you do not know how they lived or died, nor what sort of blood they mingled to pour in these veins? 'Well, what of that? Why should that distress you? As I am an honest man, I thought you had received some bodily hurt.'"

V

The atmosphere of the room stunned my spirit, yet I could not leave her. For many hours I lay across the bed, my head within reach of the dying hands. They moved ceaselessly in my thick hair. I was full of love and pity…I gave her my physical discomfort with all my heart…I had noticed that the touch of me, for some reason which I did not try to understand, smoothed out the contractions of her face. The lines of her mouth composed themselves in the regular rhythm of sleep.

All night members of the family came in and out. Wives of the elder married brothers, whom I had never seen before, had come. Their faces were grotesquely serious. I felt as if I were living in a nightmare…. I longed for her to die—for all this pitiful farce of lowered voices and sentimental grief from people who had been cruel to her in life to end. I was astonished at the meekness and tameness of the bogies of my childhood. Alice appeared the very wreck of the tyrant of whom every one had been afraid. Mr. Wingfield was a broken old man. I was sorry for both of them, in spite of the repulsion that they inspired. Even the most ill-natured people are better than we suppose, and in the presence of death I understood this clearly. The undaunted forces whirling above my head caught up the sordid infidelities of the husband, the unfilialness of the daughter, and reduced them to nothing.

It was towards dawn that she cried out in a loud, clear voice:

"I think I'm going to die!"

It was then that I wished for an infinite consolation to be transfused from my head into the wandering hand...that now seemed to have terror in it at the nearness of dissolution. I heard Charlie, who was going to be a clergyman, say, "Yes, dear mother, I think you are," and begin to read prayers in the typical English parson's voice. And Milly with characteristically obstinate optimism kept on whispering in the dying ears: "No, no... you are going to get better."

The brightness of the fine November morning was heart-rending. The birds were singing for joy of the belated summer. I found myself wishing that I might die on a dreary, foggy day, when the beauty of the world was obscured, and no birds sang.

The hand had long ceased to wander in my hair.... It felt solid, tenacious. My limbs were inert and stiff, and my veins throbbed painfully. "Not another moment can I bear it," I thought, my flesh fighting the spirit that wished to bear her spirit company during its last moments on earth. "You believe in the soul, then?" cried the inner voice. Little by little the clasp of my head that had seemed so indissoluble gave way as if life were failing it. I heard a nurse say "She's going," and Milly, "I must call them." Breathlessly I seemed to be waiting for an arrival, and the dying one's breathlessness increased my own. Would not some divine voice call her now and raise her up? I struggled off the bed, swaying on my numbed feet. I clung to the bed-rail. The sunlight pouring in at the window seemed curiously white. I had lost all sense of time...all knowledge of place. Through my confused dreams of enormous endless plains under infinite white skies a rattling sound in Mamma's throat penetrated. It stopped suddenly; the glance of the grey eyes was arrested by some sight beyond me. The silence seemed to be expecting a sound.

"She's gone."

I saw the nurse step forward to close those wide-open eyes which had changed utterly since that moment of *arrest*. Immediately I was conscious that the room was full of people: that some had lost all control and were howling and lamenting. Repulsion filled my being. I slipped out of the room. It was not grief but the melancholy of one outside a closed door that thickened round my heart.

VI

"You take my house, when you do take the prop
That doth sustain my house."

I thought of those lines often during the next few days. The prop having been withdrawn, the house of Wingfield had ceased to exist. Disintegrated atoms the family seemed, with no reason for holding together any more. I longed to escape at once, and never to see a Wingfield again, but the certainty that there was something that concerned me among Mamma's papers restrained my unthinking impulse to flight before the funeral.

There was much to provoke cynical bitterness in the clumsy halo with which the dead woman's brows were now adorned…. Ripton, which had neglected Mamma living, found her a source of pride now that she was dead. She was the "distinguished artist that had dwelt amongst them," "our esteemed fellow-citizen," and so on. Wreaths poured in from people who had slighted her and snubbed her. An extra postman had to be employed to deal with the letters of condolence. A few favoured neighbours in Gorges Woods were conducted by Milly to see the corpse.

"She looks so beautiful," was the refrain of Milly's demure grief.

I was silent, because I could not agree. To me that arrest at the moment of death, as of a winged thing poised for flight, had been beautiful. But I was distressed by the dead features as composed by cunning professional hands…. That serene sweet smile had been made by them. The sunken cheeks had been plumped out to deceive such an observer as Milly into saying, "She looks so happy and peaceful."… What increased my distress was that I seemed to perceive a faint smell of corruption in the room in spite of the flowers and the spraying of antiseptics. I thought it was not fair to that poor motionless body on the bed to delay its transference to the coffin while visitors with the smallest claims to intimacy came and gazed at it with awe-stricken eyes.

Madame Pohlakoff, to whom I had telegraphed the news of the death, telegraphed me two pounds to buy violets. This provoked a discussion about the propriety of coloured flowers at a funeral.

"They always have them abroad."

I spoke with authority, although my experience of the Continent was confined as yet to six weeks in Brittany, where I had gone the preceding summer on a reading-party, and to a week in Paris with my college friend Sunny.

"The extravagance of the woman!" grumbled Mr. Wingfield. "And as I think I know why she has so much money to fling about, I would rather not have her flowers on my poor Eleanor's coffin. It would be sacrilege."

"Don't worry," I said, speaking calmly in spite of my indignant heart. "Her spikenard shall be poured out upon the ground."

"Spikenard?" said Alice. "I thought you said violets."

I did not answer. Alice then advised me to order a wreath of stephanotis and lilies, which I could get for a pound, and to keep the other pound for myself. When I protested angrily that I loathed stephanotis, and that anyhow I was not "a swine," she expressed a pained surprise that I could use such a dreadful word.

"Poor mother was dreadfully distressed at the bad language you have picked up at Oxford. And how do you think you are going to live now? You may need that pound. I meant it kindly."

For the first time I began to think of the difference that Mamma's death would make to my position. My allowance so far had come out of Madame Pohlakoff's £200. But no one but Mamma knew of that arrangement.

I felt scared at the prospect of finding myself penniless, with all those debts at Oxford unpaid. I scarcely knew the value of money. When I had it, I would give it away for the asking, or spend it recklessly. It was gone in a moment. The terrible carelessness sprang partly from never having been taught to be careful; but as the sharpest lessons in after years never cured me of it, I suppose it must also have been a trait in my character.

The day of the funeral, I strewed the violets, wine-coloured, blue and white, on the steps of the house, and on the drive. As the feet of the coffin-bearers passed over them, I felt that the fragrance of a great generous heart was ascending heavenwards.

VII

When I returned to Oxford it soon became apparent to every one that I was greatly changed. They put it down to grief at my mother's death, and never questioned me.

The Warden feared I was reading too hard. It was true that I spent all my time in my room, and if any one came in, the text-books of my special period, the French Revolution, were open on the table, and confirmed the general opinion that I was "swotting."

But for weeks I could not take in one word of what I read. Morning, afternoon and evening I was engaged in fitting together the bits of a puzzle. In vain I tried to fix my attention on the "sea-green Incorruptible," on the Girondins, on Danton and the rest. Disconnected questions would arise in my mind: "Why was my father obliged to leave England?" "What made my mother run away from him?" "Was she beautiful? Certainly she had lovely hands. He is always praising them in his letters."

A little faded photograph of my father did not conflict at all with my baby memory. He looked like an artist, or a composer, with his hair worn longer than is usual—"though not too long," I maintained—his clean-shaven face, and wistful, visionary eyes.

I thought gently of him most days, as I had thought gently of Oscar Wilde when, during my first year at Oxford, he had come to grief, and been made the scapegoat of outraged English morality, just as Byron had been made a scapegoat nearly a century before. Often I had lain awake at nights thinking of Oscar Wilde's *débacle*, and wishing that I could serve a few days of his sentence in his stead, that he might walk abroad unseen in Oxford, and see above her spires and towers "the deep sky clad in the beauty of a thousand stars." I had never known him, yet he was my friend through his works, in which I could find much that was artificial, much that was others' metal melted down and recast, often in more graceful forms; but not a word that was ignoble, or suggestive of evil, or calculated to appeal to readers athirst for indecent sensations... The purity of his *work* is appreciated now, but when I was eighteen it shared his fate of public infamy. This great sorrow that I felt for the stricken man was no idle sentiment. In it there was no desire to deny or even to palliate his offences, no pride in running counter to popular opinion. It was just a spontaneous act of love, an instinctive discrimination between what a man is and what he does.

My burning hatred of the English press as an arbiter and guide was born during Oscar Wilde's trial. The papers seemed to exult over his downfall and disgrace. They pointed the moral with a bludgeon…wrote of him with insult which no poor sinner ever deserved, whatever the magnitude of his crime. They were the spokesmen of a nominally Christian land, yet which of them was deterred from insulting and exulting all at once over the wretched by the Christian ideal: "Let him that is without sin amongst you, cast the first stone!"

VIII

I thought gently of my father, as I have said—as one flying before some mysterious disgrace, burying the child he had begotten in the sepulchre of a respectable English family, pleading that his memory might be blotted out. But as one who had let my mother go, as one whose love had not been great enough to save her, as one who apparently had been indifferent to her fate, I thought of him accusingly. It was easy, the pieces of this section of the puzzle being so much mutilated that they would not fit in at all, to defend him, even to justify him. But led by instinct alone, my mind refused to do this easy thing.

In the little bundle of letters and bits of things, marked "Joanna," without any further directions, that had been found among my adopted mother's effects, there was but one letter that was not in my father's writing. It was written from a shabby little hotel in Paris, and undated. It was what an unprejudiced reader would have called "a begging letter." It did, indeed, make a pathetic appeal for help. Even now, when I have altered my past, as Oscar Wilde says in "De Profundis" that the commonest sinner can do, when I have ceased to wander among the tombs searching for the little obscure grave in which the facts of my mother's story are buried, sentences in that "begging letter" rise before me, unbidden, and again I grow cold as when I first read them, and again I feel that shock to my whole system which ends in dizzy nausea and a profuse sweat.

"If my child is still with you, of which I am not sure, I implore you for her sake to send me ten pounds." The trifling sum asked for increased my anguish. "I have never known what it is to be without luxuries…yet here I am hopelessly ill in this dirty, squalid room, without the means to buy any food that I can eat. It does not seem as if I should get better, and indeed I don't wish to, as I have lost everything. Not a friend, I who have been so much loved. But a little money for nourishing food would be a relief. The doctor ordered me oysters when he last came, and suggested my wintering in Syracuse! I laughed, and asked him how he thought I was going to follow his treatment, when I owed the proprietaire here six months' rent. He said he regretted—that was not his affair. It was his duty to give medical advice. If only he had given me a few oysters instead. But, poor man, I daresay no one pays him.

"I do not send a message to John-Baptist. You would not give it, I expect. I am glad she will never know that I came to this… with hope and ambition for nothing beyond a dozen oysters.

"If you cannot grant my request, please do not write. A letter of refusal is so heart-rending to a beggar, especially to one who is as sensitive as I am…. Yes, in spite of my life which ought to have thickened my skin, I am terribly sensitive."

The letter was signed "She that was Cécilie Montolivet." Across it was written in Mamma's hand: "Considering all the circumstances, decided not to send money. Doubted whether letter was genuine."

"Then why didn't you ask me?" I spoke to Mamma in her grave, but quite gently, for I always thought of her now in her mortal weakness, and I could not be angry with her, any more than I could have struck her in her last moments. I was sure, all the same, that she had made a cruel mistake. I recognised myself in the letter, and I knew that I could have written it only in terrible straits. My mother had needed ten pounds, had needed them so much that she had brought herself to appeal to a stranger. That was genuine. It did not seem to me to matter whether her account of her situation were true or false, seeing that, whatever it was, it was proclaimed desperate. But I never doubted for a minute that every word was true…. Was it through her own fault that she was poor and forsaken? The worse guilt, I was inspired to think, is that which accumulates the deeper guilt of wealth and prosperity. I knew nothing of my mother's life, but the thought of her misery and discomfort, her untended sickness in that mean little hotel, her humility in not sending me a message, restored her to me in all her primal innocence. Had she written from the Hotel Ritz, and simulated interest in me, indulging in sentiment about the dead, distant past, while she bought new hats and attracted new lovers, and ate delicate food, how different my feelings would have been! As it was, I said "Darling, you shall never know what hunger is any more!" and rushed into her arms.

IX

In some of my father's letters to my mother there were bits of biography. They interested me, and did not hurt me so much as the expressions of his ardent love, which seemed so pitiful in the light of what had happened afterwards.

He wrote, always with the object of revealing himself to his beloved, of the conversion of his grandfather, John Montolivet, to the Catholic faith. In those days before the Catholic Emancipation Bill a confession of such a change of religion meant grave sacrifices, but John Montolivet had made them. He had resigned his commission in His Majesty's army, and had been thrown upon the world, deprived of his younger son's share in the Montolivet patrimony. His father was indignant that a son of his should have become a Papist, and would do nothing for him except undertake to support his wife and child so long as they adhered to the Protestant religion by law established. As the Montolivets had been established in England long before that religion, and as they had not benefited at all by the dissolution of the monasteries, bigotry in them was less intelligible than in most families, and probably John's act was punished harshly more because of its social consequences than because his father was rich in Anti-Popery prejudices. The only Montolivet who had distinguished himself since the Reformation had been a statesman and writer who could afford to be tolerant of warring creeds, since he had no faith himself. That great Remy Montolivet had even joined for a time, after his fall from power under a Protestant sovereign, in a plot to replace a Catholic King on the English throne, and had spent some of the years of his long life at the Court that the claimant maintained in France.

There seems to have been little of this great Montolivet's passion for intrigue, or of his overmastering ambition, in his descendant John, facing the world with nothing but a few principles, disowned by his family, forced to separate himself from wife and child, while he went into exile to live the rough life of a soldier of fortune. And all because, while guarding a party of French prisoners in Suffolk, one of them had let slip a few words which had sown themselves in the heart of the young captain of dragoons, and come up mighty convictions, for love of which he must sacrifice all other loves!

My father told the story well. I felt as if I were sitting by the fire, listening to him. I was excited and joyful when he came to the part where Captain John, taking a holiday from using his sword in the cause of the Poles against Tsar Nicholas, returned to England and carried off his young son, Remy, from his Montolivet home, from England, Eton, Oxford, and the Protestant religion by law established. "He had heard of his wife's death, so he went home to ask for his son fairly and squarely. When my grandfather refused to give up his grandson, my father came back at night and simply kidnapped him!"

After that Captain John's name had been blotted out of the Montolivet records. His disgrace was complete when he robbed his son of the advantages of being a Montolivet. How did Remy like the change, I wondered. Did he regret Eton at his Jesuit school near Vienna? Did he know that the change in his religion to which he seems to have offered no opposition had cost him £30,000? My father spoke of hardships that his father had had to endure, Captain John always being at grips with necessity. "I should never have had the pluck to endure what they endured…. They knew what I shall never know…they won the victory over things that I should never have conquered. Thank God for their experience of life, though, or I should have been an ordinary young English fool, unwilling to learn anything from any country except my own."

Here was romance enough and to spare. It outstripped all my childish dreams—the real Montolivets were more interesting than the imaginary De Courcys—but I was struck by the fact that there was no tale of glory in it, no wonderful achievement that might have set the exiles on a pinnacle for the admiration and envy of their family at home. Captain John did not die in action, but of a lingering illness in a hospital in Warsaw; and my father said he was the victim of "damned ingratitude" at the hands of the party of Polish freedom. Remy made no mark of any kind. He married a young Polish girl belonging to an ancient family, ennobled since the Crusades, but impoverished by the Russian occupation, and the marriage was not at all happy. The final breach came in England, where he had taken her on a visit, perhaps with the idea of reconciling himself with his family. There was another visitor in England at that time—the Tsar Nicholas I. A country that could receive with honour that tyrant who had the blood of thousands of her countrymen on his hands was no place for my Polish grandmother. While the English journals of the time were appealing to all Polish refugees in London not to create a disturbance when Nicholas appeared there as the guest of Queen Victoria, my grandmother started for Warsaw to take an active part in a new rising against him. "She always said that if she had stayed she would have killed him…. If you had ever heard her talk of the atrocious sights that she herself witnessed, when the Emperor was trying to root out the Catholic faith in Poland, you would be surprised that she did not. What an event it would have been! I can almost see the letters that the Montolivets would have written to 'The Times' disclaiming any connection with the assassin!"

I felt sorry for my father because this militant, patriotic mother of his had died young, and he had lost touch with his Polish relations. I saw him drifting about the Continent with his invalid father—poor Remy Montolivet had never recovered from a bullet wound received in Poland in his youth—with just enough money to make an indolent life possible. His letters revealed a pleasure-loving, charming, and generous nature, with rare gifts lying uncultivated, and a fascinating sense of humour. They revealed one who at forty, the age when he had met my mother, was still a great child, who looked on life as a beautiful game. His tenderness for beautiful things was quite extraordinary, and was the snare in which his feet were entangled. "God and the devil fight in beauty," he wrote more than once. "There is great comfort in ordinary people to whom love does not mean a tempest in the blood. That is why I am fond of Eleanor Wingfield. You know I once asked her to run away with me? You should have seen her face! I asked her not because I loved her, but because I wanted to give her a good time…and I knew her married life was going to be a state of slavery to the end. If she had said she would come, I wonder what on earth I should have done?"

X

It was all like a large oil-painting defaced by some obliterating chemical, from which a patch here and there had escaped to create wondering guesses at the subject and colour of the whole picture.

I grew tired of guessing. My soul was weighed down by the riddles of the universe, of which my individual share seemed an epitome. If they could be solved, how would their solution help me? My position in life was anomalous—it must remain so always. For a time I thought of calling myself John-Baptist Montolivet, a name so curious that it would certainly invite the attention from which at this time I shrank, as though I were responsible for keeping my dead parents' secret. I began to feel there was much truth in the platitude, "Where ignorance is bliss, 'tis folly to be wise."

By Mrs. Wingfield's will I was left £500. That seemed to me quite fair, for the money that had been given her when she adopted me was hers, not mine.

I tore off my black clothes in the Christmas vacation which I spent with Sunny in the north, and banged the door on the Wingfields, on the Motolivets, on all problems, on all pride and humiliation of heredity. Many a time I was tempted to burn that packet of letters, and they were eventually burned, though not by an act of my own will. I trained myself not to think of the past, but to live in the moment, to become as great an individualist as I could. By an individualist I meant one who derived all from self, and asked for nothing else, and was affected by nothing else. What else was of any importance? I was myself—the only firm ground in the whole quicksand, the only fact in which I should be clothed in the hour of death. Sometimes I believed that I had dreamed my history, that it had all been scrawled by my imagination; and this consoled me, as showing how little reality it had, even if true. When my companions spoke of their relations, I invented stories of mine to match theirs, and this absurd mendacity was also a consolation. For some time I felt as if I were compelled to drag about a cage of wild beasts, a heavily screened cage. I hoped if I did not feed those savage sorrows they would die. And sometimes there would creep to the bars, and try pitifully to move the blinds, a little thing not at all wild—the thought of my mother, longing for oysters in the shabby Paris hotel.

VI
WORK

I

"You must not be depressed by your position in the class-list," said my tutor. "It by no means represents your attainments."

A week had passed since the Honours list in Modern History had been posted up at the Schools, and the remembrance of the moment when I had seen my name in the third class was still bitter. I had worked very hard at the last, but I could not make up for times when I had never worked at all. Probably the result would have been the same if I had worked evenly all along. That want of power to sustain, that working of my intellectual activity in flashing moments succeeded by long periods of quiescence, would have found a week of examination papers too long and exhausting an ordeal in any case. I had willfully destroyed what chances of success I had when, instead of "cramming" during the last Long Vacation before the final, I had gone to Russia with Madame Pohlakoff, spending some time in France and Italy with her on the way. She had wished me not to return at all, but in spite of my ardent affection for her I could not bring myself to the point of accepting complete economic dependence on her. At least this is how I explained my irresistible desire to go back to England, where my prospects were far from bright.

Most of the Marville students who had done well in the Schools in my time had become schoolmistresses. I knew that teaching was not my vocation. I knew that my ambition of going to London when I had done with Oxford, and of earning my living by writing, would be very hard to realize. Had I nostalgia for England and English people? There was no one in England at this time to whom I was strongly attached, and the loveliest landscape there seemed to me like fancy-work compared with those immense stretches of Russian earth. I never felt a stranger in Russia, and had no difficulty in understanding the people I met there, although I did not understand their language. Madame Pohlakoff praised my adaptableness, and told me that her friends liked me. I noticed that her friends were all men. The women of her own class never visited her, either in the country or in St. Petersburg.

There was a mystery surrounding my dear one—a mystery from which an unseen power was withdrawing me before I penetrated it.

"Do you see in any of the young men who come here him whom you would like to marry, Ivan?"

So she called me now, adhering to her "little boy" impression of me.

"No," I answered, with a strange sensation that these words foretold my destiny if I remained in Russia.

"Still obstinate on that point? Still resolved to live and die a virgin?"

I blushed to my forehead.

"You yourself taught me that marriage was a Schweinerei without great spiritual love."

"Well, you may find that great love…. You are young yet. A strange child. No bit what you call a prude…yet so empty of the natural feelings. Ha! When love takes possession of you, you will find you do not object to being a pig…an animal. It is such a warm, caressing child too. I feel love flowing out of it sometimes, and I cannot but ask myself who will be submerged in that beautiful hot flood. And that makes you angry, because you are, oh so English!"

"No! no!" I thought of my grandmother, who would have killed Nicholas I.—for love! Of Captain John, who had become a poor exiled adventurer—for love! Of my father, who had been ruined—for love! Of my mother, dying in loneliness and poverty—through love! I was wounded by the suggestion that I, the fruit of such lovers, could not love. I felt the passion in me rising, burning my reserve, licking my body as a flame licks wood.

"If you could understand! If I could understand myself!" I wept because it was impossible to explain, or to justify myself to her.

She comforted me, with gentle childish words. "My little boy! My Vanusha! I not mean to hurt you. You are not at all cold or English…just a little mad, c'est tout [that's all]!"

If I could have found the words I would have told her that I was frightened at the love in me—that I poured it out on the wind when it touched my face, on the earth when I lay on it, on every human being who brought me joy for a moment. But it was never the proximity of a man, as man, that called out this love. Indeed, it was just that proximity which sometimes made it suffer a complete eclipse. I had a great dread of being snared into the trap and finding that I had been wounded for nothing. How could sensual caresses, the acts of animals, interpret this infinite inebriating love? It was a great mystery to me, this prohibition that the spirit in me laid on my ardent palpitating senses.

II

You who read this may deduce from it that I was a young girl who disliked men—who, because she had less subtle magnetism for them than most women have, became a man-hater to console herself for deficiency. The deduction would be entirely false. I was at this time, and for many years subsequently, far happier with men than with women. One reason was that they seemed more intelligent and more simple. They were, so far as my experience at Oxford went, better friends—or rather better comrades, for friendship is the rarest thing in the world and I did not know what it meant until I was much older.

I have said that I can hardly recall the names and faces of the girls who were at school with me, and these undergraduate comrades of mine have also receded into shadow-land. I retain sweet memories of expeditions up the river, of teas in lovely old rooms at Christ Church and Oriel and Magdalen, with those excellent hot toasted buns that never taste the same out of Oxford, of luncheons and breakfasts during "Eights" week, and dances at "Commem." Through these innocent diversions flit faces into which I looked frankly, and which gave me back a boyish sympathy, a fresh and clean affection.

I remember one face in particular—belonging to a boy with a great love of nature. He knew all the wild flowers by their names, and no bird's note was strange to him. He was at one of the less smart colleges, and some of my other friends looked down on him. In my more raffish, excitable moods, I too had a slight contempt for him, but in quieter and better moments I preferred him to any one. We used to go long country walks together, and sit in the shelter of haystacks, or lie on the grass watching the skylarks rising "to sing hymns at heaven's gate." I found out that Oswald too was a singer. He gave me a thin little volume of sonnets, published by a bookseller in the High Street, and told me humbly that no one had taken any notice of them. They had not extracted a review even from the "Oxford Magazine." I was thrilled by their beauty, and looking at Oswald's quiet, rather mousey face, wondered how he could have written the superb closing lines to his sonnet on "Disillusionment."

"Now not a corpuscle in all my blood
But in its wonted place doth quiet go."

His father was a country parson near Oxford, so when I came up in the summer vacation to learn my fate in the Schools, he was at hand, and for a week was my inseparable companion. He was always in an attitude of submission, eager to be kind in the way that I liked, eager to comfort me in a delicate, tactful way. We often sat on the grass with our arms round each other's necks as if we were children, and walked along the country roads hand in hand.

The last day had come. I was leaving Oxford for ever. Through Sunny's influence I had got a post as secretary to a retired mill-owner in the North, who had a scheme for brightening the lives of the masses in the manufacturing towns, and was making a beginning by starting a popular museum of reproductions of the world's beautiful things in the town where he had made his "brass." He had selected me as his assistant to oblige Sunny, whose people were a power in his part of the world, and because I wrote a clear, legible hand! It seemed to me that I might have learned to write decently without spending three years at Oxford, but neither then nor at any time was the "Testamur" of the University examiners any use to me. Because of my sex I was barred from the degree, the general explanation of this refusal to allow women to reap what they were allowed to sow in academic fields being that if we were admitted to the B.A. degree, we should *ipso facto* be entitled to proceed to the M.A. degree and vote for the University Candidate. This is the first time I remember having my attention drawn to woman's suffrage, which was not to become a burning question until the next decade.

Oswald was more silent and meek than usual. We happened to walk in the direction of his home. In the distance we could see the little square tower of the church and the chimneys of the parsonage.

"So that's where you're going to end your days, Osy?"

"I suppose so. My father will leave me the living. It's his own. My grandfather bought it."

"And you're becoming a clergyman just for the sake of that snug little berth?"

"I have no objection to taking orders." Oswald never would grow nasty when I was sarcastic.

"English orders are twaddle, anyway," I said.

"That's a matter of opinion."

"No, it's not. It's a matter of fact. Even reading the history of the Reformation as told by prejudiced Protestant historians has taught me that."

Our nearest approach to a quarrel had come of discussing this subject before. I had lamented the dissolution of the monasteries. Oswald had said that if the monks had not outlived their usefulness, and become weak as a moral force through the corruption of the monastic ideal, no human power could have destroyed them. I had argued that the stories of immorality in the monasteries had been exaggerated as a salve to the consciences of the people who had stolen their property. "We have an aristocracy of thieves in England. Is it a good exchange for the monastic aristocracy, who at their worst were the friends of the poor?"

Oswald, remembering the bitterness of our discussion on that occasion, did not pursue the question of the validity of Anglican orders, but asked me why, as I had such pronounced Roman Catholic sympathies, I did not become a Roman Catholic?

The question made me strangely angry. I did not want Oswald to know that while I was sure that the Catholic Church was the only Church, and the Catholic religion the only one worth considering, I had no faith. I had good reason for believing that I had been baptized by a Catholic priest, but my education as a Catholic had ceased at the font, if there had been a font, and I hated the Church which seemed to have cast me out, and to have deserted me as my parents had deserted me. Once or twice since I had read my father's letters, many of them containing touching allusions to his faith, I had gone timidly into the Catholic church which abutted on to our garden at Marville, and had stood at the back, wondering at the beauty and stateliness of the ceremonial which obliterated the ugliness of the building, and silenced criticism of the poor oil paintings of the Way of the Cross, and the vapid plaster statues. I had never stayed more than a few minutes, however. My attitude was one of profound terror mingled with hatred. Here in this church I felt that they believed in God, and in a beloved God. The lights and flowers, the continuous stately movements of the priest before the altar all proceeded from love, a love which I did not understand and could not share. What a horrible thing it would be to love One Who had allowed me to grow up ignorant and unenlightened, and had not missed me in that congregation of the faithful! It was then I would slip out of the church, like some savage humiliated by his darkness and nudity for the first time, and I would take the earliest opportunity of going to an afternoon service at Magdalen College Chapel to restore my irreligious content. Here there was no invisible Beloved, but the respected but unloved divinity of the English people. It was all about as devotional as a banquet at the Mansion House. Thoughts like these made me silent when Oswald questioned me as to my Catholic sympathies.

"I suppose you don't approve of clergymen marrying?" We were walking back to Oxford, and the moment of farewell was near.

"Oh, Oswald, why do you start that again! You know it makes us quarrel."

"I have a particular reason." He stood still in the country road, on which the day was closing in. I am sorry to say that I noticed that he wore cheap, ill-made boots as he scraped the dust together with them into little heaps.

"I want you to know that I care enough…in fact, I want to marry you." He never looked up, and continued to take great interest in his dust-hills.

This was the first proposal of marriage that had been made to me since my childhood, and I took it very seriously. I was really fond of Oswald. He was simple and humble, and although a time was coming when I was to be false to myself and to my ideals of what people ought to be, it was natural to me to love and admire simplicity and humility. I was nineteen, still on the threshold of life, but I had already suffered cruelly, and I was terrified lest with each succeeding year I should grow in the power to suffer. My third class had made me more doubtful than ever of my ability. I was not convinced by my tutor's opinion that I should do better in the world which lay beyond the Isis and the Cherwell. The lot of the undistinguished professional woman stretched before me, full of all those mean discomforts which I loathed. I loved the country, and Oswald would minister to that love. He would shelter me from the consequences of my character and history. He need not know of the existence of John-Baptist Montolivet.

While I made these rapid calculations Oswald looked at me timidly.

"You might say something. You don't know how it hurts."

I was touched by this, yet it alienated me. My brain felt as clear and cool as glass, reflecting the future of a curate's wife, reflecting me constantly "hurting" Oswald, provoking him at last to retaliation. It reflected, too, the meanness of marrying him to escape from life. It reflected the word "Schweinerei."

I was suddenly seized with horror of Oswald. The dear comrade had become offensive to me. And still I said nothing, but walked on to the grass at the side of the road, and looked away from him over the low hedge at a field of waving corn. He lumbered after me, and put his arm round me. He kissed my cheek in a frightened way, and murmured: "Do say something. I love you…I love you so much."

"Osy…I beg you not to say any more." I groped for words that should not wound him, and found only these: "I don't want to marry."

"But you're fond of me."

"Of course I am."

"There isn't any one else?"

The silly turn that the conversation was taking exasperated me. "Can't you believe me when I say quite simply that I don't want to marry?"

"But why? You may change your mind."

"Don't waste your time in hoping for that. Come, let's go home."

We walked back to Oxford in silence. I felt miserable because I had hurt him; I wished that he was vain, for vanity would have made him angry.

"Good-bye, dear, dear Osy." We had reached the gate of Marville. He smiled at me pathetically, like a sick child who has been told that he may never play some game any more.

"Don't be unhappy. I could not be unhappy if I had written those sonnets."

"I would rather have you than be Shakespeare."

The expression "have you" grated on me.

"You want me, without caring what I should bring? You would be content to love me though your love made me sick?"

"No, no," he protested. "But I would be content with very little. I just want to watch over you, to save you from being hurt by life, to leave nothing undone that could make you happy, to protect you from unpleasant things.... I can't bear to think of your working for your living."

"My dear boy! I expect I should have to work fairly hard even if I married you! The profession of a poor man's wife is not a very well paid one either, so far as I can see.... However, we needn't discuss that, because it has nothing whatever to do with it."

My fear of the lonely road had vanished. It beckoned to me now with a gesture far more passionate than any that Oswald used. I saw myself grappling with necessity and throwing her easily. I saw bright superb things waiting for me, things that were worth fighting to reach. Some words of Keats's comforted me as I left Oxford the next day to begin the fight. "I was never afraid of failure, for I would rather fail than not be among the greatest."

III

I had thought it would be easy to write when the day's routine work was ended, encouraging myself by great examples: Charles Lamb, producing the exquisitely concentrated beauty of the Essays of Elia while a clerk at the India House; Rousseau, achieving immortality while copying music for bread. Yet during the next four years my first novel made little progress. I succumbed to mental fatigue. I never could keep myself out of the work that I had to do for others, and reserve my strength for my own.

Then I had not that firmness of will, that rigidity of purpose, that heart-whole determination to succeed, which characterize those who win in this world. I was easily distracted either by melancholy thoughts of the vanity of adding to the huge unnecessary book population, or by my youthful desire to enjoy myself while I was young and healthy and strong. At Larkscoe, where I labelled and catalogued and classified, and wrote letters for Mr. Forran, I often spent my free time in walking miles over the bleak and barren Derbyshire hills, and was happy because the heather was under my feet, the sky over my head and the wind on my face. I never saw a labourer going home from work without being filled with envy of those whose destiny was to toil in heaven's air, who ate plain, coarse food without demur, who had no aspirations gnawing at their hearts, who were not oppressed by the monotony of existence, and to whom a pipe, a newspaper and a drink brought a satisfaction that I should never know.

On Saturdays it was my duty to drive into the big manufacturing town, always wrapped in a man-made night, where Mr. Forran's museum for the people was situated, and attend there to "be of help" to the visitors. I was extremely shy of the few weavers who did come in, and could have burst into tears when the mill lasses mimicked my Southern accent and good-naturedly made game of me. It puzzled me that I, who had so much fraternal feeling for those who laboured in the abominable darkness of this wretched town, who felt the injustice of their producing wealth for such insufficient reward as a "living wage" on which none could live beautifully, could not get on terms with them. I used to think with a pang on envy of how Martha Ladde would have "jollied" them, although behind their backs she would have spoken of them as "the lower classes," and considered that poverty and discomfort were their due, as luxury and pleasure were hers.

Mr. Forran lived in a fool's paradise of press-cuttings, and never seemed to doubt that his scheme of teaching the workers to appreciate art and nature was a success. When *The Times* devoted a leader to his praise, and a philanthropic Princess promised to come and "open" his museum, although it had been open in the ordinary sense for months, he grew in self-importance before my eyes.

But the words of a sturdy young silk-weaver made a great impression on me. I had begun to converse with him in the section devoted to the wild birds of England, and, thanks to Oswald, I had been able to tell him a little more about some of them than appeared on the labels on the cases. In his opinion, which he expressed with all the wealth of the Northerners' dialect, all these notions of improving their taste were no good.

"It's like locking the door when the horse is stolen," he said forcibly. "Like spending money on big places for consumptives instead of trying to remove all that means consumption; like being kind to cripples made by lead-poisoning, instead of taking the poison right out. To my mind that's what's wrong. Ned Forran and the rest spend their brass on making it up to the sufferers, instead of trying to root up the evils that have produced them. It's like this, you see. When we've got decent houses, and are working under proper conditions, and have more leisure, we shall want all this"—he waved his arm at the cases of stuffed birds—"we shall have as much taste as you. But I don't hold with its being poured into us by the rich. It's got to be a spring, not a cistern. I'd like things to be worse so that they can be better. I'd like landlords and capitalists to be harder, and to offer us none of these pretty little sops. Then the worst sheep among us would become lions, not to be deceived. So I'm not grateful to Ned Forran for coming down here and trying to brighten our lives. Let 'em get darker and darker. Then there'll be some hope of dawn."

I have not attempted to reproduce the young weaver's rich idiomatic dialect, but I have reproduced his wisdom, which made a lasting impression on my mind.

VII
STRUGGLE

I

The next few years were the darkest in my life, and by "my life" I mean always the history of my soul. It is this history which we miss in the "biography famous." We read of what a man did, of events in which he was concerned, of people that he met, of women that he loved; but of the one thing necessary, the one thing of immortal interest, we are usually left in ignorance.

Life is often compared with a play, but the play to which it bears greatest resemblance is one which has never been written, where each act is divided into two scenes, the first dealing with the actions and speeches of the characters, the second reproducing the interior and hidden life from which those words and acts arose, and showing the spirit in conflict or in union with the visible drama. What a strange reversal of the judgements and emotions created by the first scene would be provoked by the second! How often would greatness appear little, and virtue vicious, the lie a truth, and success failure! But the only dramatists who could write the second scene are the recording angels.

Mr. Forran dismissed me, on the ground that I was not interested in his work, and that my want of interest made me careless and inaccurate—charges that were more or less true. The charges that I could have made against him were those that can usually be made by a sensitive person occupying a dependent position in the house of a rich man. I dined with him and his family as an equal, unless there were visitors. Then I was banished from the dining-room, and had meals in the schoolroom with governess. In a hundred ways I was made to feel that the work I did was overpaid, and that I did not show enough gratitude for the advantage of earning my living in such pleasant and delightful surroundings. Mr. Forran lived in a narrow circle of sycophants, with his wife as leader of the chorus of adulation. The spectacle of this little tyrant of a little world exacting sacrifices from every one roused my hostility, and my enforced silence made me sullen.

With what joy I left Larkscoe for London! The shrill screaming of the engine as the train approached Euston sounded to me like the noise of real battle. I had been to London before, with the Gosboroughs, and later had stayed there with Oxford friends, but it was a very different London which now swallowed me up. Its immense indifference to arrival of a new victim roused my defiance. "I shall conquer you yet," I thought.

After a few days at common lodging-house for decayed gentlewomen, generally known as "The Catteries," I set out to look for lodgings. I had a few bits of furniture stored at Oxford, and when I had found two low-ceilinged attics in a quiet eighteenth-century street in Westminster, and put these bits there, I felt for the first time in my life that I had a home. My prints looked far better on the panelled walls than they had done at Marville. How welcome was the silence after Mr. Forran's booming voice! How delightful it was to sit down at night to some "comestible" bought from a ham-and-beef shop round the corner, and make my own coffee as Madame Pohlakoff had taught me to make it! I looked out on a wall dating from Norman times.... I could see a bit of the Abbey, and the big dormitory of Westminster School.... I was alone, but my solitude was peopled with beautiful shapes. Ambition stirred in me. Here surely I could write, as already I could dream.

Everything went well at first. Through an introduction from an undergraduate friend I got a post as proof-reader and doer of all kinds of odd jobs in the office of a weekly literary journal. I sat in the outer office with the office-boy, and wrote paragraphs which were mercilessly cut in the inner office, and passed all the articles for press.

Unfortunately this continual reading of other people's work affected my individuality. I strove to imitate this writer and that in the articles that I sent to other papers, thinking that in this way I should give satisfaction. And I was encouraged in my wretched course by the fact that anything that was accepted was always one of these imitations, while what was truly my own thought expressed in my own way was invariably rejected.

My undergraduate friend who was still "up" at the University did not think my position as a sort of a superior office-boy did him credit, and he sent me another introduction, this time to his uncle, who was a newspaper proprietor. I called on the great man without delay, for I was finding it increasingly difficult to live on my salary, and I wanted a new pair of shoes.

He was busy writing when, after an agonizing period of waiting at the "Enquiries" pigeon-hole, I was at last conducted to his room. He jerked out, "Sit down," and went on with his work. Suddenly he looked up and fixed me with a peculiarly terrifying dark eye.

"So you know my young scamp of a nephew?"

"Yes."

"Is he in love with you?"

"Good Heavens! No!"

"Then what has he written this for?"

He picked up the letter of introduction, and let it drop scornfully.

"I suppose he wanted to help me. He knows I have to earn my own living."

"He doesn't say that," said Mr. Ling-Roberts. "He says you're one of the most talented people he has ever met."

I thought this was generous of young Ling-Roberts, yet was afraid that his praise was making a fool of me in his uncle's eyes.

"Talent is important in journalism, no doubt, but a rhinoceros hide is still more important."

My heart went down into those worn-out shoes which I was longing to replace.

"Well, what can you do?"

I nearly answered "Nothing." Then I said in a stilted way that I thought I could write well on any subject that interested me.

"Does music interest you?"

"Very much," and again my sincerity tempted me to add, "But I am totally ignorant of it."

"Well, it happens that we want a musical critic on *The Guide*." He named his halfpenny evening paper. "Notes on concerts twice a week, running to half a column. Two guineas a column. I don't interfere with my editors. If the Editor of *The Guide* isn't satisfied, he'll tell you so. But you can try it."

I forgot my incompetence for the job and thanked him whole-heartedly.

"That'll do," he said sternly. "Never be grateful and never be frank—in a newspaper office at any rate. Leave your address downstairs. Good-morning."

I went out into the fog with a radiant heart. I thought of new shoes, and of being able to afford to go out to dinner sometimes instead of eating cold sausage at home. I gave the blind man near Westminster Abbey all the money I had in my pocket, although I had been told that he was not really blind.

II

Now indeed, had I been the beast or god who loves solitude, I ought to have been happy. Alone I sat in the office of *The*

Weekly Digest, except for the occasional company of the office-boy; alone I attended concerts for *The Guide*; alone I went to the pit at the theatre, when I had half a crown to spare; alone I had dinner in little foreign restaurants in Soho; alone I walked about the streets, stopping a long time at the second-hand booksellers', and reading books in the shelves outside until a cold look from the proprietor at an unprofitable customer would send me away shamefaced at not buying anything. Alone I swelled with pride when I opened an evening paper of greater repute than *The Guide*, and found some verses printed in it, bearing the signature of "J.B. Montolivet." Although I still kept the name of Wingfield for the traffic of daily life, I adopted my own name as a pseudonym—a strange reversal of the usual custom. I tried to believe that my loneliness was sweet, but there were times when the sweetness was sprinkled with gall. Independence had always allured me. Now I had it, and melancholy would overtake me because there was no one to care about my goings-out and comings-in.

I applied myself feverishly to my novel. I did not want to write like the English novelists, even the best of them. I revolted against their fidelity to detail, their exasperatingly minute descriptions of everyday life and everyday people. The exceptional moments in the lives of exceptional people seemed to me the right stuff on which to work. However much the novels I reviewed for *The Digest* might differ in subject and in craftsmanship, they all resembled each other in being poor in definite, simple things. They admitted the commonplace too freely, and shut the door on the heroic. Then they did not discern the greatness in little ordinary things, as did Balzac. They were content to reproduce them. With what immense relief I used to turn from the jejune chatter of the average English novel to the splendid poetry of Dostoyevsky, of Turgenev, of Tolstoy and of my compatriot Sienkiewiecz. The strange orchidaceous beauty of Gabriele d'Annunzio's novels also compelled my admiration. Whatever might be urged against these foreign novelists, they dealt with huge things, with beautiful truth not with ugly truthfulness. They achieved universality through poetry. What Russian, what Italian, what Frenchman could read the English novel, with its parochial interests, its avoidance of psychological mysteries, its degradation of love into flirtation and coquetry?

So I meditated in my youthful insolence, and stood before the walls of epic achievement, thinking that I could storm them with my imagination. Often I had reason to remember Madame Pohlakoff's prophetic words: "The poet's heart will give you great suffering without the poet's genius." There is no melancholy like that of the mind that can apprehend its own powerlessness to do the thing it would do. I fell into what the Church calls "accidie," wilful sadness, and lent my ears to the voice of the tempter that whispered that I must live before I could hope to write.

It was at this critical moment that the Gosboroughs came back from Italy. Lord Gosborough had married again; Arthur was now in the Guards; Lettice and Violet had changed greatly since the Crupples days. They had lost their youth, and were not bearing the loss gracefully. They were a curious pair, admiring each other extravagantly one minute, and quarrelling bitterly the next. Both of them loved me, not very warmly or unselfishly, but enough to make them want to see me. They came to London for the season now, the second Lady Gosborough thinking that this was the way to get Lettice married; and through them I again began to see something of "life." My ascetic solitary existence was invaded by Lettice and Violet and their friends. I rejoiced at the invasion. The part of my nature which loved pleasure and delicate food and the companionship of those who shared my tastes, if not my aspirations, conquered the part which welcomed hardships and suffering and loneliness.

I lost *myself* in these days, adopted the views of others, dulled my anguished desire for creation by sharing so far as I could the freedom and idleness and comfort in which the Gosborough world lived. I was never really naturalized in that world, but I took pleasure in sojourning there, in feeling that I was able to absorb its manners and its peculiarities. My pride often rebelled at being patronized; I was disgusted to find that I was never taken on my merits. It was all right for anyone in this world whose position was secure to be shabby and dowdy, but for the "doubt-fuls" it was obligatory to dress well. I strove to dress like Violet and Lettice, and soon got into debt.

I threw away my precious inheritance, a love of simplicity and humility, a joy in innocence and purity, and began to cultivate a sort of Pagan belief that pleasure was the object of life, and that those who lived for pleasure were those who lived best. Of all the acquaintances that I made in this aristocratic Gosborough circle there was not one who was living for anything else. It is true that some of them dabbled in charity, but if they had been asked to make any real sacrifice for the poor, for whose benefit they would sometimes sing and dance, they would have refused, I know.

Often when I drove from my poor little Westminster street, through streets more squalid, to the stately mansion in which the Gosboroughs lived when they were in London, I felt an insensate hatred for the rich, and for myself who sat silent at their table while they expressed their prejudices and discussed their amusements as though poverty and failure and disgrace and suffering were no concern of theirs. With a few exceptions these people were more innately vulgar even than the "middle classes," for whom they had a scorn all the more intense because they never expressed it.

The worst fault of the middle classes in England is that they are the people who keep alive the fiction that there is some special distinction about the English aristocracy. It is true that those members of it who came under my observation at this time did not indulge in the *niaiseries* [silly things] of those born and bred in less exalted circles. Their very sureness that they were the salt of the earth prevented them from fawning on those a step above them in the social scale, and we must not forget that there is no definite top to this ridiculous ladder. The steps increase in number as they decrease in steepness when the middle has been left behind. But I maintain that the pathetic frankness of middle-class snobbishness, exasperated as it may be, is far less odious than the reserved snobbishness of the fashionable world.

I was always hearing the word "well-bred," but what I understood by it, and what people whose breeding was beyond dispute understood by it were things entirely opposed. Good manners among these people appeared to be manners which were friendly only to equals. If these good-mannered aristocrats came across any one of whose credentials they were uncertain, their attitude was one of frigid or insolent condescension. Even their pride was of doubtful quality, since it would melt like wax before the influence of wealth. Wealth appeared to be the passport of the climber. Then if he wished to take out papers of naturalization, he had to adopt the habits and the jargon of his new compatriots. He too had to learn to value every one for what they have, not for what they are.

When I recall my own adventures among this rude, arrogant aristocracy, I blush for the servility with which I endured their condescending kindness, and for my efforts to absorb their science of values. The favourite remark on hearing my name was: "I knew some Devonshire Wingfields." And as I was not a Wingfield either from Devonshire or Tottenham, the conversation dropped. Old Lady H. said to me frankly: "Do you know why I am so polite to you, my dear? Sophia, Lady A. (mentioning a famous old Victorian marchioness recently dead) had this maxim: 'Always be civil to a young girl. You never know if one day she won't be a Duchess.'"

There must be a conspiracy to keep alive the tradition that there is some refined and noble odour of rank as there is an odour of sanctity. We laugh at the caricatures of the nobility in books and plays, but we do not realize what a caricature of humanity at its noblest is the reality! Most of our landed proprietors began badly, as I had told Oswald, by stealing the property of the Church or receiving its stolen property. But the Reformation did more than enrich and ennoble brigandage. It destroyed that great and humbling idea of spiritual equality which the Church imposed on those who were rich in material possessions. The most highly honoured members of our mediæval nobility were those who embraced the religious life, who, like St. Francis, himself a noble, took poverty to be their bride. Proud the old-time aristocracy may have been, rich it may have been, but it recognized that above it was an aristocracy of poverty and humility. The English, we say, dearly love a lord. When they dearly loved a saint, they knew better what was the value of social distinction.

III

"My friends, show me my friend." I stood on Battersea Bridge gazing at the sullen, swift current of the river. "Here is my friend," I thought. Yet tears came into my eyes at the pity of it. I was young—only just of age. I was strong and well, yet I wanted to throw myself into the Thames. Destitution stared me in the face. I could not live, although in spite of everything life was sweet.

Disasters had overtaken me in swift succession. First I had been peremptorily dismissed from *The Guide* because I had written a libel. In an interview with Mr. Ling-Roberts I had protested that what I had said was true. "Your truth has cost us £80," he replied. "That is what we have had to pay the young lady whose violin playing you did not appreciate." "But why not fight it?" I clung desperately to the honesty of my convictions. "Because it would cost us more than £80 if we won. The words complained of are 'posing as a prodigy.' The girl's father says he can produce her birth-certificate, which will disprove your implication that her youthful appearance is assumed for the platform."

"It may have been bluff on his part."

Mr. Ling Roberts looked at me with a sardonic expression.

"I don't want contributors who cause trouble. Whether you were justified or not doesn't matter."

"Won't you give me another chance?"

"My dear young lady, you're not sufficiently valuable to my paper for me to risk your costing me another £80."

I thought that this was quite true. My musical criticism amounted to very little as criticism. If my notices had been headed "Impressions," and signed "Ignoramus," I could have defended them on the score of their honesty and their freedom from the usual *clichés*. As things were, I could think of nothing in their defence. I ceased to put up a fight, or to plead for reinstatement. I pulled my hat over my eyes, from which the tears were now flowing freely, and left the office of *The Guide* for ever. I thought that those tears showed that I was unfit for the world's battle; and I was humiliated by my weakness. Yet now those tears, with many others that I shed during my years of struggle in London, seem to me the one offering of any worth that I made to the hidden heavens. When I scorned myself most, I was most blessed: "*Beati qui lugent, quoniam ipsi consolabuntur.*" [Blessed are they that mourn, for they shall be comforted.]

The loss of my work on *The Guide* involved me in another disaster, from which I emerged with less credit. For some time I had striven to model my style on that of the most success-ful contributors to *The Literary Digest*. During this anxious time, when I had only twenty-five shillings a week as a certain income, I carried this imitation too far. I was accused of plagiarism, and peremptorily dismissed. I have never been able to determine whether the punishment fitted the crime, if crime it was, but I am quite sure that my fear of being myself in my writing de-served this sharp lesson. I took the disgrace greatly to heart; it seemed to me like a sentence of death. I was wounded in the only place where my life-current flowed strongly; the garden of my aspirations towards literary achievement and fame was laid desolate. I walked about the streets of London for days, desiring death, yet afraid to seek it. I lunched and dined occasionally with some of my aristocratic friends, and succeeded in concealing the anxiety that was gnawing at my vitals.

Violet Gosborough gave me five pounds to buy a new coat and skirt for the summer. I took the money, and lived on it for some time. Once or twice I tried to tell her that I was nearly destitute, but each time I saw that she could not, or would not, realize the desperateness of my position. She was quick to tell me that she also was hard up, and apparently she did not see the difference between my poverty and hers. The bitterness of going to the Gosboroughs and other rich people increased as I came nearer and nearer to the end of my money. I was in the same position as the thirsty man adrift at sea. There was money, money everywhere, but I could not contrive to get any. Ever since those evil days I have been able to imagine what the poor feel when they drag their empty stomachs and tired feet along the streets of the West End, and witness the spectacle of ex-pensively clothed people coming out of shops and restaurants, where they have spent as much money on some unnecessary trifle, or on a single meal, as would keep the outcast's head above water for a considerable time.

As I walked backwards and forwards on Battersea Bridge, I became conscious that a man was watching me closely. I had had some experience since I had lived in London of a detestable class of men who seem to have enough time on their hands to follow young girls, and enough impertinence to accost them if they show any sign that they recognize that attention is being paid to them. I had soon learned not to fear the silly creatures, and had never had any difficulty in shaking them off, but the persistent way in which this man watched me and followed me struck me as strange, even though it left me quite indifferent. I was, if anything, rather consoled by his presence, because it gave me an excuse for not taking that plunge into the river which frightened me and tempted me at the same time.

"I wouldn't do that if I were you," said the man.

I walked rapidly away from him when he spoke, but he caught me up easily.

"You'll forgive me for speaking to you, I hope," he went on. "I see you are in some fix, and that you are thinking of jumping into the river. Don't be a fool. You're young and not bad-looking. Life has a great deal to offer you."

"Kindly leave me alone." I was indignant with him for speaking to me; my one idea was to escape. It was difficult to place him socially. He was well dressed, he had an air of refinement, but his voice was quite common. His words were not at all insolent, but his look was worse than insolent. He appeared to be valuing me, to be weighing my physical advantages and disadvantages. He looked at me exactly as the pawnbroker had looked at my gold chain the day before. My resentment at that look filled my mind to the exclusion of any other emotion. I entirely forgot that I had intended to commit suicide.

"Be a sensible girl. Come and dine with me at Kettner's and we'll see what can be done for you. There is always a future for a woman, as I can prove to you. She need never want for anything."

With immense relief I saw an empty hansom approaching. Ten shillings represented my entire fortune, but I hailed the cab and jumped in.

"Is the gentleman coming too?" inquired the cabman through the trap.

"No," I said angrily. "Drive on, and as fast as you can."

"Where to, Miss?"

"Anywhere."

The man drove in the direction of Sloane Square. We passed through Cadogan Gardens; outside some of the houses carpets were spread from the door to the road, so that the rich people who were going out to dine might not soil their shoes by contact with the pavement as they walked to their carriages. I myself had walked on such carpets, and been watched enviously by a hungry passer-by. Now it was my turn to watch and to be hungry.

I paid the cab at the corner of Cadogan Square, and wandered along the pavement past those opulent houses in which lived the women who were protected from the world's dirt and squalor even to the hems of their garments and the soles of their feet. One of them came out as I passed. A butler preceded her. A footman waited with a rug at the open door of the carriage. She stared at me without recognizing me, but I recognized her. It was Lady Martha. I had a wild idea of stopping her and begging her help, but I was chilled by her expression. I realized in that moment how very insensible prosperity and pleasure make people. I hoped that I might never be so near to anguish and misery and have no pulse to vibrate to their appeal. I had no claim on Lady Martha except that I had once loved her with all my child's heart…but I was hurt that she did not know me again.

Since my meeting with the man on the bridge I had abandoned all thought of self-destruction. I had been humiliated when he had read that thought and had tempted me away from it by indicating that there was a future for me in the evil things of life. There had come to me then a certain conviction that I had a glorious future, and that I must patiently bear suffering for its sake. God was with me, although I was not with Him. He used an evil instrument to save me from taking my life, and then let it have no power over me.

Often now at night, when I see the face of some poor young prostitute under the street lamps, some girl about the age that I was when I stood on Battersea Bridge, I say to myself: "There but for the grace of God goes John-Baptist Montolivet."

IV

It was from the hand of a stranger that I received help a few days later. During those few days I learned to know what hunger was and the approach of night when a refuge was uncertain. My landlord had threatened to turn me out if I did not pay the two months' rent that I owed him. One meal a day was all that I could afford, and I had gradually reduced it to a bun and a cup of coffee. Yet there was nothing in my appearance to show that I was in distress. I still took pains to be clean and tidy. My hair and complexion were as brilliant as ever, perhaps more brilliant from my enforced fasts. Often I had noticed the dishevelled hair of the outcast women who slept on the seats on the Embankment, and had wondered if I should ever come to the state when I should not mind having an untidy head.

It was by a mere chance, as I thought then, that I went into that old-fashioned bookshop kept by a very old and surly bookseller. It is a shop frequented chiefly by collectors, for its wares are not the latest novels, but fine editions of standard works, beautiful old printed books, and expensive new publications in history and biography. Externally the old bookseller, with his grim face and horn-rimmed spectacles, his air of being accustomed to wait on distinguished customers only, was forbidding in the extreme. Yet I hung about the shop while he talked to Baron F——, whom I knew by sight from having seen him at the opera, as if I had business there. I became absorbed in Charles Lamb's Letters, a new edition of which lay on the counter, and was roused only by hearing both the collector and the bookseller at a loss for a name. I supplied it—what it was I have forgotten—and the bookseller looked at me keenly, not through his spectacles, but over them. When Baron F——had gone out of the shop, the old man came and talked to me. In a few minutes he was in possession of my story, and, looking as disagreeable as ever, he came round from his side of the counter and dropped five sovereigns into my coat pocket.

"This to go on with, till I find you some work," he grunted. "How would you like to learn typewriting and shorthand? A woman to whom I was once foolish enough to lend money, is at the head of an office where these accomplishments are taught. Instead of repaying me the loan, she can teach you."

I accepted the offer gratefully, believing that "these accomplishments" would make me of some practical use. During the term of my apprenticeship, Mr. Hardy, my old bookseller friend, found me many odd jobs, such as indexing, copying, cataloguing, addressing envelopes, which kept me alive. I drudged away patiently, but there were days when this drab life of uninteresting labour was loathsome to me. I had a frantic desire for pleasure. I wanted to exercise the strength of my youth in other ways than in clicking out letters and specifications on a typewriter at a salary of 15s. a week. I wanted to travel all over the world and steep my soul in emotion. I had such a thirst for the cup of life that I felt I must drain it even though bitterness and poison were in the draught. My face was calm, my brow still like a child's brow, but in my heart were disorder and rebellion and chaos.

It was at this time I read Nietzsche for the first time, and became impregnated with the idea that strength was glorious and weakness the only sin. I tried to persuade myself that everything was lawful, and that it was through believing in prohibitions that people became weak. In my first and last novel, on which I was still fitfully at work, there are many traces of this artificial lawless spirit which I absorbed from the "Anti-Christ" and "Zarathustra" of Nietzsche.

I strove to incorporate much of myself into the hero of this novel, and found him an easier creation than any woman in the story. I did not understand women, I thought, because they loved to attract love. They desired *to be loved*. I felt in myself a burning desire to *love*, to be the active one who gave, who held the world's record for giving. To be content to receive, to be passive, to be the beloved, was not my aim. I saw myself always as the lover.

My friends, those friends who were always confiding their love-affairs to me, those friends who knew nothing of that moment on Battersea Bridge when in a sentence the whole infamy of the world seemed to have been revealed to me, those friends who had not picked me up when I fell by the wayside, for the excellent reason that they did not know that I had fallen—my friends, as I call them half in affection, half in scorn—would often tell me that I could not write until I had "fallen in love." I would answer lightly that I could never remember having been out of love. It seemed to me, on looking back, that I had always been in love with something or somebody. Then they would wag their heads mysteriously and say that "it" was quite different, as I should know well enough when "it" came. And, although I was scornful of the mystery which I believed to be no mystery at all, I was angry at their assumption that I was inferior to them because I had not had "it" in my life. I would argue that imagination and instinct could enrich a nature far more than experience, and I poured contempt on the theory that I was ignorant of love because I had never yet loved any man. Still in my hidden heart I was vaguely troubled, and could not keep myself from wondering if this was the explanation of that famine within me, the pangs of which were far more cruel than the disappointments which attended my struggles to become rich and famous.

"To love and be loved affected me most if I could enjoy the person that loved me," says St. Augustine in the "Confession." I recognize myself in that confession. In childhood and youth a caress as a caress never meant very much to me, but where friendship existed between me and another it meant everything. The touch of a hand would penetrate to my soul when words left me unmoved. I could not show myself to any one who was physically repellent to me. My hands and my heart seemed to move in unison, and if my hands found no response, but were repulsed either through indifference or through a dislike to such demonstrations of affection, my heart immediately withdrew to its fastnesses. From this I deduced that the senses were intimately connected with the spirit, and were dangerous only when they tried to hide what they were intended to reveal and to die in revealing.

Just before I met Jerome Sales I had been strangely impressed by a saying of Cicero's quoted in Montaigne's Essay on Friendship: "Love is an endeavour to contract friendship through the splendour of beauty." I held fast to this. Love was a road to union. In this love there could be no disillusionment, because it was not a state which one expected or desired to be permanent, but a progress towards the more grave and more beautiful relation that existed between the friends of antiquity. Bearing this in mind, I was not shocked by the revelation that in these noble friendships there had been an element of sensuality. I regarded that as the gate through which men must pass before they found what they were seeking. I thought that if they were base they remained on the threshold and were transformed by their passions into beasts, but that if they were noble they passed on and transformed their passions into something very spiritual, very noble.

I had no idea of what was in store for me when Mrs. Sales came up to my little garret one autumn evening, and begged me to lunch with her the next day. She had been asked to call on me by a mere acquaintance of mine, one who seems to have appeared in my life as a servant does in a play—to set the action going. I was not restless or anxious, or shaken by a fatal presentiment, as Mrs. Sales spoke of her husband—of Jerry, as she fondly called him. "I am simply longing for Jerry to see you. You and he will have a lot in common. You are just the kind of girl he likes." It was with words like these that I was drawn towards my destiny.

From the first moment I was fascinated by Jerome Sales. I was twenty-two at this time; he must have been about forty-seven, but he did not seem to me at all old. In appearance he was rather flamboyant. You would have guessed him Italian rather than English but for his splendid physique. He was not very tall, but so well built and well proportioned that he seemed the perfect height. His dark hair, thick and crisp, was like hair in statuary; his skin had that luminous warm pallor which is rare in the English, and his clear greenish-brown eyes with their black rims were also impregnated with Southern heat. His moustache gave him the appearance of a mousquetaire or rather of a condottiere, as did also a sort of insolent assurance of being a splendid fellow that streamed from his whole personality. Most people thought his exaggeratedly ceremonious manners theatrical, and it is true that had he been less simple and less virile he might have passed for an operatic tenor.

I soon found that he was immensely lazy. When he was not taking violent exercise—he had a great fondness for sport—he was generally taking a nap. His mental gifts were very great, but he had never exerted himself to use them. He talked charmingly, all his expressions being salted with a delicious humour, a quality which made it impossible for people to be angry with him, even when they had most cause. He belonged to a very ancient and distinguished family, and he assessed the privilege at its right value. There was something about him that reminded me of my father as revealed to me in his letters. He had none of that stiffness, those carefully cherished class prejudices which had offended me in the Gosborough circle. Jerome was an *enfant terrible* in his frankness. I had not been in the house ten minutes before he asked me to take off my hat. "I hate hats, however pretty; I prefer hair, and I know before you take off your hat, which isn't pretty, that you have nice hair." We became good comrades immediately; I felt before I went home that night that he loved me, and I found it easy to love him. His simplicity made me lovable.

It never occurred to me that a time would come when Nellie Sales would be jealous. I liked her too, and at first was just as happy when she was with us as when we were alone. Then I fell ill with the first serious illness of my life, and during my convalescence I began to be conscious that our relations had changed. Jerome's anxiety about me irritated Nellie, although she was untiring in her devoted care of me. I felt that she was suspicious and uneasy, and I longed to be well enough to do without her attentions and her show of affection, which hurt me because of her distrust.

I did not blame Jerome. I have never blamed him; even though I see now that he, older and more experienced, was in a position to see the danger ahead more clearly than I, who was young and entirely innocent, in spite of the instinctive knowledge that I had of the affairs of love. People with natural moral principles, and people who are taught by religion what are the laws of good and evil, will find it difficult to believe that I hardly knew that I was doing wrong in returning his love frankly and whole-heartedly. He himself was puzzled by me. He did not find me cold, but warmly and passionately anxious to give him all I had. Yet I was grieved and disillusioned by his passion. I saw the ugly, devouring beast in it; he could not drown my thoughts in his kisses. Lawless as I was, I was always conscious of a prohibition that we must not violate; there was something in me that remained aloof, reproving and despising the ardent blood in my veins that thrilled when he was near.

Who watched over me in this hour when I walked through the fire and was not burned? Who kept my heart pure in spite of the fact that I had no reverence for purity? I can say now that it was "no other than Thyself, O God!"

V

I came back from the country with the weak chest which my illness had left me entirely cured. During my absence from London Jerome wrote to me every day—fine, simple, friendly letters, advising me so wisely about my future that again my hopes burned high that he who must not be my lover might become my loving friend. For the first time in my life I felt the joy of being cherished and cared for, of having some one as an intermediary between me and life. It was a joy to see Jerome at the station on the day of my return, to drive back with him to my humble lodgings, and find that in my absence he had had the walls repainted, and had put new plants in my window-boxes. His thoughtfulness in such little things endeared him to me more than ever.

We sat side by side on the window-seat that he had made—he was a great carpenter—and for a long time did not speak. He did not look like a human being at all, but like some faun, a creature of the forest, feline and gentle at the same time, nourished by the roots and herbs which apothecaries used to gather to make their love philtres. Not for the first time I saw that white fire invade his face. I knew that he was dominated by the madness of passion, utterly careless of my safety. I too was careless this day, for I had understood from him that Nellie had declared war, and as I felt myself innocent of having injured her, I was indignant at the outlawry into which she had driven me. So long as she had trusted me, I would have died rather than betray her trust. Now that she had done with me, I felt myself released from any obligation to consider her. Such morality as I had was all the morality of generosity, but unfortunately I had not learned that there is no great merit in behaving well to those who behave well to us.

In that burning silence the whole world seemed to vanish like a shade. I hardly thought at all. My one desire was to love. When our lips met, I had no sense of being subjugated. I gave of my own will. I would have given all, ruined myself most willingly, if I had felt that it was for my soul, and not for the pleasure of a moment, that his eyes were consumed by so cruel a fever. But soon I felt the illusion that this was love, and this was beauty, slipping from me as he held me, and at the same time the warmth slipped from my body. The chill of death crept down my back. I became strange to him—deaf, far off. It seemed to me that the closer our embrace the further we receded from one another. I broke away from him and gazed upwards. "Come back, my soul!" I cried.

VI

Men and women are not animals. Therefore they can never be happy when they are indulging the passions of animals. Their infinite souls must wake when the effects of the drug of pleasure have passed off. What a terrible melancholy there is in human love, however sweet its appearances! I felt no antagonism to Jerome, no hatred of his desire; I do not accuse him of having rubbed the bloom off my innocence. What I did to myself was far worse than anything that he did to me. But I was always infinitely sad in these days. I knew that, even if he had been free to devote his life to me, even if he could have come to me untroubled by the petty deceptions which he had to practise in order to see me, I should have suffered as much, perhaps more.

It is difficult for me to describe what was in my heart. It never occurred to me to bewail the obstacles which prevented our union. I was almost glad that they existed, so that I might never know what it was to see love, the flame of life dwindle and suffer a dreadful change into cold ashes. It was with relief, not with chagrin, that I heard Jerome confess that he would never ask me to run away with him, because by doing so he would cause more pain than he could ever hope to give joy. He liked to speak of the agony of this prohibition—to tell me how ardently he wished to have a child that should be my child, a daughter that should be dearer to him than any of his sons. I listened to him tenderly, for I understood the aspiration that I could not share. There was no hunger for maternity in me, any more than there was a desire to be loved as men love women.

I knew that Jerome had been in love many times during his married life. It was not the first time that Nellie had had cause for jealousy. This knowledge did not hurt me at all; I had an instinct that I too should love many times before I found the perfect love, love having to be learned like a language. I made progress in the language under Jerome. First I learned to be generous, to make no reproaches, to stand aloof from those who curse and lament. I learned that even for a moment's love one should be humbly grateful—that one should never regard the gift as a reward, but as a wholly unmerited blessing. I learned a delicate reserve in speaking of such a blessing. When I hear a woman boast of the love that she has inspired, or a man exult in his conquest of some heart, I am shocked as by some vulgar act of immodesty.

I do not wish to make myself out fine and well-bred in the conduct of this, my only love affair, in the ordinary and normal sense of that expression. I did much that was wrong and foolish. Undoubtedly I ought to have broken with Jerome directly his wife frowned on our friendship. But as at that time I should have done so only from a motive of respect for human conventions, renunciation might have been more barren of good than retention. When Jerome began to drift out of my life, the anguish that I suffered was more for the loss of his friendship than for that of his passionate love. It was as comrades we had been most happy. All the virility in me responded to him. All the docile child in me felt the benefit of his guidance. All the humour in me was roused to laugh at life through his humour. He was a man of the world, yet not a bit worldly, and through him I lost my last shred of respect for worldliness. Naturally expressive and simple, I had acquired in the Gosborough circle a certain artificiality and self-consciousness, a certain stiffness. I had tried to imitate the reserve in others which wounded my own impulsive spirit, and to be meticulously careful in avoiding the extraordinary. Jerome knocked all this out of me. Gracefully and easily he interpreted himself, and taught me the folly of trying to think other people's thoughts, the only thing that was interesting in man or woman being what was their own. He was an individualist, and many a time he has quoted to me these lines:

"O Seigneur, donnez-moi la force et le courage
De contempler mon corps et mon cœur sans dégoût."
[O Lord, give me the strength and courage
To contemplate my body and soul without disgust.
Charles Baudelaire]

The prayer had certainly been answered for Jerome as far as the "corps" [body] was concerned. He had a frank admiration for his own physical perfection. I used to wonder why he loved me, as he thought more of the beautiful body than of the beautiful mind, which in my pride, and with no eyes then to see how it was defaced by ugly thoughts, I believed that I possessed. He never flattered me as a rule. Perhaps that is why I remember so well his expression: "Beauty you have of a sort, and I love the sort." I remember, too, that he told me that he had always thought Oscar Wilde's favourite description of hair as "honey-coloured" absurd until he saw mine. He gloried in my strength and activity, and when we played at castles in the air, always chose for his the sea off the coast of Majorca, where we were breasting the waves together. He would tell me that my shoulders and breasts were made for swimming—although, in fact, I had never excelled as a swimmer. He said that Aphrodite and Artemis were the types into which all women could be divided, and that he had always been attracted to the Aphrodite type until I had come into his life.

I recall a familiar line, which I cannot verify, and do not really wish to verify, to the effect that "man's love is as a thing apart: 'tis woman's whole existence." It is, no doubt, very flattering to man's vanity to think that while he loves and lives as well, a woman's life consists entirely in her love for him. It confirms the theory that women exist only to give themselves to men. It has always been thought natural that man should love and ride away, and that woman should sit at the casement watching and waiting, with the sad refrain on her lips of "He cometh not, she said." The ideal woman, disappointed in love, takes up the womanly attitude of patience on a monument, and sits there eternally smiling at grief. There are women, however, who do not correspond to this ideal, women who are in love with love, and know how to cut their losses. There are women again to whom a love-affair is merely incidental, women to whom life and the love of men are not equivalent terms. When shall we cease to generalize about women, and to assume that sex is more powerful in determining their actions and emotions than the soul which has no sex, and differs in every human being born into the world?

Slowly Jerome and I drifted apart. Was it because he grew tired of Artemis and longed for Aphrodite? I never knew. I missed him cruelly, but I never felt that life was impossible for me without him. True to the one principle which was law to me, I made no reproaches. If quarrelling be a proof of love, Jerome and I never loved. No bitter words ever passed between us; no "scenes" disfigure my memories of him. The very last time we met, we spoke to each other and embraced each other as on that first day when I had taken off my hat to please him. We had no idea that it was the last time; we were unconscious that we were kneeling by a deathbed. In perfect innocence we closed the eyes of that which had been our love.

VII

"It is in the brain that everything takes place." I understand that very well. The worst effects of my endeavour to contract friendship with Jerome "through the splendour of beauty" I felt in my brain. It was in my brain henceforth that I committed sins against that purity which Jerome had not been able to undermine. Up to the time I met him I had hardly been conscious of a passionate temperament. Now it was revealed to me, and the revelation seemed to be written on my forehead. I found myself inspiring degrading passions; for the first time men who did not love me "made love" to me. I was humiliated by this, for I had not resisted conquest by one in whose passion there was much that was good and beautiful and humane, to fall a victim to the parody of it, which was often coarse and silly and brutal.

Why should I recall this period of my life? I think of it with horror, not so much on account of what I did as on account of what I became. I worked by day, but the evenings, which once I had been content to spend in solitude, often found me in the company of some man who had taken a passing fancy to me. I dined with him, went to the theatre or music-hall, sat up late in my rooms with him, smoking and drinking. I became nervous and excitable, thirsty for wine and pleasure. The danger of my way of life was in itself an attraction. I enjoyed playing with fire.

There seemed to be two natures in me: one which was happy in senseless amusement, which was not offended by coarse jests and indelicate allusions, which gloried in its shame; the other which suffered agony at this ignoble sowing of the wind, which austerely reproved any story depending for its point on some impropriety—a nature which was still as white as unsmutched snow. One nature made excuses for me, said that it was right that I should enjoy myself while I was young, and lured me into wasting my time and my talents with the unworthy; and the other condemned me, reproached me incessantly, drew me towards heights which were cold and barren of pleasure, scourged me when I strove to drug its persistent activity in the close warm atmosphere of the depths.

To those who knew me at this time I must have appeared a wild, undisciplined creature, whose utter carelessness of anything but the pleasure of the moment would end one day in disgrace and shame. The impression, if I made it, was accurate as far as it went, but because of its inadequacy it was not faithful. I was redeemed from being what I appeared to be by my suffering.

VIII
IN THE THEATRE

I

Through the theatre I escaped damnation. I find pleasure in writing this paradox, for I know that the stage is still regarded by a great number of people, perhaps by a majority, in all European countries, as "a very dangerous place and fatal," the Goodwin Sands of life, where much virtue and innocence lie buried. In England the Puritan idea that the theatres are the "devil's chapels" is not confined to a small class, and even among those who patronize the devils' chapels either for amusement or for intellectual recreation there are many who think that virtue stops at their side of the footlights, and that actors and actresses are all depraved. When any member of an ordinary English family takes to the stage as a profession, it cannot be said that it is considered a matter for congratulation. The social position of the profession has improved; alliances between members of the aristocracy and actresses are less rare; actors are knighted and go to court in cocked hats and buckles; but all these changes have left the roots of the prejudice undisturbed.

I know from experience that to some extent suspicion of the stage is justified. The temptations to impurity are not exaggerated, but I believe that they arise from a condition of things which could be remedied, and which even now is by no means universal. We should also remember that the fact that the player practises his art in the public eye makes him less reticent than most people about living in the public eye. He does not hide his frailty under a bushel. Through this open, almost childish, disregard of secrecy, he has suffered in reputation, not after his deserts, but much more. When he takes his art seriously, and the religious rapture of the artist seizes him, he lives a cleaner life than many a well-reputed citizen who escaped calumny because he has escaped notoriety.

II

To me the stage was a teacher of good and beautiful things. It was the theatre which knocked the nonsense out of me, which killed the pedantry that had crept into my system at Oxford, which made an end of my self-consciousness, which turned me from a student of books into a lover of mankind with a great compassion for human frailty. I learned lessons in humility and in rhythm. I never rose from the ranks of the "supers" while I was on the stage, but I found that to be a good "super" meant hard work, and I was not content to be a bad, lazy "super." In those small dumb parts I found a vehicle for expressing some of my latent passion. In my young dreams of the stage I had seen myself as a second Siddons. There were no limits to my tragic powers. Yet in the reality, as a pierrot, a servant, a clerk to the court, a drummer, an insensate shouter in a crowd, a peasant, or an attendant, I experienced no shock of disillusionment. To me these assumptions of unregarded and unimportant characters in the play were a terribly earnest undertaking. Night after night I made up my face and put on the dress allotted to me with as much attention to detail as though the play depended on my individual appearance. Night after night I stood in the wings with my heart quaking in my throat for fear I should not do well. Sometimes I would say to myself: "I have the actor's temperament, and I cannot act. I have the poet's heart, and I cannot write." And often a deep melancholy submerged me…until the cue came for the entrance of the mummers, when I would dash on to the stage as a pierrot, shouting, laughing, and turning somersaults with an agility that was entirely a stage creation, for nowhere else could I perform such daring acrobatic feats.

III

How did it happen? What made me go on the stage? My ambitions in this direction began the day I first saw the great Shakespearian actress Louise Canning, but they were not realized for many years, and then they had almost burned themselves out. But apart from my brief and undistinguished career on the stage, my meeting with the actress had great significance in my life, and as I did not mention it in its proper chronological place I feel I must return to it now...even at the cost of returning also to the house of Wingfield. Yes, once again I must walk up that detestable winding drive, pretentiously designed to look longer and grander than it was, and face that stone "mansion" with its castellated bow windows smothered in shrubs. I must face that breakfast-table covered with a cloth that never looked clean, the scratched leather chairs, and the walls covered from floor to ceiling with poor oil-paintings. I must experience once more that sensation, as of fog descending on my merry morning mood, and growing thicker with each fresh arrival at the breakfast-table. To this day I cannot dissociate marmalade from gloomy, discontented faces and a heavy silence broken only now and again by some querulous complaint.

The Wingfields seldom went to the theatre, but the visit to Ripton of Louise Canning and her great partner Mark Washington was an event in which they took an interest. In those days the famous pair were seldom seen in the provinces, and when they did appear there the theatres were patronized by people who were not play-goers in the ordinary sense of the word. Indeed, many of them disliked the theatre, but they wished to be in the fashion, and it was the fashion to go and see Mark Washington and Louise Canning in Shakespeare.

I had always instinctively loved the theatre. All the games that I played by myself as a child were dramatic art in its first stages. I represented the adventures of imaginary people, fought battles in which I acted both the victors and the vanquished, invented dialogues between the lover and beloved. When the curtain rose on "The Merchant of Venice," at the Royal Theatre, Ripton, I felt that I was in a familiar atmosphere, only now I was looking at actors instead of being an actor myself. This must have been after my first visit to Crupples, for I remember thinking as I sat in the theatre how wrong Lettice Gosborough had been in saying that Shakespeare was spoiled when he was acted, and that she preferred to read his plays at home. I knew directly the first scene between Shylock and Antonio was over, that I might have read it a hundred times without seeing for myself what Washington revealed. I felt that there was a great deal more than the written word in Shakespeare's plays, stupendous as the word often was.

I was fascinated by the contrast between the actor and the actress. His method was difficult, thorny and painful; hers as easy as the singing of a lark, or the blooming of a flower. His was the art of sorrow, hers of joy...but they resembled each other in that they both expressed beauty. I heard people round me saying that the scenery was lovely, and that the canal was just like a real canal in Venice, but the beauty I saw was in Shylock's face when he returned from supping with the Christians to find his home desolate, and in the light, gay, caressing movements of Portia's hands.

IV

Louise Canning was no longer young when I first saw her play Portia, but her whole being was still impregnated with grace.

Her walk, her diction, her merriment were all graceful. Her entrance into the Court in the Trial Scene suggested to me the entrance of an angel into a naughty world. It was this angelical touch which charmed my nature, athirst for something alien from the joys and loveliness of earth.

V

I flew to meet the actress with the wings of my soul unfurled. She was quite ignorant of the approach of the poor childish dove. Night after night I stood with one of the Wingfield boys in the crowded pit, and afterwards went round to the stage door with a beating heart to watch her leave the theatre. I wrote her long letters, in which I laid all my dreams at her feet. She answered curtly, thanking me for the flowers and fruit that I sent with the letters, but not referring to the letters themselves. The night before she left Ripton I managed to get a word with her. I was mortified because she treated me like a little child. I felt that I was making no impression on her at all. "I know I am ugly," I thought, "but I have an original face." Then immediately I was doubtful even of that! I wanted her to remember me; I clung to this idea as I stood in her dressing-room, awkwardly twisting my hands, and incapable of expressing anything.

"But I sent you those," I murmured, almost in tears, as she selected a bunch of violets from the flowers of which the room was full, and gave them to me.

"You can't be John!" she said, laughing. "These violets come every day with a letter, signed 'John-Baptist.'"

"That's my name," I answered timidly.

"But child, you didn't write those letters! I thought they were from some silly young man."

I grew scarlet, and she, seeing that I was near weeping, grew serious suddenly.

"The letters are not at all silly, but still…don't wear your heart upon your sleeve. For one thing it's not a ripe heart yet, as I could prove to you if I had time. But I must really go home now."

She stooped, with the grace with which she knew how to invest the most ordinary movements, and kissed me. I did not see her again for years, but often during the intervening time, when I was wounded by some snub to my impulsive expression of a genuine feeling of love or admiration, I had reason to remember her warning. Yet I was never ashamed of giving myself away. It was a great comfort to me to find that in this I resembled my Polish grandmother. In one of my father's letters he had quoted an expression of hers which had impressed him deeply, an expression which I, in my turn, was never to forget. My grandfather had criticized her for using exaggerated language about her sufferings in England, and she had replied to the charge in one masterly sentence—"Whatever I have written of my sufferings, I have lived them more." I know now that those simple words constitute the *motif* which runs through all the varying episodes of my emotional life, and binds them together. Those who have letters of mine know with what burning intensity I have often expressed myself; no doubt, if they happen to read those letters now that I have passed out of their lives, they wonder if I could have meant half that I said. I know that I meant a hundred times more than I ever expressed, and that my fiery words were ice itself compared with the flaming heat that consumed my heart.

VI

In ten years Louise Canning had not forgotten the queer little girl in the red coat who wore an unripe heart upon her sleeve. I had long ceased to write her impassioned letters. It is difficult to keep up a one-sided correspondence. But my greatest pleasure during my years of struggle in London was to go and see her and Washington act. It used to be said that the public regarded the Blackfriars Theatre as a church, and assisted at a performance there with the solemnity of people witnessing a religious ceremony. There was some truth in the gibe. In all Washington's productions there was a greatness which forced his audiences to reverence and their knees. In Louise Canning's acting there was a touch of spirituality, of aloofness from the common ways of women—and this as much in comedy as in tragedy—which appealed to the desire existing in every human being to look up and away from ordinary experience, to the religious instinct in fact.

Just as some men have become saints, not through doing extraordinary things, but through doing ordinary things in an extraordinary manner, so Mark Washington and Louise Canning attained their position and their influence not through appearing in very remarkable plays, but through doing remarkable and lofty work in plays which, outside their Shakespeare repertory, were of no great account. They never did things on the stage which made their worshipper say, "That is just what I should have done." Both of them outstripped the observation of the commonplace mind of the majority. Through this singularity they made enemies, especially of people devoid of reverence. To those incapable of a reverent attitude appreciation of Washington and Louise Canning was an impossibility.

It was through my capacity for reverence that I met Louise Canning once more. On the very night that the little house in Westminster in which I had lodged ever since I had come to London was burned to the ground I had been to see a new production at the Blackfriars Theatre. As I walked home, I remembered that it was Louise Canning's birthday the following day, and I was determined, if I had to sit up all night, to try and express some of the immense gratitude that I felt for the lovely incarnation of Shakespeare's Imogen with which she had ushered in her fiftieth year.

In the omnibus I had heard two young girls, pretty in a coarse style, commenting on that wonderful performance. "She's looking very old now, isn't she?" said one. "And getting so fat!" said the other. "I think she ought to give up acting young parts now." I gave the offending critics a look which should have blasted them, and jumped out of the omnibus, preferring to waste my fare rather than travel in such company. I heard them giggle as I nearly fell in the road—the omnibus was travelling at full speed—but it seemed to me honourable to have excited the derision of those who had not recognized the beauty of Louise Canning's Imogen. I was more sorry for them than for myself, yet there burned in me a desire to make reparation for their blindness.

I turned the corner into my quiet little street, and was amazed to find it full of noise and commotion. A huge crowd had gathered and were watching a fire. I could smell the smoke; the air was thick. I saw a fireman's helmet gleam above the heads of the crowd. It was then that a dreadful conviction seized me that the fire was at No. 20, where I lived. My thoughts flew first to the manuscript of my novel, on which I had been working for nearly four years…then to the new riding-habit which Violet Gosborough had just given me…then to my mother's letter…I thought of her letter before any one of my father's. That little bit of crumpled, faded, blue paper was all I had of her, all that I knew of her. I stood in the crowd, trying to remember every word. I kept on repeating: "'In spite of my life, I am still very sensitive.' Yes, that was it. No, it was not quite that. What was your life, mother? Who says you were wicked? I do not say so. I am like you…am I wicked? If I were beautiful….I should never think of anything, but love…. Mother, why didn't you send for me?… I could have brought you those oysters for which you longed in your last illness. Now you are burning, and I cannot save you."

"There's nothing of any value in there," said a man near me. "That's one good job."

"Whose house is it?"

"Only a lodging-house. The lodgers were all out, except an old gentleman on the ground floor. He got out and gave the warning."

"They're sure there's no one in there?" said a woman.

"There isn't much left of them by now if there was."

By this time I had edged through the crowd to the barrier which the fireman had erected. It was a dark night, and the street was ill-lighted, but the flickering gas-lamp fixed to the wall opposite showed me the gaunt black skeleton of the house shining with the water which the firemen were still showering on it, although there was no sign of a flame.

I forgot myself and my losses for a moment in pity for the poor little house that had stood there so bravely for more than two centuries, only to be destroyed utterly in a few hours. Then, with that anxiety to evade sorrow, characteristic of me in my youth, I turned and ran away. People told me afterwards that if I had waited and spoken myself to the salvage men, I might have recovered some of my possessions from the ashes. I did not think of this. My one idea was to escape. I ran into Victoria Street, crying bitterly as I ran. Then without any effort on my part my tears dried up. My mind became cool and calculating. I added up the advantages of my situation. I had been stripped of everything, but the pathos of my nakedness receded and became a hazy sentiment. Soon I found myself experiencing an immense relief that those troublesome witnesses to my identity had been burned; that my furniture, which had absorbed too much attention from me, could never exact it any more; that my novel could never again plunge me into depression and humiliation. I was released from the obligation of tinkering at its base metal. I thought of this with pleasure as I walked into the region of the Cadogan Estate.

I had broken down at first like a child. Like a child I had cried "Mother! Mother!" In my new-born hardness I gloried at having nothing left in the world but myself. I remembered a saying of Nietzsche's, "The noblest only is perfectly hard." I sought shelter, indifferent to the strangeness of the hour, indifferent to my chances of a welcome. I was not resigned; it was a hard, bright satisfaction that I felt rather than resignation.

And I earned at this time a great reputation for courage! I remember now with amazement what sympathy the loss of all my possessions brought me. It was the "bodily hurt" of Iago which could be understood; at no period of my life have I ever received such kindness. I was grateful, yet in my gratitude there was an element of contempt which I tried in vain to repress as criminal.

VII

The owner of my haven that night was a plaintive little woman whose goodness to me had often crystalized in the words. "Will you dine with us to-morrow?" She had married young; her husband was as dry as the scientific works by neglected German authors which he translated as a recreation from professional life. She had children; and the most malicious and suspicious observer would hardly have questioned her right to the title "an excellent wife and mother." Yet I knew that for years she had had a lover.

The romance of this conventional, respectable little lady affected me to continuous surprise. She had confided in me easily, without any fear that I should be shocked—it was the habit of every one with whom I came into contact to say "You will understand"—but I never grew accustomed to her secret. It was a disagreeable tenant of a room in my mind, perpetually reminding me of the absurdity of drawing any natural conclusions about virtue. If Rachael could carry on an intrigue, what reason was there for thinking that any wife was above suspicion? I distrusted the world's "good" henceforth, and hated my distrust, which was hostile to my instinctive desire to think the best of people rather than the worst. As I floundered about, I caught hold of this: "Finer to be with those who believe and are proved wrong than with those who distrust and are right."

Rachael, I remember you because in your house I found pen, ink and paper, with which before another dawn I transfixed my wandering sonnet to Louise Canning. Was it only prose cut up into lengths? My riper judgment laughs at its reference to grace as "golden." What a predilection I had for that adjective in my early twenties!

But whatever the sonnet was, or was not, it brought me into touch with Louise once more. I thought it all chance, because I was blundering through life at this time clinging to nothing except my admiration for the strong who could hew a way through the obscure, incomprehensible forest of the world.

I attributed all my failures to my own weakness of purpose. The virtue I reverenced most was fortitude: the ideal of conduct I pursued most strenuously, "Let me never complain of anything. Let me never desire pity."

VIII

The sonnet provoked an invitation from Louise Canning to go and visit her one night at the suburban theatre where she was playing a special week. I went down there on my bicycle, which I still used in the London streets in spite of many nerve-shaking escapes from serious accidents in the traffic, and one genuine disaster from which I had emerged with a fractured knee. It was a warm evening in March, and I felt a freshness about me that it is impossible to describe. I vibrated with hope, was spurred on to my destination by a sense that something was now going to change my life, and relieve me for a time of that terrible ache for beauty to which my recent misfortunes had served only as a temporary counter-irritant.

A thousand new energies were kindled in me as I stood at the stage-door waiting for the answer to my timid inquiry for Louise Canning. I found myself wondering why she was not acting with her great partner Washington, and remembered rumours of a quarrel.

By the time the dresser came to fetch me, some of my excitement had died. It was my first experience of "behind the scenes"; the queer austerity of everything attracted me after the first shock of surprise. The dresser and I had to pass across the stage to reach Louise Canning's dressing-room. I trod in it with awe, fascinated by the dangling ropes (a scene was being shifted), by the army of carpenters, by the determined and vigilant young stage-manager supervising every movement from his standpoint against the curtain, by the pert call-boy rushing upstairs with many cries of "Second Act, please!"

I was bewildered, but pleasurably bewildered. That strange immaterial entity—*the theatre*—as distinct from its parts, the play, the actors, the actresses, the scenery and the rest, called to my blood, and my veins made rapturous reply. In Fleet Street I had always felt a stranger, and I had disliked all journalists and writers with whom I had come in touch. Here I felt the presence of a life which exhilarated me—a vehement, savage, ingenuous life, where vulgarity and delicacy, counterfeit and reality, soul and body were jumbled together obscurely and forcefully.

Yet Louise Canning thought, I knew, that I was feeling some repugnance to the theatre at close quarters! Neither that night nor at any time did she understand me in the least. A thought persisted in my heart that I was disappointed in her, although I kept it inactive with ardent assurances that I was not! The thought did not rise because she looked older and less beautiful than I had expected to find her. Although I could see in her face the traces of the years that had passed, I was not shocked. It was wonderful too how, as she sat at her mirror, she recomposed the illusion of youth with the aid of the little pots and bottles of ointments and washes and powders with which the table was covered. Although she was too fat—I admitted it—her body was still a miracle of grace, still able to obey the dictates of her ever youthful heart. Her vitality, out of which she could have fed fifty ordinary natures, and still have had enough left to dazzle and fatigue those round her and to defy the threats of time, seemed to me superhuman.

I sat in the corner of her dressing-room, feeling like a timid bather in a buoyant sea, as the waves of her exuberant temperament broke over me. It seemed to me that she was all temperament— that heart and soul and intellect in her were all submerged in something which was all of them and none of them. In this vast temperament I detected an Olympian quality. I was reminded of those gods and goddesses in Lempriére's Classical Dictionary, in whom the noble and the trivial, the fine and the base, the generous and the mean, were inextricably mixed up. Louise Canning seemed always to be making harlequin leaps in her conversation: it required some mental agility to follow her; and if you had anything to tell her, you had to be very patient, for she was as slow in grasping a point as she was quick in making one.

IX

During my years in London I had heard many things against her reputation, and now that I was in her presence I wondered if they could be true. From her personality rose all kinds of exhalations, but there was no breath of impurity among them. I felt this at once, and experience was to confirm my instinct later on. It was not because I was young, and she was cautious, and we were not intimate, that Louise refrained from a kind of conversation with which I had become sadly familiar from mouths which would have condemned her. Neither than night nor at any other time did I hear her say anything nasty or suggestive. She had a mind that was clean, innocent, and almost childlike in its simplicity; a homely Rabelaisian jest was not alien to it, but she simply could not see the point of a subtly improper story, or else she ignored it deliberately.

Louise was disconcertingly frank. She could make vain people feel very uncomfortable, and as I was still vain, and very self-conscious, I suffered from her frankness. I suffered too from her restlessness, for I loved tranquillity—not apathetic tranquillity, but the shimmering quiet of a mind at white heat. I found her as insensible to the tender love that my heart longed to pour into her soul as on the day we had first met. And when I watched her act from the wings that night, my instinct told me that her lovely art had become a little fussy and over-elaborate. It was not so virginal as I remembered it. But there was still no doubt as to her hold on the public's love. She knew how to establish an understanding between them and her. This flattered their self-esteem, and made her a "popular" actress in a very real sense. But I had still too much of the intellectual ass in my composition not to be affronted by this popularity.

For years I had longed for this meeting, and now it had taken place, now the cherished dream had been realized, I was surprised to find myself sick at heart.

She was playing this night one of the parts in which I had seen her at Ripton, the part of a young girl "who stoops to folly, and learns too late that men betray."

Perhaps it was in response to my unspoken thoughts that she said suddenly:

"It's absurd for an old woman like me to be playing a part like this, isn't it?"

I denied the absurdity strenuously, calling to my help all my theories that in acting assumption is half the battle, and that it would be preferable to see a sixty-year-old actress of genius as Juliet than a sixteen-year-old girl without any art. But I knew all the time that there are some parts, and this was one of them, in which years count.

"Although in many ways I am younger than my daughter," Louise added. "You don't know my daughter yet, do you? She's my greatest care and my greatest comfort. You must know her. Lizzie! Go and call Miss Sally."

I had already seen "Miss Sally" on the stage, and had noticed how much of her mother's grace of movement she had inherited. She was playing quite a small part, but she had invested it with a curious distinction; and she, more than any one on the stage that night, had contrived to give an eighteenth-century impression, from her lace cap to her red heels. There was something foreign about her long dark eyes, set wide apart, and her almost indolent expression.

I learned subsequently that she felt small sympathy with her mother's crowd of girl adorers, and that it was not by accident that she had avoided me. She came into the dressing-room now reluctantly, and gave more attention to the mitten that she was mending than me. I shook hands with her in spite of her warning to "mind the needle," and hardly felt the prick that followed because of the greater prick to my self-esteem that her attitude gave me. I longed to shake her out of what seemed to me a self-complacent certainty that I was just another foolish girl "from the front." I almost hated her for not seeing at once that I was not "another" of any type with which she was familiar. I did her an injustice with my heart's cry "Disdainful!" Sally's disdainful air sprang from shyness rather than from contempt. I diagnosed her thin lips wrongly too, those lips which prevented her generous wide mouth from resembling her mother's. "She's an acid creature," I thought. "She despises her mother for giving herself away...but she is too cautious to give away anything, especially love!"

Yet, inexplicably, there moved in my heart as I made these mental notes a great wave of sympathy. It broke, and was succeeded by another wave, and another. All that I observed, all that I thought, was submerged in a sense of complete harmony with the strange dark girl. Or, to use another metaphor, I read the word "affinity" by a flash of lightning!

Yes, I had taken fancies to people before. I have recalled earlier in these pages that when I was asked if I had ever been in love I used to reply with some truth "I have never been out of it!" Often physical beauty had arrested the wanderer, the seeker, the sufferer in my heart, and at the very moment of being charmed I had seen that it resembled the iridescent stuff that shines on the surface of a stagnant, ill-smelling pond. I had known what it was to love some one deeply for one little kind and graceful action—even for a hand outstretched at the right moment, for an understanding glance, for a tear shed over some sorrow not my own, for some welcome sign that there were people in the world who had visions of the heart of life and were not afraid to suffer for the privilege. But the wind of circumstance had speedily blown out these lights so unexpectedly kindled, leaving a greater darkness, in which I was tempted to doubt the holiness of my rapture, to see it as a silliness to be scorned.

The quality in Jerome that had attracted me most had been his "good sense." Sally had the same quality, but in an even higher degree. Her taste for beautiful things was governed by this "good sense"; so were her affections. People who loved her mother's open-hearted ways, her ebullitions of warmth, were alienated by Sally's coldness. They complained that she looked at them critically, and accused her of being deficient in the "Canning charm." Some of Louise's light-hearted buoyancy had all the same been transmitted to her daughter, in spite of that serious demeanour which chilled the commonplace observer. And although the mother had the warmer manner, I divined in a few minutes that it was possible that the daughter had the warmer heart.

Sally, who was soon to be my Sally in a very special sense, made no effort at all to put me at my ease, yet I felt at ease with her at once. It was a novel sensation, for in my relations with human beings I had always felt more or less uncomfortable. We said very little to each other that night, yet everything that we did express seemed to leave streaming in its wake a comet's bright tail of comprehension.

I had gone to the theatre thinking only of Louise. I left it thinking only of Sally.

IX
FRIENDSHIP

I

A few months later Louise Canning left England for an American tour, and Sally and I set up house together. Since the fire I had been drifting about, staying with people, or taking a furnished room when I was weary of being a guest, or felt that I had outstayed my welcome. It was delightful to have a home again, and a home with Sally had none of the dullness of domesticity! We both spent too much on the decorations of our little house, or rather Sally spent too much, and I incurred fresh debts in trying to do my part. Almost from the first we lived beyond our income, but we were too happy to think of the rod we were pickling for our backs. We were as happy as a newly-married pair, perhaps happier; and we certainly disproved the tradition that women are incapable of friendship.

I used to wonder which was the husband and which the wife in the *ménage*! Sally looked after me with a care that was almost maternal. Without preaching, she made me feel ashamed of many of my habits. She broke me of asserting myself a Bohemian by drinking beer and wine to excess which never really tempted me, of working late at night, of going out to dinner at restaurants with a class of man whom she disliked and distrusted. In fact, it was Sally who guided me away from all to which the stage is supposed to lead. With my hand in hers I felt no difficulty in turning my back on these things. I had been in the habit of excusing myself for my recklessness, especially as regards my association with men, by saying that "one must live." Sally thought this nonsense, and she converted me to her views.

We fought sometimes, but we loved—that was the great point. Even our fights were interesting, and our reconciliations bound us together more closely. I grew angry sometimes at what I chose to consider Sally's "superior" attitude. She was always finding fault with me, and she was generally supremely right, as my good sense told me after I had flared up and denied her right to criticize me.

The quarrels were worth while because they revealed a sensitiveness and tenderness in Sally which I was too dull to perceive until I had wounded both. At ordinary times she showed a tendency to lord it over me, but when she became conscious of her power to make me suffer, she would immediately abandon it, and be so gently suppliant for forgiveness that she was hardly recognizable. I often caught myself admiring her when she was in a rage. If only I had not been the cause, I should have loved to see those dark eyes shine with the glint of battle, and to watch the flames that seemed to stream from her personality. It was then that she became the tragic actress which she could not be on the stage.

Her deficiencies as an actress were hard to define. Perhaps it was her abnormal personality, hard to suit with a part, which fought against her. She herself never spoke of her disappointment—she seldom spoke of anything near her heart—and declared that the *décor* of the stage interested her more than acting. At the time we first met she was designing costumes for the theatre, and making experiments in producing plays. She was always busy over something, and that something was always connected with the theatre. Her capableness and her industry were touched with a genius which was seldom recognized because she never "pretended." She did not use big words about art and colour schemes and the rest, but when she was given an opportunity she never failed to use it.

Her freedom from personal vanity was extraordinary. (I write of Sally in the past tense for convenience's sake. She is still, thank God, a part of my life.) She was *really* indifferent as to what she wore or how she looked or what people thought of her. When she dressed up, either for a part on the stage or to go out somewhere, she did it swiftly, with an unerring sense of what was decoratively fit, but without any vain fussiness; and when she was pleased with her appearance, it was for its own sake, and not because she hoped to attract men or make an impression on women.

Her attitude towards men in general resembled mine to a certain extent. She liked them if they "behaved well," as she said, but she had no special tests for man's conduct. She had a way of finding people out with her penetrating brown eyes, and no decent human being, whether man or woman, found her antagonistic.

Unfortunately all men and women are not decent human beings, and Sally had many enemies. I used to remonstrate with her for being too uncompromising, and too merciless in her judgments, but I had to admit that she seldom put these into force against the weak. For the weak and the unfortunate she had a beautiful predilection, and both the men she came near marrying had a physical disfigurement.

Did she love me because I was a waif and stray? What attracted her to me? She never told me. The foundation of our happiness together was a harmony of character...or even of thought. Indeed, we thought very differently about many things. But wherever we went together, to theatres, picture-galleries, "antique" shops, gatherings of people, we saw the visible world with the same eyes. I recognized, however, that Sally's eyes were keener than mine, and her joy in the visible more complete. To me it always brought a certain weariness. I knew in my heart that I did not think the world such a nice place as she did. She was always happy to the very end of the little "sprees" we had, either at home or abroad; I, after enjoying myself feverishly and incoherently, would grow suddenly dejected, even at times intensely depressed, by the lively recklessness of the actors, actresses and painters who were Sally's friends.

She did not care a rap who people were, or what they had achieved. It never occurred to her that it was desirable to know people for the sake of their distinction. I have never met any one with less respect for wealth, or position, or anything which is supposed to make human beings socially valuable. I was ashamed, feeling myself a snob in comparison with her. But the shame cleansed me of snobbishness.

It astonished me to find that the general opinion was that Sally was hard and cold. I knew her to be very soft and warmhearted, very maternal. If I had the smallest physical pain she would mother me as your ordinary pretty little feminine women, who are supposed to be so gentle, never can mother any one, even the children of their own bodies. If I want to conjure up a picture of maternity, I think of Sally with her brother's children.

At first I was always anxiously analyzing her and trying to explain her to myself. She was a sphinx where her interior life was concerned. But perhaps the sphinx is quite simple in fact, and it is only eternal thinking about her that has made her a riddle. Sally would keep silent and smile, an interesting, enigmatic smile, when her mother spoke of marriage with enthusiasm. She could not be induced to express her views on this subject, but I knew that she did not think that matrimony should be the object of every woman's education and the end of every woman's desire.

She was exceedingly patient with the romantic strain in me, although she had small sympathy with it, and found my swift alternations from exultation to despair puzzling, if not a little foolish. She was much more sane in her attitude towards life. "Why can't you be more contented?" she would say sometimes.

"You always want too much." It was true, yet a very little would throw me into a state of rapture to which she was a stranger.

Three years of this intimate friendship passed as quickly as a summer's day. Storm-clouds there were, but the fair sky was never wholly overcast. As was only natural, Louise was jealous; when she came back from America she wished Sally to come and live at home again. I said to Sally, "If you are going—and perhaps you ought to go—go now...before I forget how to live alone." I was wounded and perturbed by the thought that I was robbing Louise of her daughter. Sally faced the situation calmly.

"It's nothing to do with you, and mother knows it. When I was a little girl I made up my mind that I would leave home when I was twenty-eight. I think women ought to do it, whether they marry or not."

"But your mother wants you at home," I said, pleading bravely for what was going to make me desolate.

A little cruelty showed itself in Sally's smile.

"You don't know mother. She wants me because I have gone away. When I lived at home I hardly ever saw her...partly because she was never there, and partly because she can never bear to be with any one for long at a time. Please don't think I mean she doesn't love me. Of course she does—tremendously; at the same time she has all sorts of ideas and sentiments that she doesn't really wish realized. One of them is my living with her and looking after her. No one can look after mother."

"But I don't like people to say I have taken you away from her."

"As you haven't, what does it matter? If I tell you that I shall be of far more use to mother, and ever see more of her, if I go on living with you, won't you believe me?"

I did believe her. It was a habit of mine to respect Sally's judgment, and I had often been surprised by the wisdom with which she steered her course. Her hand never faltered under criticism or calumny. She had her own way of being a devoted daughter, and if it was not the approved way, it must be remembered that her mother was not of the approved pattern. In a very short time Louise overcame her dislike to me, and ceased to treat me as an interloper. She recognized that I was quite ready to step aside and leave the road clear for Sally's return to her, and immediately she did not wish me to step aside. I found myself treated as a son-in-law might have been treated. Louise and I discussed Sally's health, Sally's talents, Sally's looks, Sally's clothes. I became the willing slave of both mother and daughter. My life became most intimately bound up with theirs. Had I died and been born again in another world I could not have been more completely severed from my old associations.

How strange and narrow and insincere that former life seemed now! How dull and uninteresting those exclusive personages who had deigned to patronize me because I was that desirable thing "a lady!" It was good to be with people whose thoughts were their own, whose speech was sincere, whose human kindness was not crippled by the strait-jacket into which that mysterious authority known as "society" puts its victims.

II

"This is perfect," I often thought during those three years—"this fills up my life." All my troubles and sufferings seemed to have flowed away, and I never had any fear that they would return. This ideal friendship intoxicated me. I read all the literature of friendship, and in every word my own experience seemed to smile at me. "Nothing is worth what Sally can give me. Nothing is worth this certainty of never again being alone until death."

III

I have compared my three years of happiness to a summer's day. There are summer days in the tropics, I believe, on which night descends in a moment. This was how my night descended.

Of course I was the last to know that Sally was in love. Many people might have told me, might have warned me. But if they had, I should not have believed them.

One horrible moment…A bomb hurtling through the serene air of my Paradise, exploding with a noise of devils' laughter, tearing up immemorial trees by the roots, laying waste the greenery of hope and faith—then filth, stench, corruption—then nothing, no suffering even—nothing.

"Yes, I care for him," said Sally. "I want to marry him."

"That deformity!" I cried, and for a moment I saw myself outside myself—not beautiful certainly, but straight-limbed, clear-skinned, with hair and eyes still shining as they shine in youth. "Then—then—"

I pressed my hands to my heart, and ran out of the room. I was burning in the fire of my own wrath, and had a kind of ecstasy of desire for death and annihilation. Yet behind my hot forehead my brain felt like ice. I remembered clearly a bottle of cocaine lotion in the bath-room, which had been prescribed for my ear-ache. I went in and drank it without a moment's hesitation. The effect of the action was to put out my wrathful fire. I became weak, timid and sorrowful. I had often thought I should not be afraid to die if Sally could be there, close to me, holding my hand. She had such a comforting hand. I burst into sobs, thinking that if that hand even caressed me again it would break my heart.

I put on my hat and went out. It was an April evening soft and damp and warm. My veins throbbed painfully in my limbs, which seemed to grow more torpid with every step I took. My fury with Sally had departed completely; I did not even associate her with the anguish in my heart. But all the numberless things that I had suffered in my life seemed to be nourishing it. "It is inevitable. I must die."

I saw London darkening as I had seen it a hundred times. The shops were being lit up…the gold street lamps sprang up in the dusk like stars. The sky where the last streak of daylight remained glittered like a long pale sword. I hailed on omnibus, and climbed to the top. I noticed that my limbs no longer felt heavy, but strangely indefinite and light, and that all the life in the streets below was a phantom life that made no noise. Yet I was still perfectly conscious. Was there perhaps in the crowd some equal, some brother soul who could share my hopes and aspirations? Was there living in the world somewhere at that hour some one who needed me, and was I doing that life a wrong by dying? Certainly there were actions to be accomplished, conquests to be made. Yes, there must be heroic reasons for life.

All these years I had had that desire by the side of which the desire of love is pale—to finish one great work. The desire had never left me, nothing had killed it, or even drugged it to sleep. Well, at twenty-four I had finished a work. I had published a novel, not an ordinary second-rate novel, but a book animated with violence, vibrating with youthful force, a book destitute of the rhythm of art, and destitute of the compelling charm of originality—an impetuous, silly, fervid thing, thematically worthless, yet showing in flashes a passionate knowledge of the holy things of the heart. I had created nothing, yet the book had some marks of the creator. I forced myself to acknowledge this, even though the poor unwieldy Frankenstein of my brain had caused me much bitterness by not being that "single great work" which was the end of my desire.

From the top of the omnibus, my mind swayed to and fro by a dissolving terror, I looked down on the immensity of life, and saw that even the "single great work" could be nothing in it. Was it not foolish to make it a reason for living? I thought of Æschylus with his hundred tragedies, of Sophocles with his hundred more.... Yes, such work as that, work vast as a cosmogony, was a heroic reason for life.

I noticed a woman coming out of the post-office at Knightsbridge to her carriage. Every one near was instinctively arrested by her beauty. People stopped to look at her, not surreptitiously, but openly. The brow was wonderful like a fine manly brow, the dark eyes had that burning quiet which you hardly ever see in the eyes of an Englishwoman. I was sure she was not English if only because of the austerity of her clothes, and the next second her noble free carriage reminded me of olive-gatherers in Tuscany. Her pallor too was Italian—warm with an inner flush of tawny rose. I gazed at her with fixed, wide-open eyes. The vision filled me with an immense self-pity.... What case was like unto my case, what sorrow like unto my sorrow? The creative feeling mind without the power of creation.... I had just been groping after my identity with that...and now I saw this physical perfection, and realized a door shut on me as a lover as it was shut on me as a poet. With what passion could I have spoken that line of Cyrano de Bergerac's (and a heaven-sent Cyrano nose to assist me):

"Molière a du génie, et Christian était beau."
[Moliere had genius and Christian was beautiful.]

"O Lord," I thought, "all my life has consisted in stepping aside, in seeing some Molière or some Christian pass me. No doubt they were worthy and I was not, yet I have had such thoughts...such witty audacious thoughts, and I have loved greatly. Well, now the end is coming...without an hour of crumpling my laurels in my hand to give perfume to another…without an hour of love." So I rambled on, still gazing at that disdainful red mouth, which seemed heavy with an ungiven kiss. The love that was in her veins seemed to be rising towards me…yet I knew that this strange fiery flower of a woman had no care but for her own good, and that her love, like her blood, was flowing back to her own heart. It was as if the Hellenic myth which created the ideal form of the Hermaphrodite had been manifested to me as another heroic reason for life. And indeed Giovanna Ludini was to make me rejoice a few years later at my preservation from death on the night I saw her for the first time. It is also true that she made me sorry I had not died.

IV

That beautiful tragic face rising above what seemed a belt of stars was the last thing I saw. My eyes closed against my will; I sank into sleep. With my last moment of consciousness I thought vaguely of God. Although I had professed not to believe in Him, and had often said that if you did not believe, there was no obligation to be good, and no such thing as virtue, I had often prayed, and always in the same words: "O God, please make me good." And now, though I was suffering neither remorse nor terror, though I did not think that this might be the sleep of death, I said, "Dear God, I am sorry I have never been good." Perhaps many poor wanderers from the eternal goodness and beauty, too ignorant to know the hideousness of their wandering, have made similar acts of contrition at the last.

V

I woke next morning in a hospital ward. I was not altogether surprised to find myself there, because during the night I had a dream of being carried through a crowd up some steps to the door of a big building. I had seen the faces in the crowd very distinctly, and had recognised one man as an actor in Washington's company whom I knew.

Some nurses in blue cotton dresses and white caps were sweeping out the ward. I wanted to call one of them and ask what I was doing there, but all my life I had been shy of asking for information, and in this case I shrank from being enlightened. I felt quite well, yet I might be dying.

I was a little frightened at this possibility, but my dominant emotion was shame. What I had done was shameful. However infatuated Sally might be with—with that *thing*, she would not be able to avoid remorse if I died. I was appalled at the monstrous selfishness of love, at the mortal hatred and cruelty that it conceals. I had always prided myself on seeking Sally's advantage before my own, often in opposition to my own; but I realized now that I had demanded some reward for this "unselfishness," demanded it as a right. I remembered Nietzsche's cynical saying. "Even God becomes a terror if He is not loved in return." I remembered another saying not less cynical:—"L'amour est de tous les sentiments le plus égoiste, et, par conséquent, lorsqu'il est blessé, le moins généreux." [Love, of all the emotions, is the most selfish, and, therefore, when injured, the least generous. Benjamin Constant]

VI

The nurses began bringing back the flowers into the ward, and a ray of sunlight fell across the polished wooden floor. Screens were moved back from beds, displaying patients, newly washed and cheerful, sitting up in bed in their red flannel jackets. All this life seemed to me prodigious, and very sweet. I noticed a woman opposite me studying the temperature chart hanging on the wall above her bed. It occurred to me that there might be something about my case over mine, and I turned over on my side and raised myself to look. I read that I had been brought in at eight o'clock the evening before, suffering from cocaine poisoning, that my pulse was so-and-so, my heart so-and-so, and that I was "rapidly sinking."

A nurse noticed my movement and came over to my bed.

"Well, how do you feel now?" she said with rough geniality.

"I feel all right," I answered. "Except for my wrist."

I looked at it as I spoke, and saw that it was scarred with one or two little red marks.

"That's where they injected morphine into your pulse last night. It had nearly stopped. What had you been doing to yourself?"

"I had ear-ache, and I put some cocaine in my ear."

"That was what your friend said; and Dr. Briggs said you ought to have a nurse look after you, if you used cocaine as recklessly as that."

"My friend! Do you mean Miss Fraser? Has she been here?"

"I should think she had! She was in a way when they couldn't bring you round. She stayed here till Dr. Briggs said you were all right. I never saw such a recovery! Well, I expect you feel hungry now! Would you like some breakfast?"

I was sitting up in bed eating a boiled egg, and trying to reconcile the fact with that "rapidly sinking," when Sally came.

"O Jackie!" was all she said after she had kissed me. And again, "O Jackie!"

I clung to her in silence.

"Aren't you a naughty baby to have given me such a fright?"

"Yes," I whispered.

"Why didn't you tell me your ear-ache was bad?"

"I don't know…I was upset." But I took the cue from her. Docilely I repeated, "It *was* bad!" And all the time I was thinking of a pain that had not been in any of my members.

"Did Lucas Sands tell you I was here?"

"Yes," Then Sally looked at me in amazement. "But how do you know?"

"I saw him on the steps as I was carried in."

"But, Baby, you were unconscious…and in the police ambulance. It is covered…You couldn't have seen him."

"I did see him."

At that moment the doctor came. I had to endure his genial loquacity for a long time. He advised me to study the connexion between the ear and the throat, and not to put deadly poison into my ear in huge quantities in future. All the time I thought: "They want to hush it up. They know I drank it. Sally knows."

We discussed my vision of the actor, Lucas Sands. Dr. Briggs said it was "a good story," and that he had never heard of an unconscious patient being able to see through thick canvas.

"I saw him. I saw the whole crowd." I stuck to it obstinately. "I could describe all their faces, but Lucas Sands was the only person I knew."

"Second sight!" said the doctor amiably. "Well, I can believe anything of a young lady who has recovered as you have! I don't mind telling you now that when the porters carried you up to this ward yesterday evening, you were dying. And now I'm going to discharge you."

"I can take her home now—at once?" asked Sally eagerly.

"Well, this evening. There's nothing the matter with her. But tell her not to do it again. She mightn't get off so easily another time."

We went home. I humbled myself, ashamed. I said nothing, but every act of mine silently begged for pardon and oblivion.

In theory I was now quite willing that Sally should marry Robin Long. I can write that name without a shudder, that name which once I could not hear without nausea.

"Now not a corpuscle in all my blood
But in its wonted place doth quiet go."

In theory I submitted. Then I would see him, and my heart would clamour: "It can't be. It shall never be."

I imagined that my opposition was disinterested. Perhaps it was to a certain extent. Robin was a painter, with nothing first-rate about him except his conceit, which was sublime. He was sickly, stunted, and had a disfigurement which made sensitive people avert their eyes quickly from his face. But he was not sensitive about his affliction. He seemed to be proud of it, to brazen it out; to wear it as a *panache*, which made compassion for him difficult.

For weeks after the day I left the hospital, neither Sally nor I mentioned his name. I knew that she saw him constantly. We lived as before, yet not as before. I found out that Louise hated him as much as I did. This gave me hope, a hope of which I was ashamed. As Robin had no money, and Sally was dependent on her mother, they could hardly leave Louise out of their reckoning. Would Louise stop Sally's allowance if they married? This seemed to me unlikely, but I thought it quite likely that she would reduce it. The vision of all the squalid discomfort, of all the grossness of matrimony in such circumstances, threw me into violent anguish. Often I was seized with a desire to interrogate Sally…but I dared not, for fear my voice should tremble in uttering that name which was for ever rising in the silence between us, for fear that those troubled furies who had made me their prey on the night I had tried to take my life should re-assert their hideous existence.

Yet one day the words came quite easily to me. We were sitting side by side in the garden of the cottage to which we went sometimes as a refuge from the whirl of London life. A feeling of infinite repose came from our beloved still marshes. Human pain seemed powerless here. The calm was full of a promise of joy.

"I suppose you will marry him?" I heard the hardness of necessity in my voice.

She laid her hand on my arm as if to beg me to stop.

"No, speak to me. I am not afraid of suffering. Let me hear what you are going to do. It's only fair. Are you going to marry him?"

"I suppose so." She spoke in a suffocated voice, and with no great joy.

I had felt so calm, so good; my heart had been lifted high for sacrifice. Yet in a minute a malignant demon scattered my purpose.

"No! he shall not have you!" I remember saying this, and many more insensate things, laughing, a sharp, unresonant laugh, recalling most meanly all that I had done for her, all that I had sacrificed for her. Every trace of goodness and tenderness in my nature seemed to be wiped out.

Sally tried to quiet me, but I was impatient at her gentleness. Her balsams acted as irritants. Then she too grew impatient.

"One thing is certain: you can always be trusted to behave badly."

She rushed into the house, but I remained for a long time in the same position, staring into the immensity of the twilight. The darkness swallowed up all forms and colours—a darkness one with my heart's darkness.

Then Sally came out again, with that dear timid look which had the charm of unexpectedness on her strong reliant face.

"Aren't you coming in to supper?"

I bent a little towards her shoulder, sought for my voice to say… "Forgive me!"

VII

How it ended I never knew. Sally did not marry Robin. Her love-affair fizzled out. She never spoke of it, she never explained. Her heart was not broken. Perhaps the hearts of people who have work don't break. At this time Sally threw herself with immense energy into arranging a long tour for her mother. I joined the company as a "super," and travelled with it all over England, Scotland, Wales, and the United States. During the long rehearsals I used to write plays in note-books. I became convinced that the drama was my medium of expression.

Sally was a severe critic of my early efforts. She knew that baffling thing "the theatre" as I felt that I should never know it. When I heard her rebuking the electrician with many allusions to "steel blues" and "floats" and "ambers," to "pin-lights," "frosts" and other mysteries, I was deeply impressed by her knowledge and my own ignorance. At first when I showed her a play I was chagrined at her curt condemnation: "Impossible on the stage," but when I subdued my vexation and listened to her reasons, I was quick to see that she was right. She was as quick to see that I had a natural instinct for writing dramatically. She was not at all discouraging, though sometimes my vain sensibility accused her of making me despair. Half my despondency was due to vanity, but I did not know this for many years. I have learned that the artist who despairs convicts himself of pride. Why, after all, should he expect to do such great things? If he has endeavoured manfully, why should he be cast down at the first word of adverse criticism? The only criticism to be resented is that of the critic who says in effect: "This should not be a chair; you ought to have made a table," or "This man should be sitting down; he should not be standing." It is for the artist to choose his work; it is for him to say "I have done this." The critic is concerned only with the manner in which the work has been done.

VIII

What is success? "What is truth?" said jesting Pilate, and did not pause for an answer. Success may be a bauble, and truth the holy Grail, but both are equally difficult to touch and feel. Success means to some artists the recognition of their work by the many; to others its recognition by the few. There is a condemnation which fixes attention on the condemned, and means another kind of success. There is the reward of finding work profitable even to the extent of making a fortune out of it—yet another kind of success. There is the growth of reputation. There is the steady faith in the quality of your own work, in its inevitableness, in the reality of its message, a faith not at all affected by the reception of the work. That again is a kind of success.

As I look back on the last ten years of my life, when, relieved to a certain extent of the necessity of drudging all day at some mechanical labour for a living wage, I have been able to do a little creative work, I cannot see that success in any of its forms has come to me. Sometimes I have thought, "I have no luck." But my preponderant reflection has been that I have not deserved "luck." I have never devoted myself heart and soul to the business of expression. When my first play was produced, and it was written of me that I was a "born dramatist," I saw myself speeding down an exhilarating vista to a commanding position in the world. And perhaps I might have attained it, or what we take to be it—for such positions have no real existence—had I "shunned delights and lived laborious days," had I been more stubbornly set on achievement, more conscious of a special responsibility.

There were moments during these ten years when myself, *my task*, ruled imperiously, when I thought it would be fine to trample on everything else. My natural repugnance to such egotism seemed to me like a sickness. When I ran to others to serve them with my gifts, I did not congratulate myself on a sacrifice, but felt that I was shirking a vocation, escaping from distant frightful worlds in which I was called to dwell, worlds where there was no good-nature, no gentleness, no unselfishness, only cruelty to everything and every one except the work, the deed for which I was fitted.

IX

O the warfare of those years! The profound suffering! "Let me serve!" for ever fighting with "Let me rule!" And the struggle complicated by a love of sensual ease, and a devouring hunger for love! I still loved my friend, but my ideal of friendship had been tarnished. I saw that I was never to know a human relationship in which I was to be the "only one" to the "only other."

Perfect friendship, says Montaigne, is indivisible, and I had found it so. I had given myself up so entirely to Sally that I had nothing left to dispose of elsewhere. No wavering affections ever distracted me from her. I was never happy out of her company. But from the day my certainty of her intentions and opinions, my confidence that her heart was laid open to me, were shaken, I found myself almost unconsciously seeking nutrition elsewhere for my hungry heart.

The hearth was still there, but it was not sacred. The Penates were no longer decorated with flowers. Out of this changed, neglected house my romantic soul roamed forth, stung to wandering by the desire to give itself, to prostrate itself before some unknown love.

X

These wanderings seem to me now all anguish and darkness and humiliation, yet at the time a rare moment's joy would plunge my suppliant soul in such ecstasy that I felt ready to endure I know not what ignominy and cruel disappointment for the sake of being submerged once more in those radiant deeps.

There are hard-headed rational people who complain of the preponderance of the theme of love in books and plays. Love, they say, occupies much less time and space in mortal lives than authors represent. These rationalists plead for the exposition of more important passions—such as those of patriotism, commercial enterprise, the pursuit of knowledge or of glory, and for the description of all those actions which men perform between birth and death, and in which love is not directly and evidently concerned.

The generalization that love in a man's life is a thing apart, "'tis woman's whole existence," is one of the strongest links in the chain of proof that woman if inferior to man. Yes, it is considered very fine and manly to pursue the business of life, to govern other men or conquer other countries, to discover new worlds, new stars, new forces of nature, or to amass money, to write books or paint pictures, to improve social conditions, or to talk about improving them, and to regard "love" as a childish toy to play with for recreation, or a temporary madness which in your true "man" is soon cured.

Yet the masterpieces of the world have always been inspired by "love" in some aspect or other. Strip the world's literature of love, and it will find it difficult to cover its nakedness. Those who have had the clearest vision of humanity have realized that it is in the agony and exultation of love that the human heart is laid bare. Love is almost as merciless as death in beggaring us of all artificial advantages, in reducing us to one possession—that of our own soul.

Those who scorn love lightly very often have no clear notion of what they are putting in its right place. They have whittled down the holy name to fit the passion of man for woman, of woman for man, and by intimating that woman is quite complete without such passion—good women should be content to receive love, at the most to respond to it!—they have still further narrowed the scope and meaning of love. To them, in fact, love is the desire to *possess*. To possess what? Something that will gratify an animal instinct? Is it that desire which interests us when we read the history of lovers, or of all the acts now sublime, now dreadful, and again both, that have been done for love? It is only the monsters of mankind, people made callous and coarse and heartless by frequent indulgence in pleasure, who identify love with such desire, and even they, living up to their theories, have never been satisfied, for the simple reason that the lowest sensualist cannot transform himself into a beast—although he may make himself lower than the beast by the attempt.

If love is terrible on earth, and often it is most terrible in the finest natures, it is because of our duality. A violent craving of the spirit seeking to satisfy itself through the flesh! Let us be compassionate to this tragic search, and at the same time acknowledge it to be the cause of the strange domination which love exercises over life itself, and over the expression of life in the chronicles of humanity.

XI

People kill their beloved ones, I believe, because their failure to find love in the beloved one drives them mad. We should be sorry even for them.

XII

I return from these byways to the road of my own life. Outwardly my life has not been passed in loving. It has been spent in doing more or less inefficiently a variety of things. I continued writing, more because I had to write than because I loved it. I wrote articles weekly for a second-rate lady's newspaper. I wrote plays, as I have related. I wrote books which did not appear under my own name. And it was as "'le Nègre" [the Black man] that I made most money. It was as "le Nègre" that I earned most appreciation for my style.

Style has always been a mystery to me. I had from the first a certain sensitiveness to the magic of words. It was impossible for me to use "any word," even when I was writing for that lady's paper. But often I wrote ungrammatically, and awkwardly. I have never read anything of mine in print yet without a sensation of disappointment. Eager to find an excuse for my inability to be masterly in the English tongue, I have sometimes attributed it to my foreign blood. My manner of expression reminds me, when I am in a judicial mood, of a translation from the Polish or the Russian.

XIII

When I had made some money through my work as a ghost, I never saved it. I was desperately extravagant, and lived for the time as if I were a millionaire. I recall that I was ironically nicknamed "The Millionaire" by Violet Gosborough.

I loved to give people presents. There was no method in this madness for giving. It would have been kind and sensible to have given to the poor, to those who needed to be enriched or cheered by some gift. But with a curious and quite undeliberate perversity, I seem always to have lavished my gifts, as I lavished the treasure of my love, on those who already had much.

In "De Profundis" Oscar Wilde writes of going down the primrose path to the sound of flutes, of throwing his soul into a cup of wine. There was never a moment when my downward path did not wound my feet. Instead of sweet instruments of music, the sound that accompanied my mad pursuit of pleasure was a lamentation faintly chanted by the pure and austere spirit of my guardian angel.

Pleasure! The word suggests the evil things of life.... We have to prefix it by "innocent" when we wish it to have a good savour. So the word may rouse in minds that have an unhealthy curiosity about these things expectations of a description of my contact with evil. I shall disappoint the prurient. To put it in the blunt way of common speech, I never went to the bad. There was less virtue in my comparative blamelessness of conduct than the facts announce. If I abstained from the sins of the body it was more from lack of opportunity than from horror of them. In my brain I often sinned. In my brain I was for the space of two years the slave of ignoble passions. In this dream-iniquity I experienced a kind of ferocious satisfaction. After all, I thought, I am the only being capable of responding to my own devouring love.

Mercifully for me, others fled me, despised me, misunderstood me. Since I had tasted the joys of friendship with a woman possessing many attributes that are generally praised as "manly," I had lost all desire for the friendship of men, and for their love I had never cared. Besides, I had drifted out of the ways which men frequent, and the freshness of my youth, which once had attracted them in spite of their antagonism to my boyish independence of spirit and to my complete immunity from the influence of sex, had passed. This caused me no regret. It is not an idle boast, but the plain truth, to say that if men wanted nothing of me, I wanted nothing of them. I was never in my life curious of the admiration excited by other women, although I have wondered sometimes why they excited it, and striven in vain to understand the power of the "man's woman." Indeed, the "man's woman" and the "woman's man" were precisely the products of their respective sexes for which I had a natural dislike. It has always been to men who are not ashamed to be womanly, and to women who are not afraid to be manly, that my heart has been attracted. The noblest qualities of human nature are neither male nor female.

Yet I admit that until I was thirty I thought that men were to be envied for having been born male. Through that accident of birth they appeared to have a fairer field for the development of those noble qualities which I did not believe to be essentially masculine. Above all I envied them their prerogatives as lovers.

XIV

Stendhal says that he did not seek to record events so much as the influence which events had upon his soul. When I read this it made a profound impression on me. In it is to be found the explanation of my omission in these pages of many events in my life, and of many people whom I have known.

XV

I am travelling to Cologne with Giovanna Ludini. Her beautiful head rests on my shoulder. I can read every line of that perfect face, and read calmly, as I cannot when she is awake, and the expression in her dark eyes troubles my veins. She seems to me like an incarnation of the genius of Gabriele d'Annunzio, like "a rose of heaven death-cankered at the heart." Yes, I have called her *Rosa mundi* [rose of the world], have spent a fortune on buying her roses; the rose has always been dominant in my imaginative thoughts of her. The hour is approaching when she is going to pass out of my life for ever. What has she been to me? What has she done for me?

I answer these questions impetuously. In a passion of resentment I assert that she has corrupted my soul, beggared me of every penny—what were my pennies when her whims needed satisfaction?—forced me into despicable disloyalty to all those old familiar friends to whom I owed faith and allegiance, inspired me to cruelty, humiliating folly, and petty deceit. Often during these five months that I have known her I have hated her, yet I have not been able to tear my soul away from her. And then another voice in me answers this fiercely accusatory one, telling me that it is I myself who have brought myself to this pass. Giovanna never sought me out. It was I who insisted on knowing her.

At first there was no such thought in my mind. I used to gaze at her fixedly—we often saw each other by chance in the restaurant of a famous hotel—with no aim but that of securing a lasting impression of her beauty. Then I grew glad that she was not disturbed by my look, but seemed to welcome it. I found myself growing angry if a companion depreciated her looks, or suggested that her eyes were evil. I remember thinking for the first time in my life that Sally was stupid when she said "I am sure that Ludini has a very low mind. Her refinement is only skin-deep."

Every one in London called her "Ludini," and seemed to be interested in her, but no one could tell you who she was or where she came from. She was seldom to be seen in the company of others, either men or women. Her demeanour in the restaurant was irreproachable, but there streamed from it a kind of contempt which I found very provocative. And a senseless determination to overcome that contempt invaded my mind.

She always dressed very plainly. There was something about her which reminded me of Madame Pohlakoff, yet I knew instinctively that she had none of that simplicity which had distinguished the noble-hearted Russian, and has stood before me all my life as a great sea-mark towering above the affected good manners of the world.

"No," I would say to myself, "you are not well-bred, like Madame Pohlakoff. There is something in you coarse and rough. Your father may have been a prince, but your mother was an Italian peasant. I can see you with a coloured handkerchief tied round your head, eating *polenta* with huge appetite—you who are now toying indolently with oranges which you have made the waiter bring in absurd quantity to your table. How beautiful you look with those golden fruits piled near you! You are own sister to them. The same tawny sunshine ripened you."

While I made these mental notes I would talk to Sally and others with my lips, and turn away my eyes from Giovanna Ludini, but all the time I felt her eyelids vibrating in my blood...the dense shadow of her eyelashes seemed to reach to the innermost part of my heart.

I had written her verses and sent her roses long before I spoke to her. I never thought of what she might be, as others did; I argued with myself that I needed this beauty to fructify my spirit...and I was angered at the disapproving silence with which Sally received the news that I had made the acquaintance of the lovely Italian.

"What is it? Why do you object?"

"I don't object."

"I should like you to meet her too." The habit of sharing everything with Sally was still strong, although our lives no longer kept an even pace together, and I could not forget that she had thought of resigning herself to another.

"I don't wish to know her."

"Why not?"

Sally answered with another question: "Why should one want to know people of that kind?"

"Of what kind! You are trying to insinuate that she is a bad woman, I suppose. I know she isn't."

I remembered that Giovanna had said the day before: "No doubt your Miss Fraser thinks that I am a *cocotte*. Do not defend me. Do not speak of me to her…do not speak of me to any one. The very day I discover you have discussed me with any one, and I shall discover it easily enough, I finish with you."

Although I did not seek to violate Giovanna's prohibition, it excited my antagonism. From the very first, disgust and hatred and contempt had mingled themselves with my devotion and admiration. I fought against them, as against enemies who were striving to destroy the idealism in my hidden soul. But they were always near, lurking above my caresses, putting poison into my cup of pleasure.

She had never even cared enough for me to try and keep me. Over and over again during these five months we had quarrelled, and it was always I who had crawled back, begging forgiveness… entreating to be allowed the privilege of emptying my purse for her on flowers, or on a motor drive, on an opera ticket, or on some hat or coat which she lamented she could not afford.

Why has she allowed me to accompany her abroad now? Is it not chiefly because I am saving her expense? I hope she will not feel my tears falling on her face. She has never had anything but insults for my tears.

Yet it is unfair and unchivalrous to blame her for my wretchedness. Perhaps it has been to save me that she has been so ungenerous. Perhaps she has withheld herself from me because she is contaminated with innumerable unknown loves. Yet how fair and innocent is her white forehead! I caress it despairingly with my fingers. She opens her eyes and gazes at me with that look which first bound me to her—a look of election and of promise. She whispers in her deep Italian voice, "Giovanni, tu m'ami? Carissima! Tu m'ami?"

XVI

That very night in the hotel at Cologne she abused me like one demented. She called me "common," "mean," "weak," "foolish," "intolerable," and in Italian and French showered words on me that were more abusive but less wounding than those English ones which indicated my possession of qualities which I disliked and despised. Her features were convulsed with rage. And why? The immediate cause was her discovery that I had forgotten to bring some curls that she had commissioned me to fetch from a Bond Street hairdresser's the day before we left England.

In my dreams I had thought: "This last day and night will pay for all. All that has been hostile and obscure and impenetrable will vanish. She will give me a moment which I shall remember all my life. It will be so sweet and so noble that, although outwardly I shall return to England a beggar, I shall possess an inward treasure cheaply purchased at the price of this frightful torture."

"Only one moment!" It was for that I had come. With that I had extracted sweetness from the bitterness of my blood. And now I was conscious only of blows aimed at me by a firm, calm hand.

Yes, Giovanna was firm and calm at the station, when she left for the watering-place where she was going to do a "cure" for that ailment which was as mysterious as everything else about her. It was I who wept, careless of our surroundings, careless even of her displeasure.

There was some compassion in her attitude at the last minute. She kissed me on both cheeks, and exhorted me with many a "Courage, chérie." But I detected on her face an inexorable "finis." She could afford to be kind because she was getting rid of me, and I had no claim on her—except that spiritual claim of having given freely all that I had, which might have wakened some sense of responsibility in a less selfish nature.

XVII

Three hours had to be passed somehow before I could return to England. I went into the cathedral. It seemed to me far more beautiful than in the morning, when I had hurried through it with Giovanna. I remembered that, just as the solemn grace of it all had begun to penetrate my being ,and my mind had ascended with the springing arches, she had touched me on the shoulder and said, in a voice suffocated by anguish: "Come, let us go away from here. It reminds me of everything that I want to forget." In that moment I had seen a lightning-like apparition of her tragic history, of the prince of the Church who was her father, of the mother in the small Italian town on the hills, the mother whose humbleness was a more poisoned prick to her proud flesh than the sin of which she had been born. In that moment I had ceased entirely to think of myself and my own wounds. I saw in her physical beauty the same poverty that I had often seen in great possessions. The beautiful and the rich are alike poor. I saw to what terrible things she had been condemned by her character and history, and how hard it was for her to rise from the depths of her own personality.

I had lost that compassionate love in the hours that had followed, but now it returned to me. I wept, but without bitterness.

I no longer cried "Why? Why?" The cathedral seemed to teach silence, to promise peace in time. I did not know then, but I was to know hereafter, that I was blessed because I was still athirst, that I was most happy because I did not curse the insensate attachment of which I had been the victim, nor yield to hatred and despair. As I knelt in this glorious dwelling of the Most High I groped painfully after the truth that this shame and ignominy had not hurt my powers of loving, but had made them more beautiful and strong. I bowed my head to the humiliation of having been denied the chance of renouncement, of having been forcibly sundered from beauteous evil; and through that one little humble act, so small that no human being would have counted it of any merit, I think that my deafness to the call of divine love was pierced for the first time.

XVIII

I am writing to Roxane. I pause and wonder why I am writing to her and why I have written to her so often for five years.

I am not a facile letter-writer. Never in my life have I sat down to "write letters," although it seems to be the chief occupation of many people that I know. Indeed, I have the reputation of never answering letters, and when I am abroad, the last thing that I want to do is to send a long narrative of what I have seen and done to some friend in England.

Yet I write easily to Roxane. I tell her all manner of things about my life, my work and my soul, and about the impressions that I have received from people and from works of art. This day—it is some time after my return from Cologne—I swear that I will never send Roxane a gazette again. Better to have a heart heavy with unexpressed love than to lighten it of its load by casting it at Roxane's feet. But I know as I swear that I shall break my oath.

At the time I knew Giovanna, I was always reading Gabriele d'Annunzio. The poet of my relations with Roxane is Rostand. It has been through her that I have been able to get inside the skin of Cyrano de Bergerac; and when she has wounded me by her reserve, by taking as a matter of course that she should receive my devotion without responding to it, by her interest in me as a curious revival of a medieval swineherd, adoring from a distance an inaccessible princess, by her never volunteering to bridge the gulf fixed between my world and that world of 'smart' people where she enjoys supremacy, I have caught myself repeating those lines in which Cyrano sums up his life—those lines which first wounded me with their beauty when I believed myself to be passing out of life:

> "Pendant que je restais en bas, dans l'ombre noir
> D'autres montaient cueillir le baiser de la gloire!
> C'est justice, et j'approuve au seuil de mon tombeau;
> Molière a du génie, et Christian était beau!"
> [While I remained below, in the dark shadows
> Others climbed up to pluck the kiss of glory!
> It is just, and I agree, at the threshold of my tomb;
> Moliere had genius, and Christian was beautiful!]

I wonder if Roxane would give me something more than a charming patronage if I were something more than a dweller in "l'ombre noir"...I will not think that I could unlock the door of her life with a golden key, although she is most often found in the society of rich people. But *prominence*—that is another thing. I think she would be proud of me if I made a mark.

Nothing can kill this force in me, I decide, as I go on with my gazette. I am older—oh, so much older!—since Cologne, but not at all wiser. I still hunger and thirst for love. I still love, and cannot restrain myself from expressing love.

Had Roxane laughed at me, as most of the fools and gluttons and idlers in her fashionable "set" would have laughed; had she chosen to ignore the little pot of nard broken at her feet...expensively shod feet which have walked only in the pleasant places of life...she never would have known a Cyrano de Bergerac. But there is in the nature of this spoiled child of fortune, this glass of fashion, this winner of the race for social honours, some touch of divine simplicity which from the first forbad her to refuse or scorn or belittle what I gave.... Do you know, Roxane, that it is as guardian of that precious pearl that I am significant in your life? Others admire you for your quick wit, love you interestedly for your worldly advantages, are impressed by your success in whatever you undertake. But you have held me, who have neither natural affinity with you nor acquired freemasonry, by that pure spring of water in your heart which has not been poisoned by the pride of life and the deceitfulness of riches.

Yes, I owe much to you, although the debt cannot be calculated by algebra. We have met very seldom, and when we have met you have not made me insensible to what you would never call "our respective positions." No, you would never *say* that you, an aristocratic woman of the world, with enough of wealth to satisfy your expensive tastes, and enough of social engagements to keep you from thinking, are my superior. I do you wrong to assume that you would think it, for you have a noble nature. Yet in your kindness I have detected condescension. Do you know what a great educator it has been of my humility?

You too, Roxane, you more than any one, have taught me that love can exist without egoism. You have often said that my devotion touches you beyond words, but what have you substituted for the words you could not or would not speak? A caress from you! It would surprise me as much as if the stars left their courses and made themselves into a diadem for my head.

Once or twice at parting you have said "Bless you!" I have taken those two words into my soul, and found they were worlds, not words—twin worlds of gentleness and sweetness in which I could wander for a long time dreaming and gathering flowers.

Again I say I owe much to you. There was no *reason* for my being attracted to you…and you have never given me any beyond that one you give every one in the world by living and being beautiful. So you have educated my faith as well as my humility and self-effacement. It has been very hard sometimes to believe in that living spring of water. In spite of you, rather than because of you, *credidi et amavi* [I believed and I loved]!

X
RESPONSIBILITY

I

It was the first anniversary of Mark Washington's death, and Sally and I had gone to the Abbey to put rosemary for remembrance and laurel for honour on his grave.

This was the only great man of the age to whom my soul had gone out in hero-worship. I had admired him living, I loved him dead. I loved him the more because during the last few years of his life he had lost his hold on the public, on the fickle mob-public whose support means money. Many of the great actor's friends and followers thought it tragic that he should have died poor. I regarded it as the crown to his existence, the seal on his greatness. For he had lost the allegiance only of those who had not really loved his art, but gifts that he offered with his art—fine productions carefully considered even to the meanest detail, solemnities unique in stage ceremonial, an atmosphere of dignified illusion. When or why the public lost a taste for this sort of thing I cannot say. Perhaps all tastes are naturally limited in their extent and duration. Perhaps Washington's powers of developing his own lines were limited too. He was much blamed for not trying other lines, as a great horseman might be blamed for not exchanging his horse for an aeroplane. But he knew that this objection to the material in which he worked was fantastic, and to the end he continued to present himself in familiar parts in familiar plays. What did not become familiar was the genius of the actor in these parts. I never saw him act without experiencing an exquisite sensation of surprise. He could not disappoint you because he was always at the height of the particular situation. If he acted a rogue, he was a great rogue; if a saint, he was a great saint.

He died, and his body was hardly cold before jealous fangs opened to snap at the justness of his reputation. By a man's enemies you may know him. It is a bad sign when the whole world is his friend. It is not easy to love a truly great man. It means humility; it means taking trouble; it means reverence; it means self-effacement; it means comprehension of the values of failure and success. Few people loved the afflicted Napoleon dying at St. Helena.

There was a great commotion outside the Abbey. I asked a man why there were so many policemen.

"It's because of these women who want the vote," he answered.

For some time Sally and I had been living in retirement at the cottage on the marshland, where burning questions did not intrude.

"Woman's Suffrage" was to me only a discordant expression, standing for a dull and ugly Thing, a Thing connected with "politics"; and "politics in their turn conjured up grotesque memories of my childhood when grown-up people used to fly into a rage at the bare mention of the name of Mr. Gladstone. At Oxford I had known Liberals and Conservatives, and discovered that their differences were quite unreal, and that their convictions were not perennials, but "bedded-out" plants. If their party were in opposition they had one set, but when it came into power they made a clean sweep of opposition opinions, and substituted those which became a Government. I found it impossible to interest myself in the intricate game of party politics. It seemed to me an unreal business, as unreal as the business of international politics.

I had a leaning towards Socialism, because its aims were more comprehensible to me, because it seemed to have no horror of the unpractical. "A practical scheme," the Socialist argues, "is either a scheme that is already in existence, or a scheme that could be carried out under existing conditions. But it is precisely these conditions that are wrong and foolish, conditions that assume the necessity of oppressors and oppressed, of the monstrous exploitation of the weak by the strong, of the right of the few to enjoy comfort and beauty and the luxuries which science has placed at the disposal of mankind, while the many remain in barbarism, of the giving pennies and moments to the affairs of peace, and pounds and hours to the machinery of war." It seemed to me that the mere *doubt* as to the necessity and inevitableness of such conditions was inspiring.

But I was disheartened and discouraged when Labour began to be represented in the House of Commons, and the representatives of the poor and the oppressed appeared to become very like the representatives of prosperity and oppression. Whatever their good intentions, these new members, sprung from "the people," were quickly caught in the party gin. Their claws were cut, they were incapable of doing anything.

So my "politics" had become vaguer and vaguer. In my soul there was a great desire to stretch out my hand to those who were sunk in the gulf, but I sought no opportunity of testing the sincerity of my desire. I had but one answer when I was asked if I were a Liberal or a Conservative. It was the answer of Olivier in "Jean-Christophe": *"Ni l'un ni l'autre…J' suis pour les opprimés."* [Neither one, nor the other…I am for the oppressed.]

I suffered when I thought of *Them*, the only party to which I owed allegiance. They were in England, engaged in repugnant, unclean, dangerous and monotonous labour at a "living wage" (which was not at all the same "living wage" as Roxane's); they were in Armenia, being done to death with horrible cruelties; they were in Finland with a suffocating hand at their throat; they were in my dismembered Poland, denied a place on the soil of their fathers, flogged without mercy for devotion to their faith and language; they were in terrorized Russia; they were in those far-off countries, preyed upon by rapacious Europeans in search of gold and rubber. And from them all there rose a cry to which it seemed inconceivable that the greater part of humanity could be deaf. What does it matter to us?...It is no concern of ours. A Polish child is crippled for life because it refuses to learn the catechism in a foreign tongue; an Indian in farthest Peru is flogged to death because he has not collected enough rubber (to the great peril of the "living wage" of those who have rubber shares); little girls with their mothers' milk scarcely out of them are outraged, sometimes by their own fathers; young maidens are seized in the light of day and sold to a "company" formed because the organized gratification of vice is a safe and profitable investment. What has it to do with us? We are not the oppressors, we are not guilty of these abominable crimes. Even the knowledge that such things are done under heaven should be kept from people, as there is no object in shocking and paining them needlessly.

This argument could not convince me. My heart burned with the truth that we are each responsible to all for all. It would have been useless to tell me that I was not to blame, and that anyhow I could do nothing. I wept when I read of what had been done to Marie Spiridinova. The words *they tortured her from one to seven* forced me to choose my "party." "If I say this is no concern of mine, I am as cruel as any one of those Russian officers who for six hours were as ingenious in brutality as schoolboys with a stray cat. (But the stray cat is to be envied because it is not a woman.) If on the contrary I feel that it is my concern, that those officers are pressing their hot cigarette-ends against my flesh, I am at any rate not their accomplice." Yes, it became clear to me, from the day when the details of the revolting torture to which that young Russian girl had been subjected reached England, that the hands of all those who were inflicting suffering all over the world were my hands, so long as I refused to exist in the hearts of those who suffered.

258

II

Those policemen outside the Abbey made me wonder if these "women who want the vote" were also my concern. I did not want a vote. So far as I had thought about the extension of civic rights—and I had thought about it only with that vagueness characteristic of me when my brain has not been illumined by the light of a fiery conviction—I had decided that in England citizenship was not the road to light and liberty. Poor men had been admitted to the franchise, and the result had been the triumph of bureaucracy. Votes had done little for the workers, beyond giving them an excuse for their refusal to suffer for their cause.

Then the principle of my life had been that humanity is more important than sex, and through the rise of this troublesome question of woman's suffrage I saw my principle being thrust on one side. I heard more talk of men and women, women and men, in these days than at any time in my life.

Sally was quickly converted. I lagged behind. I found it difficult to say whether I was for the Suffragists or against them. Certainly I was very sensitive to the ridicule that they excited, and their own happy indifference to it seemed to me to arise from conceit rather than courage. Their pride in the odious title "Suffragette" was another stumbling-block, their exultantly optimistic speeches another. It was very difficult to see their connexion with my party, the oppressed of the earth, in spite of the policemen. Yet sometimes when discussion arose as to whether women ought to have votes, I was surprised to find myself defending their cause with more passion than any one present.

When I went to suffrage meetings in the character of a sympathetic onlooker, I found that the "suffragettes" were not a race apart, but a collection of ordinary wives, mothers, sisters and daughters, with all the virtues and faults of ordinary women;

and I decided that the attempt to represent them as an insignificant body of disappointed and soured spinsters who had manufactured this agitation by way of venting their spite on a world where they were not "desired" would not do. It seemed to me to speak well for the agitation that its enemies had to resort to such an unworthy weapon as misrepresentation to fight it.

Old women, young women, plain women, pretty women, well-dressed women, ill-dressed women, the idle rich, the hard-working professional classes, the married, the single, athletic women, aesthetic women, clever women, silly women, steady women, excitable women—I recognized them all, as I might have done at a large evening-party, or at a concert, or at any place where women gather together. There was nothing at all exceptional about them—which was in a way disappointing. There were some who regarded "the movement" as a more exciting game than hockey, there were others to whom it meant only the serious side of life; to some it was a movement towards better wages, to others a movement towards better morality. There were a few who did not see beyond "a vote" in the purely political sense, and a few who were dominated by a desire to prick the bubble of male superiority.

I was disheartened by the speeches that I heard. The thought was platitudinous, the expression colourless; there was a lack of lucidity and simplicity. These women orators were wonderfully fluent, but their language had in a very short time become the language of their particular convention. It was so well understood by their audiences that the end of every third sentence was lost in applause.

While others admired the leaders of the movement—and indeed they deserved admiration as fanatics whose genuine readiness to suffer for their principles distinguished them at once from charlatans—I could not help seeing that they were one and

all inferior to the force on which they had been born to prominence and authority. I could understand the criticism directed
against them; when I came in contact with them I felt, in spite
of my desire not to criticize them, that they were consumed by
vanity as well as by faith, that they were shockingly indifferent
to the sufferings that were endured without glory by the rank
and file of their followers, that they were thirsty for advertisement, and not over-fastidious in their methods of obtaining it.
Vulgarity and sublimity, folly and good sense were well mixed
in their counsels and actions—which proved, after all, nothing
except that they belonged to mankind. There were jealousies and
schisms in this movement, as in all movements; there was an
ungrateful and parochial egotism in the policy of each particular
"union." You could discern this, and be more sensible than ever
of the magnitude of the current on which the Suffragist unions
and their leaders were drifting. It was the *current* which knew
where it was going, and could never be stopped.

I can't remember when I first recognized the current. The
recognition came from within, and was not caused by any personal influence. Once it had come I never had any doubt again.
I had to be a Suffragist.

What was this momentous recognition? I saw, in spite of the
dust of controversy, that this struggle, carried on directly to
gain a material interest, had indirectly an immense spiritual significance. Never, since the derided ragged regiment of the first
Christians had defied the power and splendour of Pagan Rome,
had a more remarkable challenge been thrown down by the
foolish and weak things of this world to the strong. I don't think
that any woman had a notion of the extent of a man's belief that
the battle is to the strong until this struggle for the vote began.
Then, forgetting that it is those who are despised, those who *are
not*, who are chosen to defeat those who are, he thought it was

enough to say "I don't wish you to have a vote and that settles the matter, as I am stronger than you."

I made it my business to find out why he did not wish it, and experienced great difficulty in getting at the truth. I was bewildered by the number of red herrings dragged across the path of the question, irritated by irreconcilable contradictions. How was it possible to assert with hand on heart that you honoured your mother, and owed everything to her; that you loved your wife and regarded her as the partner of your existence; that you had a deep affection and admiration for your sister; that you loved your daughters as your sons; that you were ready to admit that women as a whole were more moral and law-abiding than men, and then to swear, with your hand still on your heart, that if these respected and beloved creatures were admitted to citizenship, it would be the ruin of your country?

This attitude was so absurd that it made me laugh, but it made me weep as well. I followed the scent, in spite of the distracting red herrings, and discovered that the belief of man in his *essential* superiority to woman was far more universal than I had supposed. Some of the foundations for this belief may be insecure and shifting; but this one—the exclusion of the finest woman from a position accessible to the paltriest man—is a solid rock. No wonder that the dogged Englishman's hostility has been roused by the attack on this last and best proof of woman's natural inferiority!

Was it possible that the violence of his opposition was due to causes quite unconnected with the safety and prestige of the British Empire? I pursued this, and saw in a flash that the equality and fraternity of spirit between men and women which would sooner or later arise from their new relationship as fellow citizens would be a danger to another kind of imperialism—the imperialism of vice. Under the new *régime* vice would exist...but it would not, it could not, claim so many victims to whom all free will in choosing it or refusing it has been denied. When I saw that it was round the right of every woman born into the world to exercise that free will, rather than round a vote, that this struggle was being carried on, I could not stand on the bank and give tea and comfortable advice to the swimmers. I plunged into the stream. No one who has not taken that plunge has any notion of the strength of the current of prejudice against the women who are fighting for the principle that their existence should not be limited to certain episodes in the lives of men. That principle is the life-blood of the woman's suffrage movement.

III

My vigorous individuality, at this time disfigured by my pride in an intellectual equipment that I deemed "masculine," recoiled before the prospect of joining one of the many societies that had sprung up to "secure the granting of the vote to women as it is or may be granted to men." Others might profit by being chained together for combat, but I felt that I should lose by it. Was there no other way? Apparently not, as before many weeks had gone by I had enrolled myself a member of the most advanced of the "militant" organizations.

I thought that they would be pleased to gain an "artist," even one with my humble record of achievement; but I soon found that they distrusted artists, and even despised them as people who could not give the "cause" all their time, as people who might show unwelcome originality.

"Pauvre liberté, tu n'es pas de ce monde!" [poor liberty, you are not of this world] I was revolted by the way the committee of the union that I had joined abused their powers. In its early days this union had been conducted on democratic and representative

lines. Now it was ruled by a dictatorial bureaucracy, whose policy was to get rid of any one on the executive who disagreed with them. It must be admitted that the union flourished under this able tyranny, and that is was its fanaticism, admirable or detestable according to the point of view, which brought the question out of the drawing-room into the street.

IV

Already I can hear the impatient groans of the friend who has followed my life so far with the interest that the record of a soul's voyage must always have for other travellers, provided it be faithful. And I myself share your impatience, friend. There is nothing more tragic about "woman's suffrage" than its dullness. I went out to see martyrs in "shirts of flame." I found poor little shrinking women, dressed in ill-fitting clothes, whose "violence" was as drab as everything else about them. Have revolutionaries always appeared like this to the looker-on? Have the cries of rage, with which their attempts to gain their end have been greeted by those who hate change, never been very fearful in fact...only humiliating in their flouting, jeering vulgarity?

No one will ever know what it cost me to take a part in violence which was derided rather than feared. The faith of the women round me was a reproach to me always. I walked with downcast head in the flaring light of the torches that it kindled. I found soon how much I lacked the qualities of a "good suffragette." Yet I stuck to the work of a recruit with some doggedness of purpose...and in the process learned how brutal and how kind Englishmen and Englishwomen can be.

I never had a ready retort for the hard-featured women in smart clothes who abused me when I sold Suffragist "literature" in the streets. (It was always called "literature," although there was little that was literary in these pamphlets and newspapers advocating our cause.) I distributed handbills announcing meetings, chalked "Votes for Women" on pavements, heckled Cabinet ministers when they addressed their public, and knew what it was to be flung into the street by six or seven stewards, who tore my clothes and thumped me on the back with a mad-dog violence that astonished me. I understood that I had infuriated these men and must "face the music," but I smiled to think that "chivalry" is a very easy virtue. It is easy for a man to be chivalrous to a woman in fair weather, when he is not irritated or annoyed. It is easy for a man not to hit a woman when he has no provocation. But when he is provoked…it is then that a woman finds the worth of the chivalry of romance.

Later I stood on a lorry in the Park, on a chair at street-corners, on the platform in public halls, and was not a complete failure as an orator, chiefly because my stage training helped me to hold an audience and to make myself heard. But I knew that my comrades thought little of my speeches, and would have been better pleased if I had given more glory to "the union" and dwelt less on principles of justice and humanity. I tried sometimes to use the expressions of the union's professional speakers, but they stuck in my throat. Even my voice did not sound like their voices. Often I caught an almost hostile expression from my fellows on the platform. They seemed to suspect me, yet I was loyal and my soul was like a sword drawn for combat.

I had a taste of real warfare when, stifling my dread of crowds and my sensitiveness to publicity, I joined a deputation to the Prime Minister. I knew quite well that this deputation or "raid" was a farce as regarded its ostensible objective. We were not intended to fight our way to the House of Commons; no one expected that we should be able to force an audience on the head of the Government, who already knew what the leaders had to say. And to some of us the emptiness of the pretext for "soldiering" was very galling. We were told that the time had come for defiant deeds, and that words were paltry compared with them; but in practice the deed appeared senseless, and the suspicion that it was planned for spectacular effect made it, to me at least, very distasteful. But I strove to have confidence in the policy of which the deed was a detail. We were called foolish, misguided and hysterical, because we were ready to obey orders quietly, to say, with the Light Brigade, "ours not to reason why." But for everything we did, as for every motive that inspired us, there was some sneer in the capitalist press. Our physical courage was hysteria, our devoted obedience weak-mindedness, our willingness to incur the risk of arrest and imprisonment a love of advertisement.

I pushed through the crowd of onlookers on the pavement in Whitehall into the road, which had been cleared by the police, and saw a row of mounted police barring the way to the Houses of Parliament. I realized at that minute how much overrated is the courage of the soldier. Had those police been cannon with artillerymen behind them I should have gone forward with the same calmness. The only thing that came into my head was "Any cause is good enough to die for." I seized hold of the bridle of one of the horses and turned his head towards Westminster. The policeman made the horse rear, and I was carried off my feet. In a moment three policemen on foot left the pavement, where they were keeping back the crowd, and threw themselves upon me. They jerked my wrist from the bridle and "arrested" me. I rejoice to this day to think that the Japanese lacquer armour that I was wearing underneath my coat prevented them from handling me. Some women who have taken part in these "raids" have not been so fortunate—or so wise. It is often the same thing. "The lucky cat watches."

V

I was tried for my offence. I stood in the felon's dock, and was sentenced with a hundred more criminals to a month's imprisonment. On a point of law, however, we were given leave to appeal, and the appeal being decided in our favour, I never saw the inside of a prison.

The incident that I remember most clearly in the whole affair is that the day before the raid I was asked by an official of the union to state my religion. I answered "Roman Catholic," and then wondered why I had not said "Church of England," as all the others did, to save trouble, and ensure having recreation together in prison. Why could I not deny the religion that I had never practised, and of the doctrines of which I was entirely ignorant? I could not answer this question.

VI

In the autumn of that year during which the Suffrage movement had absorbed all my energies—a hungry monster it has been to many, devouring time, money, health, talent, artistic fever, powers of loving, powers of rebelling against injustice—I went to Rome, and my short and inconspicuous career as an active revolutionary came to an end. I am ashamed to confess that I was glad to be free from the coils of the question. I looked forward to returning to the theatre, to writing that one play which should pierce the deafness of the world. When the "comrades" reproached me with desertion, I took up the old position that I had for the time abandoned, and argued that it was my duty to do well what I could do. They thought this the excuse of a *fainéant* [idler]. Had I succeeded in writing a masterpiece and getting it produced on the stage, a work compelling recognition without any damning reservation "very fine for a woman," they would not have considered my service as valuable or as honourable as that of the meanest among them who had broken a window as a protest against tyranny.

What inclined me to agree with their estimate of values was that the broken window was a reality, the masterpiece less than a possibility.

VII

I do not know whether in my time the Government of England will admit women to the franchise, but I do know that it is not in the power of men or governments to repress the ideas which have sprung from this agitation. We can no more restore the slavery of white woman than we can the slavery of black men.

Slavery? Men indignantly deny that women are enslaved. But what other word describes the position of those who are told that if they have wrongs they can be redressed by—masters; if they want benefits they can obtain them through—masters; if they want to rule the world, they can do it by cajoling—masters?

There is a sense in which slaves are better off than free men, and it is probable that for generations after women have gained their object and are recognized as one of the essential parts of the machinery of the state, they will find life a hundred times harder than in the golden age of their subjugation. I am afraid that this accounts for the bitter hostility which many of the spoiled children of fortune among women have manifested to their sisters who would put away childish things.

VIII

The slave is after all to be compassionated less than the slave-owner. Servitude may breed such virtues as lowliness, humility, patient endurance, gratitude for kindness; but what virtues are born of irresponsible power? Only the exceptional man has been able to resist the brutalizing effects of his right to dominate woman, to be her "superior." The moral elevation which will result from the extinction of the idea of the essential superiority of the male as male will be seen first in the soul of man. We shall not see then the sweet lovable man-child transformed after a few years' contact with the world into an insufferable and exacting fellow, despising his sisters because they are women, giving the mother who bore him indulgent patronage or open scorn because she is a woman, buying his wife with a home, ignoring his responsibility for the prostitute and the outcast, regarding the sacrifice of women to his pleasure as natural and inevitable. How many of these fellows have realized during this last decade that the "Suffragette," the subject of vulgar joke or rude attack, has been the instrument of a force which has for its supreme and sublime end *their* regeneration?

IX

"La plus sublime idée restera sans effet jusqu'au jour où elle devient contagieuse, non par ses propres mérites, mais par ceux des groupes humaines qui l'incarnent et lui transfusent leur sang. Alors la plante desséchée, la rose de Jéricho, soudainement fleurit, grandit, remplit l'air de son arome violent." (Romain Rolland.) [The most sublime idea will remain without effect until the day it becomes contagious, not through its own merits, but through the men who make it incarnate and transfuse it with their blood. Then the withered plant, the rose of Jericho, suddenly flowers, grows, and fills the air with its violent aroma.]

The "idea" of the woman's movement never became contagious until the militant suffragists, "the wild women" as they have been contemptuously called, made it incarnate. When you seek to remedy one injustice, however, you risk creating another, and this has been the case with the "militants," who have committed many acts contrary to justice and charity. Of course these acts have been castigated even by those who believed in woman's suffrage when it was a "plante desséchée," [withered plant] an academic theme, an object in a museum, a swathed mummy in a case, at which no one outside a small circle of specialists ever looked. Of course we have been told that these violent acts have ruined the cause, and brought it into contempt. But from this kind of ruin and abasement dart vital beams penetrating the dull indifference of the crowd.

X

You are horrified and shocked that women should do such "unwomanly" things. Are you not more horrified and shocked that there are legalized brothels in your midst? or that young girls in respectable families are educated to regard marriage as a trade? O hypocrisy, thy name is Englishman!

XI

This moral epidemic, as I call the movement of women to obtain recognition as *human beings*, continues to spread, in spite of a powerful and immoral opposition. No generous creature, whether male or female, is able to resist its contagion. No one who has ever profoundly, dininterestedly held the *credo* of the movement has been driven into unbelief by the follies or weaknesses of its active fighters. Ah, it is so easy to be wise and sensible if you rest passive and immobile!

Is it an illusion that this is one of the great movements of humanity which from time to time renew and regenerate this old world? That question will be answered in time, but never to the complete satisfaction of the old world. To the children of darkness light is ever an illusion, though experience prove it truth. Witness, *Christianity*.

PART II

THE CELL OF SELF-KNOWLEDGE

I

LIGHT

I

I sat in the restaurant of the Gare de Lyons waiting for the Rome express, and an extraordinary sensation gripped me.

It was that of one who is drowning and sees his life pass quickly before him in a kind of myriorama.

For the first time I realized that all these events, now flashing past me in pictures, had transformed me into a cruel, selfish, absurd creature. I seemed to know myself for the first time, to see where my easy lawlessness had led me. My poverty and the necessity for work that poverty had imposed on me alone had saved me from degradation. But I had grown into a monster of pride and bitterness. For years I had not given a thought to my dead father and mother. I had become intolerable in daily life. A word of criticism, wounding my vanity, would throw me into a passion of anger. I could be kind and merry and friendly abroad with mere acquaintances, but with Sally, in the intimacy of the home, I was a devil.

As I made this fierce "Je m'accuse,"[self accusation] I was conscious of coming in touch with some mysterious beauty and happiness. I did not understand it at the time. I explained the strange feeling as premonition of death.

"I know I shall never return."

I kept repeating this sentence to myself. I varied it: "I shall never go back to London, to the old life, to Sally." At the thought of Sally, tears came to my eyes. I reproached myself for having parted from her with so little sorrow. All the hasty, irritable things that I had said to her lately came into my mind.

I shivered. I had taken this journey to Rome against her wish, against every one's wish but my own. Perhaps there was a curse on it. Then why this sensation that I was travelling towards an exquisite blessing?

I was plagued by the riddle. Why was I going to Rome? There seemed no justification for it. The money that had paid for my new clothes and for my ticket belonged of right to Sally, for she was going to bear all the expense of settling into a new home in London which I was to share. I had left her, as I had often left her before, to do all the dirty work.

Then there was my writing. I had painfully picked up the threads that I had dropped when I had been absorbed by the "Cause," and now I was dropping them again. It was shameful weakness.

Marya needed me in Rome, it was true, but Marya had no claim on me, and I knew that I was not going to her from a generous motive. "What is the meaning of it?" I thought. "Am I going merely because I hate England, and Italy is an allurement to my spirit of adventure? No...I have been summoned. I have been sentenced to death. I shall never return."

By the time I reached the Italian frontier this sense that I was obeying some mysterious command left me for the time. I gave myself up to the enjoyment of the fine-featured country through which the train was passing. Its face was noble and classic after pretty Switzerland. Italy! Italy! The name that has intoxicated the world—the name that is inseparable from beauty!

No more practical French or economical Swiss to be seen at wayside stations, but carelessly graceful people wearing rags with distinction; expressive, gay people in whom poverty has not bred misery.

In the autumn dawn the mountains were the colour of beryl. The sun touched their peaks where the eternal snows rested. Snow and stones and flowers had all changed their aspect since we had left Switzerland. They were transfigured by the Latin soul.

I gazed almost in a state of beatitude at the fluttering gay garments hung from the windows of the houses to dry, as the scarlet garlands of dried tomatoes with which those houses were adorned. All the necessities of daily life "turned to favour and to prettiness"—that is Italy.

I heard my fellow-travellers complaining of the length and tediousness of the journey, saw them reading English novels. I thought that strange, considering that all the books that had ever been written had never been able to express the beautiful images which were scattered over these hills and plains.

II

During my first visit to Italy with Madame Pohlakoff I had not seen Rome. I was filled with mingled terror and rapture as the train drew near the city predestined to rule the world. I was already half way through my earthly existence; the "subtle thief of life" had stolen thirty-three years from me, but I felt as if I were being born again with the Roman morning. A sharp sense of *newness* pervaded my being.

There rose now in the landscape relics of Imperial Rome, ruined aqueducts, massive arches under which legions of soldiers had once passed. Now carts drawn by white oxen swayed through them, or men in black cloaks, thrown over one shoulder with the sure touch of a toga-wearing race, walked indolently on the russet-coloured roads. Tawny too were the unnavigable rivers flowing swiftly over boulders of gray stone to feed the Tiber. The air was filled with glittering gold-dust which gave bronze tips to the leaves of the dark immutable ilex trees.

III

The English tourist confesses to disillusionment at the first sight of Rome. As if Rome could be spoiled by tramcars and immense tenement-houses and other features of the life of a modern city! Rome from the first moment pours a crystalline stream of poetry into the soul which is ready to expand with Latin flexibility, ready to see superbly with Latin eyes.

IV

There was Marya on the platform, charmingly dressed as always, her pale gold hair, like that of a Carpaccio angel, gaining deeper colour from the imperial purple of her hat…or was it Rome that had intensified not only her hair, but everything about her?

I admired her as I had never admired her in London, where her wealth and prosperity had alienated me, creating in me a feeling of superiority over her who had never grappled with necessity, or endured discomfort, or been bound by material narrowness.

She was a Pole, married to a rich English manufacturer of buttons; but in her Mayfair drawing-room, queening it in her Paris gowns over a rubbishy court of young men of the "tame robin" type, and second-rate fashionable women who wore their lax morality like a *panache*, whether they were married or *demi-vierges*, she had seemed to me an ordinary English butterfly with wings singed and tarnished by countless trivial love-affairs. But now, as we jolted over the cobbles outside the *ferrovia*, past that gross robustious fountain which is the first fountain you see and hear in Rome, I perceived a subtle complexity, a duality, in her temperament, entirely Slav.

I knew that Marya had left her husband and children in the summer for the sake of one of the tame robins, and that her husband was going to divorce her. I knew that for the time she and her lover had been forced to separate. At his mother's urgent request this very sensible son had consented not to "ruin his career" and resign his position in the diplomatic service, and he had been sent by the Foreign Office to an Embassy as remote from Marya as could be found.

I was greatly surprised to find Marya altogether different from what I had expected. She was really glad to see me. She was not lying when she said so. Her amber eyes glowed, she kept on laughing. She was greatly excited by my arrival, and could not stop chattering.

Before we had reached her apartment near the Pincio I knew everything that had happened to her since she had run away. Whatever event she described, and she had a charmingly direct and confiding way of describing things, she was always the heroine of it. She was now making the very most of her tragic separation from her "little prince," as she called him, of her comparative poverty, of a "dastardly conspiracy" which was afoot to prevent her prince from marrying her.

I listened to her patiently. She was very sensitive about everything that concerned herself…but as regards the feelings of others she was obtuse. In all her words and actions there was the most intense egotism. I don't think that it ever occurred to her that her prince was a traitor, but it flashed on me directly I had read one of his very literary and insincere love-letters. From that moment I had a tenderer feeling for Marya. She became to me, although she did not know it, one of the "opprimés" of the earth, bound to me by a fraternal tie. Yet there were times when her abjectness made me miserable and indignant. She did not love her prince as a free woman loves, but as a slave.

V

I had been in Rome ten days, ten calm autumn days. I felt as if my mind were in a state of arrest. I never consciously thought of anything all that time, but fragments of thought floated through my brain; light seemed to come and go.

By day we wandered through the streets. Marya was a delightful companion. She noticed everything. We went in and out of churches, spent long hours in the Borghese Gardens, climbed up the Janiculum Hill paved with the gold of the fallen plane leaves. Marya had a horror of "sight-seeing," and we never made any plans. I felt a sweetness in my heart that I had never known. When I was alone in my bedroom I would stand for an hour and more at the open window, from which I could see the whole vault of heaven unfurled over the domes of Rome. Our flat was high in the air. The statue of the Blessed Virgin on the top of the column of the Immaculate Conception was on a level with my window. I used to watch the birds flying round her head and perching on her diadem of stars. The noble, gracious figure attracted me most at night. The nights were fresh and motionless. My expectant feeling grew in their marvellous silence.

VI

I woke because some one had kissed me…I thought of my mother. "Yes, it was her spirit." I embraced the air, and cried out "Mother!" I sat up in bed longing irresistibly to kiss her, to tell her that I loved her, and had loved her all my life, although I had not known it until now. And as I sat up, facing the window, I saw between me and the glimmering square of deep blue sky full of soft shining stars, the Immaculate Figure. Yes she was in the room. I noticed that her starry diadem nearly touched the ceiling, but her face I could not see. It seemed to me that a pale stream of light came from it and fell across my bed—fell on my heart linking it to hers. Something, I know, glowed in my heart, filling it with insupportable rapture. I stretched out my arms and uttered a cry.

"You have come to fetch me at last!" The idea of being "fetched" had been the fixed idea of my infancy.

Then I fell back on my bed, unwilling to cut short my gladness, yet unable to sit up any longer. It was precisely at that moment, when my eyes no longer saw Her—that I heard a sound…and I did not know whether it was a word. It passed into my ears more like an essence than a sound—a divine essence of all that I had ever dreamed of human love when it has transcended the body of speech.

I must have fallen asleep immediately, for I remembered nothing more until I woke in the sunlight. I woke saying *"Ave gratia plena. Dominus tecum. Benedicta tu in mulieribus et benedictus fructus ventris tui Jesus."* [Hail, full of grâce. The Lord is with you. Blessed are you among women and blessed is the fruit of your womb, Jesus.]

There are things incredible and true. I had never said an *Ave* before in my life, never to my knowledge heard one, never read the angelic words in any book; yet between sleeping and waking I said them now quite easily and fluently. And I said them, as I found out later, in the very form in which they are engraved on the base of the column of the Immaculate Conception.

When Marya's French maid Augustine came in with my breakfast on a tray, I wondered if it had all been a dream. I could not repeat the words, could not recapture the ecstasy of my vision in the night. My breakfast lay untasted on the tray while I stood at the window gazing at the majestic statue. I was afraid to think of what had happened, for fear my conscious thoughts should spoil it, should obscure its clarity by some interpretation.

But I felt with a certainty that was startling, almost terrifying, that something firm and stable had entered my soul and taken possession of it for ever.

I spent the day much as usual. There was an ambiguous letter from her prince to discuss with Marya. There were letters from England about her divorce. I helped her to answer them. We lunched at Constantino's on the Aventine. It was December 7, but the air was soft and warm. The sun and the stiff tawny grass of the Campagna, the divinely clear sky, the deep Sabine Hills, were all to me as things that I had never seen before, yet I was afraid of their beauty as I was afraid of thought. There are moments when lovers dare not move, or speak, or look in each other's eyes, when all the external beauty of the world is spread for them in vain. All day like a lover I had been absorbed in the task of preserving such a moment from distraction. I had a great expectation of something to be accomplished in me if I kept my heart tranquil as a deep well.

Marya said: "They tell me all the shops will be shut to-morrow, so we must get all we want to-day. To-morrow is the Feast of the Immaculate Conception, and a great *festa* in Rome."

A lover often betrays himself to a keen observer when the name of his beloved is mentioned suddenly in his presence. Those words "Immaculate Conception" had a singular effect on me. Again, as on the previous night, I felt the pull of innumerable threads holding me in contact with other worlds.

We made some purchases in the Via Tritone. On the way home we had to pass the church of Sant' Andrea delle Fratte.

"I often walk through this church on my way home," said Marya. "It is not particularly interesting, and very dirty, but I love to see the people praying there."

She walked in with her quick gay step, and I followed slowly, almost reluctantly. From an altar on the left side of the church a river of tremulous light from a multitude of candles flooded the floor. Many people were kneeling here, with rosaries suspended from their hands. As I stood outside the circle of light, a little detachment of students from the Polish College—I knew them by their green sashes—walked quickly past me, genuflected all together with the precision of soldiers saluting, then sank on their knees in prayer. The earnest expression on those young faces filled me with desire to go nearer and see what drew that intent gaze.

Over the altar *She* was enthroned, the Immaculate Being who had come to me the night before—the same, yet not the same, for she was younger and slighter, of mortal height and build.

Marya had turned back to see why I had not followed her.

"I think this is a very nice modern Madonna, don't you?" she whispered in my ear. "Quite a good picture."

A picture! I had not thought of Her as a picture at all, but I agreed with Marya with greater sweetness than I had ever used towards her. Then I thought quite simply: "I think She would like me to kneel down. She is looking down," and I fell on my knees.

I am quite incapable of describing the mysterious change that took place in me in a single instant. The truth did not filter into my darkened mind, but streamed into it, flooding every corner with blessed light.

"I did not think, I did not strive,
The deep peace burned my soul alive."

One supreme Fact I was conscious of—that there behind the gold veil over the tabernacle was my God, and the Love for which I had been hungering all my life. I was so ignorant that I did not even know that it was a veil, or a tabernacle. I had never read anything about the real presence of Christ in the Blessed Sacrament of the Altar. No one can ever have been less instructed than I was in His historical life. Yet at that moment I knew Him perfectly, and understood all that He had been to me, unrecognized, and unknown.

Nearly every human soul knows the wonder of the moment when it becomes conscious that it is loved; but if all those rapturous moments through the ages could be summed up in one master-thought, how far that thought would be from expressing my moment's rapture as I knelt in the church of Sant' Andrea delle Fratte! It was literally only a moment, yet there is a sense in which it was longer than years.

The Polish students had risen and filed out of the church. And I rose too. It seemed to me that I did not do so of my own power. I felt that the gold rays from the little Madonna's hands had reached me. They were as fine as spider's threads and strong as a coat of mail. They drew me close to her, drew me inside the altar rails, drew me up to the altar itself, drew me inside the tabernacle. And again that sound which is more an essence than a sound passed into my blood. I *felt*, rather than *heard* her say: "Never leave Him."

I walked quickly and firmly away, but turned back at the door of the church, in spite of Marya's justifiable impatience. I remembered suddenly that I had never thanked Her.

"What did you find so interesting in dirty old Sant' Andrea delle Fratte?" asked Marya that night at dinner.

"God!" I answered.

She laughed. "Is that what makes your eyes so blue?"

I smiled at her. I loved her. I loved every one in the world. I wanted to beg forgiveness of every one, and to forgive every one. All the sorrow which the suffering and misery of the world had caused me every day of my life till now had suddenly been turned to joy. With strongly pulsating heart I recognized my own happiness. The extraordinary thing was that I had made no effort. I had not been seeking what I had found. When I had ached most with unsatisfied need I had never cried out: "Oh that I had faith!" Yet it was to me, who had not wanted it, that it had been given! Every hour that this became clearer to me I loved the gift and the giver more. I felt a wondrous fellowship with all those who deserve nothing, a wondrous hope for all sinners and outcasts.

VII

When I was writing of my connexion with the Suffrage movement I thought: "Here many will leave me." I could hear the criticism that the discussion of a social problem is out of place in "a work of art," or a novel, or whatever critics choose to call this book which I myself call the history of a soul. De Maupassant in the preface to "Pierre et Jean," and Gautier in the preface to "Mademoiselle de Maupin," both assert that the author alone has the right to determine what a novel is, and that when the critic lays it to the author as a fault that his work is "not a novel," he is exceeding his duty, which is to say whether the author has succeeded or failed in what he chose to call a novel. He is to demand this of the author, and this only:

"Make me something beautiful in the form which suits you best."

The author on his side says: "My aim is not to tell you a story, nor to amuse you, not to move you, but to force you to *think*, to understand the deep and hidden meaning of events."

"Laissez-moi penser à mon aise!" [Let me think at my leisure.] I cry. "It is my personal vision of life that I seek to communicate to you in this book."

And as I could not be deterred from including in it my confession of faith in woman's suffrage by a fear of being called "inartistic," or by a fear of losing readers who expected to find in the story of a woman's soul the story of her love for a man, or by any other base fears, so now in a far more intense degree I am not to be hindered from describing my conversion to faith in God and His Church, and my subsequent progress along the way of divine love, by any reflection that these things should be barred from books which are not theological works or tracts.

It is strange indeed that it should be considered "inartistic" to write of God in poetry or prose—of God from Whom all beautiful art descends, to Whom in simpler days all artists consecrated their work, and by Whom, dwelling in the soul of man, all true works of art are created.

The finest poem written since I arrived at maturity deals with the conversion of a poacher, and it has been said that its subject puts it outside the realms of art. What is this art which must avoid all mention of God, and must not offend people's taste by dragging in religion? Is it the legitimate descendant of the art which was a part of religion, which expressed the joy of man in the joy of God?

I know that I myself used to confuse religion with religiosity. I looked upon it as an interest in life for which people had or had not a "taste." From the very first hour of my conversion I saw that religion was not a part of life, but the whole of life, its beginning and its end, its source and its object, its cause and its effect. To be "religious" in the true sense does not mean being uninterested in everything except forms of worship or theology or asceticism or morals. It means that the Will or the Power or the Beauty of God is subconsciously perceived in everything, and that nothing is irreligious except sin.

VIII

In a very few hours the keenness of my first emotion at the Recognition had been blunted. I was pleased, however, when Marya proposed that we should go to mass at St. Peter's. We arrived late, and the immense crowd prevented my getting more than a glimpse of the glittering priests at the altar. I was to experience nothing during that mass except shame at my utter ignorance of the mysteries of the Catholic Faith. Every peasant woman kneeling near me during the Consecration seemed to me a queen because she had been brought up in intimacy with what was strange to me. I was what is called "well educated," I knew a great deal about a number of things; yet what was I after all but a savage child, unlessoned, unschooled, unable through an ignorance which startled me to participate in what was going on in this immense cathedral? Why, in our pursuit of knowledge, had I and thousands of others left this out of our reckoning?

"What shall I do now, I asked myself?" I was almost irritated by Marya's artistic delight in the ceremonial. It seemed to me impertinent to view this great act of faith from the standpoint of a theatre-goer.

I must learn; but how, and from whom? I wished to be a Catholic. That was clear to me. But to whom could I make clear the depths of my ignorance? To whom could I explain that I believed everything and knew nothing?

As we went out of St. Peter's into the piazza, black with crowds of holiday-makers, I thought in particular of a placid, affable-looking Italian priest who had knelt near me the night before in Sant' Andrea delle Fratte. I could see the black crown of hair round his white tonsure, his well-cut olive face, his large tawny eyes, which love for my little Madonna had turned to shining topazes. It was to a simple soul like his that I longed to make known my story…. It occurred to me suddenly that I could not speak his language.

This reflection reduced me still further in my own eyes.

In this great city of Rome, with its churches to be counted not by units but by scores, with its hundreds of priests and friars and monks and nuns to be met at every street corner, I felt like the Ancient Mariner: "Water, water everywhere, and not a drop to drink."

IX

I was still asserting myself, I see now, still wondering "What must I do?" At the very moment I made a humble effort after patience, my steps were guided to a church containing the shrine of a young Polish Saint.

I knew his name well. I knew that the blood which had flowed in his veins flowed to-day in mine. My great-grandmother had borne that very name which was inscribed in gold on his tomb of lapis lazuli.

I knelt before the tomb, enthralled by this fact. I knelt there so long that the sacristan came to me and asked if I would like to see the room adjacent to the church where the saint had died. I gave an eager assent. It was strange how entirely I had lost the sense of being disheartened, discouraged, and utterly lonely.

There in this room, fitted up as a chapel, was the effigy, in black and yellow marbles, of this boy, who, living in this world only seventeen years, had left an imperishable name. He lay on his side, dressed in the black gown of his order, his boyish face illumined by a joy which had the freshness of immortality. One arm encircled his crucifix, the other held up a little picture of my new-found Mother. I kissed his bare feet with tears, and from the past, that I had tried to forget as a thing laden with evil encumbrances, emerged a sentence written from the depths of my father's heart: "I should never have come to this if I had remembered the words of the only saint in our family—'I was not born for temporal things but for those which are eternal, and it is for them I ought to live.'"

Ah, how often I had been consumed by vague ambitions in my life! I had longed to be a poet; I had longed to love greatly and to be loved greatly in return. I had longed to drink the cup of pleasure to the dregs; I had longed for wealth, chiefly to satisfy that desire for giving which was a madness in my nature; I had longed for glory, yes, for that foolish immaterial glory...a rustle, a stir of excitement, every one waiting to *see*, and from every lip a sound—*my name!* I had longed for beauty...I had wasted my years in desiring everything that was beyond my reach, but my longings had never leaped beyond the grave.

And now, as I embraced those marble feet, every earthly longing was extinguished in me. "I want to be a Saint!" I cried aloud.

I knew that this ambition, unlike all the other ambitions of my life, was not subject to change, and I guessed dimly that if realized it would be only by a reversal of all the methods of thought and action by which men set themselves to gain their hearts' desire. It would not be enough to bear patiently the sufferings that I had borne, not with patience but at best with a proud and bitter fortitude, almost from my cradle. I must love suffering and rejoice in contumely. It would not be enough to accept failure with dignity. I must regard it as glorious. Most ambitions are gained by self-assertion. This one could be sought only through complete self-abnegation.

With what pride I had lamented my ignorance of the Catholic faith a few hours earlier! Now, prostrate at the feet of my little Saint, I was glad of this one thing more for which I could be despised.

Something that the sacristan murmured about my kinsman being the patron saint of novices made me think of Laurence Walker. I remembered having heard that he was training for the priesthood in Rome. A young actor in London, friend to us both, had told me not long since that Laurence found his soutane very awkward on a wet day. He could not learn how to hold it up when walking through puddles!

Laurence himself had been an actor and a very promising one. He was extremely handsome, and of all the young men whom I had met when I was on the stage he had seemed to me the one who was most earnest over his work and the least conceited about his attainments. For some reason he was not popular in "the profession," he appeared to live isolated from his fellow-actors, perhaps because he disliked beer and gossip. But often he had come to see Sally and me, and would listen, his dark eyes aflame, while Sally told him how Mark Washington had played this part and that. The last time I had seen him was at a public dinner given in Louise Canning's honour about four years before. It was then he had told me that he was leaving the stage. As he had just made a very remarkable success in a leading part at London's leading theatre, and as I knew he loved his work, I heard his news with some surprise.

"Isn't he a fool?" said Tony Watts, Laurence's only intimate friend on the stage. "He's taken a mad idea into his head that he wants to be a priest! He's chucking a fine career for that!"

"Do *you* think I'm a fool?" Laurence had asked me, with that earnest look in his brown eyes which had always charmed me.

"Oh no!" I had answered effortlessly: "I think you are quite right."

I did not know in the least why I thought Laurence right. But a quixotic act, an act opposed to ordinary common-sense, an act that was immediately called "mad" by people who would never know what it is to enjoy a divine release from the usual ways of men, generally appealed to me as an act that should not be judged hastily.

I was surprised at the look of immense gratitude that Laurence gave me.

"I too am a Catholic. At least I ought to be one," I added, with a shamefaced attempt at accuracy.

"I wish I had known that before. It would have made a great difference to me."

Then Tony had burst into our conversation, and I had said no more to Laurence except to wish him luck when he said good-night. He had said, with that solemn, rather pompous manner which sat so oddly on his youth, that he "would never forget me and my encouragement. It came at a moment when I was in grave doubt." If Laurence had been sincere then, how much it would please him now to hear that I was in love with what he loved! "Yes," I thought, as I gave a farewell kiss to the marble feet of my little saint, "Laurence is the person to help me…and Laurence is in Rome somewhere. He was to be here four years."

I understood the sacristan to ask me if I were a Pole? I admitted to "un quarto." He clapped me on the back with gay Italian familiarity. Childish delight beamed in his dirty unshaven face. "È facile indovinarlo. Io l' ho capito subito. Appena l'ho vista baciare il santo piede mi son detto che era una Polacca. Non ci sono che i Polacchi che lo baciano a quel modo!" (It's easy to see it. I knew it at once. When I saw you kiss his blessed feet I said "a Pole"! Only Poles kiss him like that.)

I was beginning to boast of my relationship to the saint, but the words died on my lips…I would not be proud of anything in this world any more.

X

I had to address my letter to Laurence care of Tony Watts
in London, and it was nearly a week before I received an answer,
quite a week before I stood in the bare, dim parlour of the Col-
legio Beda, waiting for Laurence to come to me. The room was
full of sofas, of varying degrees of uncomfortableness and ugliness, of tables on which books were placed in such a way that you
felt they were not meant to be moved, and of busts and pictures
of Wiseman, Newman and Manning. If the room struck coldly
on my senses, making me feel timorously ill at ease, Laurence's
welcome warmed my heart. He had lost none of his well-graced
actor's manner. He seemed to wear his biretta and soutane as
he had often worn "costume" on the stage. His three years of
student life had not dried up his ardent youthfulness. Rather they
seemed to have intensified it. A brighter colour burned in his olive
cheeks. He looked healthier, saner, less of a *poseur*. He talked
to me with that fraternal sweetness which I had often longed
for from men. Anxious lest he should think that I was going to
presume on our old intimacy and be unmindful of our changed
positions, I shyly addressed him as "Father." He laughed, and
told me I was "too previous." He was still only a deacon. "I hope
to be ordained next year."

He unfolded his plans for me. He knew some nuns in Rome
who made it their business to instruct converts. Would I be guided
by him, and go to one of them for instruction? I answered that
I wanted him to decide for me—this very young man, younger
than I was, one who in other days had seemed to me less talented than I was. I venerated Laurence Walker because he had
renounced the world and its pleasures for the sake of that crucified Lord whose bleeding Image dominated the dim and dusty
guest-parlour. Yet how merry he was, he who had rather prided

himself on his melancholy when he had been an ordinary young man of the world!

It was the first result of my conversion that I who had been very arrogant, very proud of my individuality, very fond of asserting what I thought original opinions unconditionally, very contemptuous of people who opposed them, was now anxious to renounce my own will and yield it in complete submission. I did this at once with Laurence. I did it again the next day, when he introduced me to Mother Anna di Gesù at the Convent. I take no credit to myself for this docility. It was all part of a marvellous lesson that was being given to me as freely as the blessed air of heaven.

The order to which Mother Anna belonged was an Italian order which had been founded in comparatively recent times. It was, I discovered later, an aristocratic community, with a reputation among the historic religious orders of ancient foundation of being rather full of fads and fancies in its rules and tendencies. To a child, however, a nun is a nun, and it never occurred to me in my religious infancy that there might be as many different varieties of these holy women as of roses.

Mother Anna was English by birth, but Italian by education and environment. She was accustomed to teaching the rudiments of the Catholic faith to people of mature years, but apparently she was not accustomed to pupils who had no "difficulties." She constantly asked me if I found a difficulty in believing this or that, and I was conscious of disappointing her when I answered "No." If I could have expressed what was in my heart at this time (but I did not wish to express anything, for fear of loss) I should have told her that from the moment I had been convinced of the existence of God I had been prepared for all that radiated from Him in the Catholic faith.

The world seemed very far away, and my whole life since my baptism of no account, as I sat in the convent parlour listening to Mother Anna expounding the penny catechism. If I had no dogmatic difficulties, I had my artistic ones. I did not take kindly to the music in the convent chapel; some of the modern prayers which Mother Anna thought beautiful seemed to me very sickly; there were pictures in the parlour that I should have liked to burn. I made heroic efforts to silence these accusing voices of a critical faculty; it was part of my discipline. It was part of my discipline too to go very slowly. Once my instruction was interrupted for ten days because Marya had a fancy to go to Naples, and I felt it would be deplorable if I failed in ordinary kindness to her on the pretext that I had a higher and more extraordinary duty. I took great pleasure at this time in being obedient to Marya, in doing what she wished, not what I wished.

XI

The day came at last when Mother Anna pronounced me "ready," and I went to stay inside the convent for a two days' retreat before my First Communion. For a long time now, while scrupulously exact in all the little external practices of faith that Mother Anna had taught me, while believing expressly all that I knew of the Church's teaching, I had ceased to feel the rapture of the days immediately following my conversion. I was indeed very unhappy at the coldness and barrenness of my mind as the great day of my First Communion drew near. I remembered the sweetness, the gracious consoling happiness that had been mine in Sant' Andrea delle Fratte when the little Madonna had whispered "Never leave Him," and wondered why She seemed farther off now that I was less ignorant of Her mysterious and beautiful prerogatives.

I tried to fix my attention on a Meditation of St. Ignatius that Mother Anna had given me, but "troops of vanity," as St.

Augustine calls them, kept on rushing into my mind. I took a violent dislike to the mouldering brown paper on the walls of my room. I thought that Marya might be sitting in the sunlight on the Palatine Hill, or on the Appian wayside near the tomb of Cecilia Metellus watching the lizards.

That light cautious tap on the door was Mother Anna's. I sprang up to let her in. I had grown very fond of her. She always looked so clean and sweet in her blue-and-white habit. Her delicate, well-bred face outlined by the white linen wimple showed no signs of age. She had come this time to summon me to the parlour.

"I really ought not to let you see any one to-day except your confessor, but Mrs. Delap has promised me that she will 'mother' you when you go back to London…and as she leaves Rome to-morrow I want you to make her acquaintance."

I made no opposition. Mother Anna gave me St. Ignatius on "Hell" for my meditation. She gave me Mrs. Delap. I never thought of grumbling at either. So I followed her to the parlour cheerfully, even blithely. But directly she had left me alone with Mrs. Delap, I wondered how she could have thought of the word "mother" in connexion with any one so unmaternal. Mrs. Delap smiled at me with her thin-lipped mouth, but her hard eyes remained expressionless. Her first care was to find out if I were related to the Wiltshire Montolivets, who were not Catholics, she feared. I answered that I had no idea to whom I was related.

"When you come back to London, I will introduce you to some *really* nice people."

The impertinent implication in this remark tried me sorely.

"Mother Anna is so charming, isn't she? Such a lady!"

"I love her," I replied sincerely. "She has taught me the only things worth knowing."

"Oh yes, she's a wonderful woman. You are, I believe, her seventy-ninth convert."

I swallowed the retort that came to my lips—"I ought to be labelled, oughtn't I?" and substituted: "I'm not exactly a convert."

"Really?" There was obvious incredulity in her tone. Her look said: "Do you think I, a born Catholic, don't know a convert when I see one?" But I refrained from telling her my history.

She then presented me with a book of devotions, bound in purple *suède* and told me she would pray for me. "And be sure, my dear child, that you will always have a friend in me." I was in such a state of irritation by this time (to which the feeling of that *suede* binding contributed) that I could hardly thank her.

"I feel I know you quite well through Mother Anna. She has talked so much about you. She takes the greatest interest in you. Of course now you are taking this important step you will find yourself rather isolated at first. All Protestants feel this when they are first received. And in your case I understand that there will be many undesirable acquaintances to…to—"

"To *drop*?" I flung the word at her with some scorn, but she caught it placidly.

"Exactly…. Mother Anna tells me you know Louise Canning…. When one is young in the faith one has to be very careful not to give occasion for scandal."

For a minute I saw red. My Louise! My Sally! My guardian angels in a dark and corrupt world! A door slammed on them is slammed on me! Good-bye, you holy people! Good-bye converts and nuns! Good-bye St. Ignatius, and hell, and heaven…. Let me rot in shame with those dear ones who have never abandoned me, to whose snow-white influence I owe my rescue from degradation! These and other wild thoughts seethed in my brain. I avoided Mrs. Delap's farewell "maternal" kiss, and rushed out of the parlour. My intention was to leave the convent at once. In my blazing rage I never stopped to consider how foolish it was to hear in the voice of a vulgar narrow-minded woman the voice of the Catholic Church. I knew only that I was wounded past cure!

Then as I flew up the marble stairway towards my room, I heard some one call me. The call was gentle, pleading, yet very insistent. I stopped dead in my angry flight. I stopped outside the door which led into the chapel tribune. I stopped to wonder who in the convent would call me "John-Baptist." Mother Anna had once called me "John," but this was not her voice.

"John-Baptist!"

There was no touch of censure in that call, no reproach, only infinite love.

"Who here loves me like that?" I asked. And my heart melted like wax. The little tribune door was not locked, and I pushed it open gently. There, on a level with my eyes now streaming with tears, was the great White Host in the monstrance, the Beauty, the Love, the Light of the World. There was He Who could not do without me, unworthy me, Who would not let me go. There was He Who had once been reviled for loving-kindness to sinners, Who knew all that I knew and loved, but multiplied a thousandfold, in the hearts of my "undesirable" friends. There was He! I fell on my knees and begged Him to forgive me for my impatience. I did not leave the tribune until I could think of Mrs. Delap and all that she represented without any bitterness. This was my real preparation for my First Communion.

XII

When Napoleon was asked what was the greatest day in his life he answered "The day of my First Communion"—surely the most surprising and significant words that ever fell from the lips of a hero of great earthly days. Perhaps all the deeds for which men count Napoleon "great" have no significance in the celestial records of his life. Perhaps that answer is the one thing remembered of him in heaven.

There is no excitement about great days in the life of the soul, however. They pass quietly, and we do not know what they have accomplished in us for years. Sometimes we see with remorse what they might have accomplished had we been faithful, had we prayed *"Confirma hoc quod operatus es in nobis."* [Confirm that which you have accomplished in our midst.]

I had not been guiltless of making plans for my future as a Catholic. I remember asking Laurence during the period of my instruction if ambition would still be lawful, and he had answered in his best *ex cathedra* voice that, with the exception of what was bad and useless, there was nothing that the Holy Spirit could not claim and sanctify.

So with the old habit of self-reliance strong in me I saw myself going back to my usual occupations, and living as I had lived before, when I had kept clear of what I knew now was sin. I would not fail in courtesy to my new acquaintance, the Church. I must obey her laws, of course, and they did not seem to me very exigent. Mass every Sunday, communion at least once a year, occasional confession, occasional abstinence—without altering my mode of life very much I could fulfil these duties. There were times when I viewed my conversion in a very natural and practical light. My return to the Church of my fathers was not so much extraordinary as inevitable.

This cold-blooded, formal attitude never returned after my First Communion. I had seen visions and dreamed dreams of this Great Acquaintance as a Friend, but neither vision nor dream could do what He Himself did that day. We can all recall moments when a human acquaintance is transformed into a friend—when we know that never again can we return to the formal relations of yesterday. We may quarrel with our new-found friend, be alienated from him, offend him, know the pangs of longing for him, but after that revelation of a personal bond, our heart, whatever its emotion, is always open. Unaccustomed to self-analysis, a raw student in self-knowledge, I hardly perceived the extent to which my heart had become a victim of love from the moment I had known Him "in the breaking of bread," from the moment I had been united to Him body to body and soul to soul. But whatever I schemed or planned with my natural mind, however fatigued I was in my natural body, however reluctant in my natural senses, I rose daily at six o'clock, and sought the altar of the Lord. Sometimes when I entered the church I would say to myself, "I will only hear mass to-day…I have not prepared myself as Mother Anna told me. I must not communicate unworthily." It was then that I could almost hear the laughter of a love beyond my comprehension. "What! You will not come to Me when I ask you! If you are not in a loving mood you need My love in you more. If you feel your imperfection, the more eagerly you should seek My perfection. If you are weak, what can strengthen you more than the strength of My Flesh and Blood?" And abased by such generosity I would creep up to the altar rails, each day losing my own will more and more, each day becoming more and more sensible of how little I had to do beyond receiving the divine embrace with a loving and contrite heart.

II
THE NEW LIFE

I

"And I was displeased with the business I followed in the world, and it had become very burdensome to me; my former desires not now inflaming me, as they were accustomed, to bear that heavy Servitude in hopes of honour and riches. For now these things did not yield me any delight in comparison of Thy sweetness, and the Beauty of Thy House with which I was in love."

I discovered soon after my return to London that it was not enough for me to go to mass daily, and strive to live a life of self-denial in the world. I was still Hungerheart.

The new suffering and the new darkness that this discontent with compromise, this passionate desire to give *all* and follow Him, entailed, were very different from the old suffering and the old darkness. Formerly my moods had alternated between extravagant gaiety and savage melancholy. Now on my worst days the peace that comes from faith exulted steadily in my heart. I was no longer the victim of moods. I often failed ignominiously, but it is true to say that I never abandoned the effort to resign my own will, to cast down "imaginations and every high thing that exalteth itself against the knowledge of God, bringing into captivity every thought to the obedience of Christ."

Imagine an ignorant peasant, striving to get some learning by himself, and surrounded by people who think all such learning nonsense. Does he not think longingly of some school where his companions will be those who are seeking the same knowledge as himself? So I began to think longingly of a "school for the service of God," as St. Benedict calls the monastery.

II

The supernatural occupies a very small space in the lives of most people to-day. So it is not surprising that anything so supernatural as the ascetic ideal should be for the most part disliked and despised, discredited or ridiculed. I can understand people who do not believe in Christ taking one or all these attitudes. But if they do believe in Him, how can they ignore His words about hating father and mother and wife and child for his sake, about selling all and following Him, about making oneself an eunuch for the sake of gaining the kingdom of Heaven?

III

The *perfect* way cannot be followed in the world. This would be very galling to some people who are doing their best, and living very perfectly in imperfect ways, if they could understand it. But as a rule they do not understand. I have grown accustomed to hearing monks and nuns spoken of sometimes with jeer, sometimes with surprise that men and women with such archaic ideals should still exist in these days. Even educated people know very little of the history of monasticism. It would surprise them if I were to declare that that history has been the real enduring history of mankind, the only history that matters. They will tell me that there have been sluggards, gluttons, and profligates among monks and nuns: yes, they know that, but do they know or care about the great multitude of meek and humble monks and nuns who in prayer and solitude have kept God's truth fair and whole, while the world outside has broken into thousands of fragments? We in England pay an army and navy to fight for our material interests, to protect our national greatness. That idea appeals to us, but apparently we cannot understand the idea of a body of people in our midst who fight for our spiritual interests in prayer.

IV

If we want a tragic sign of how far man, born to serve and glorify God, has put the glorification of humanity above the true purpose of his existence, we may find it in the opinion, common in life and literature alike, that these chosen ones of God, these eyes of His mystical body, are chosen, "called," because of some incapacity. What is not good enough for man and man's world is good enough for God! The idea that the monk and the nun are called into the cloister because of their capacity for a love, of which human love is a mere shadow, is rarely expressed, because it is rarely understood.

V

I went about my work in the world as usual, and in one sense with more zest, because everything that I had to do seemed more worth while now that it was connected with an immortal service. But already my thoughts secluded me from the world. My sympathies were with renouncement, not with achievement—with humility, not with pride. I had always been inclined to reverence, almost to worship, those whom I thought the elect of the world, those who had raised themselves by force of their mental honesty and incorruptibility above the crowd who think and act as it pays them to think and act, and who become base because they are always selling themselves for a price. But now my individualists, with their *"moi suel, et c'est assex,"* [me alone, and that's enough] were dethroned, and I recognized no greatness except in those who have never sought their own glory—except in the saints of God.

The saint! What is the saint? How varying and complicated are the ideals of those whom the world calls its "great men"! One thinks this, another that; one believes what another repudiates.

But the saints, with all their wealth of personality and diversity of gifts, have never puzzled us by a diversity of aim. From St. Mary Magdalen and St. Stephen downwards through the ages to this day, they have all been at one in this—nothing is to be put before the love of Christ. And on the whole their methods have the same unity and clarity. The book that they study is the great book of the Crucified. They learn from this that there is no wisdom so high and deep as the folly of the Cross, no richness so immense as its poverty, no honour so glorious as its ignominy, no pleasure so inebriating as its agony. There have never been Saints who have not thought this, and lived it too, whether their days were spent in intense earthly activity or in equally intense contemplation.

VI

Abnormal, useless, starved, pale—these are the adjectives that the world keeps in stock for the lives of those who seek to subdue their earthly nature for the sake of liberating their spiritual nature. Yet if you have known such a life intimately, and been given grace to understand that all its austerities and mortifications are only a means to an end, the end being divine love, you will see in the world's opinion of it only that truth which is the fulfilment of a prophecy: "Et lux in tenebris lucet, et tenebræ eam non comprehenderunt." ["The light shines in the darkness, and the darkness did not comprehend it." John, 1:5] If the Light itself was not understood, the saints in whom the Light shines, and all those humble apprentices in the school of sanctity who seek through disciplining their obscuring flesh to transform themselves into little lanterns, cannot desire to be understood. They would welcome even more abusive adjectives than the four which I have collected.

When I was still very far from being purged of my earthly desires, and was experiencing the truth of St. Augustine's saying that is "one thing to rise, and another not to fall," it pleased "Rabboni," as I like best to call Him, imitating the address of the blind beggar Bartimæus to whom He gave sight, and of that great lover Magdalen on His resurrection morning, to give me as the friend of my bosom one who had spent her life since girlhood in a school for the service of God. In her blossoming time, she, a merry, laughter-loving child, with no natural tendencies to piety, blessed with a happy home in which she ruled the hearts of her family by the sweet right of being their youngest and best beloved, had had that mysterious call to the religious life which in many cases is heard at first with terror rather than with joy.

It is true, I believe, that many girls who think they would "like" to be nuns are often passing through a phase of emotionalism, and it is well for them that a system based on an intimate knowledge of human souls does not encourage them emotionally, but tests them severely and thoroughly, to find out if their desire "be of God," as St. Benedict says. But you, friend of my bosom, "thou more than a brother," belonged to those whose strength and election are more sure—those who resist the Divine Lover, yet know that they must be His as surely as they know that to-day's night will be followed by to-morrow's dawn. And you are the salt of religious communities. You, more than those precocious in prayer, more than the prodigies of devoutness who are the pride of some Catholic families, are likely to make the best nuns.

VII

How can I write *about* you? It comes more naturally to write *to* you. My *vita nuova* has been lived under your eye, yes, in your presence, although you are in the monastery and I am in the world. You have taken the place of my dead mother. You are "little mother, little heart of mine," to use one of the dear caressing names that children have for their mothers in Poland. But you are also my "elder" in the sense that I have yielded myself to you in complete submission, as the beginners in the religious life used to yield themselves to their "elders" in Sinai and Athos a thousand years ago. It was through voluntarily submitting my will to you that I first began to learn lessons in self-conquest and self-mastery. All my education during the last few years has been your work. In Rome, when my instruction in the elements of the Faith was ended, I learned much by intuition, but I was in danger of having too great a horror of knowledge, of being content to worship ignorantly. It was you who first showed me that we must *walk* in the light, and learn to know what we love. You kindled in me some of your own devotion to the Church's liturgy, that great monument of divine science which is the same yesterday, to-day and for ever. You initiated me into the sacred cycle of the Church's year, and taught me that prayer said in union with the Church is "the light of the understanding as it is the fire of divine love for the heart." Besides the natural firmament of heaven, I learned through you to see another firmament clad in the beauty of a thousand saints! I had always loved poetry; my ears had never become too gross to be insensible to its harmonies. Now you my "elder" introduced me to the sublime poetry of the liturgy—to the songs of David, to those canticles and hymns which exceed in splendour the lyrics of secular poets as cups of wine in use at a feast exceed in beauty empty cups displayed for precious admiration. I had always loved music; now you made me acquainted with the purest music that the human mind has ever conceived, which it could not have conceived except in union with the Divine mind. How often, when I have heard your voice among the cantors in the choir, singing one of those plain-song melodies which spring from the words of the liturgy as naturally as leaves from a tree, have I not thought that this was what the poet meant when he wrote of a thing "not built at all and therefore built for ever."

VIII

You are my little mother and my "elder." You are also my friend. The emotion of friendship has been the strongest emotion of my life. I know that the desire to satisfy it has throbbed in the pages of my life's story as the heart throbs in the veins. The "princely passion," as some one has called it, has been a danger to me, and its brightness in my soul has often been obscured by clouds rising from my lower nature; but on the whole every endeavour that I have made to express myself in friendship has brought me nearer to the Divine Friend, brought me nearer, as a rule, through much bitterness and heartrending disappointment. "O my God, my Mercy, with how much gall didst Thou besprinkle those sweets unto me!" And in this I see such love! Was He not keeping me intact, unconsumed, unspoiled, for a friendship which should have no life outside His own Heart? It is there that you and I have learned to love each other.

When I was a child I was greatly attracted by the story of Endymion. And often now, with a *Sponsa Christi* for my friend, I feel like Endymion who had the moon for his bride.

To love in Christ! That sounds very cold to the natural ear. Yet it means loving in the light of immortality—not like human lovers, in the shadow of death.

IX

I shall never forget our first meeting. I had never seen an "enclosed" nun before, and when I went into the parlour with the friend who had arranged my visit to your convent, the grate through which we were to see you hurt me. I thought that those bars must beget stiffness in intercourse. But no sooner had you come than I understood that of all barriers that had kept me outside the courts of love, and wounded my yearning heart, this was the least cruelly substantial. Such love and tenderness was in your beamy look that immediately you cast out all fear and all constraint. I had not read the Rule of St. Benedict in those days, but when I did read it later, his lovely injunction that his children in welcoming guests are "to let Christ Who is received in their persons, be also adored in them" struck me as a remembrance.

I had been told in advance of your learning, of the power you had of mastering in a short time difficult subjects with which it took most people a lifetime to become familiar, of your insight into human character; but all these gifts and endowments and acquisitions appeared to me as nothing in comparison with the charity that diffused itself in your simplest words and actions, and illumined your face with a gracious and consoling light. We hardly spoke to each other during this first interview. The little friend who had brought me was well known to you, and you and she had much to say to each other. I remember you spoke of a sister of hers who had died in the neighbourhood and had been buried there some years before. And you said, all your inward sweetness penetrating your voice: "Dear little J—! I always feel that we are looking after her grave." Simple words, yet they roused in me a blessed faith and gladness. You had not known the dead sister; she had been a heretic; yet you spoke of her with a tenderness that brought tears to my eyes. I threw out only the vaguest indications of what my life had been, of its adversity, its sufferings and its sins, but I knew from the one look that you gave me at parting that nothing was obscure to a comprehension almost divine. What a look it was! It reflected on the earthly plane the look that Rabboni gave St. Peter after the betrayal, and again it was like that other look which led Magdalen to Simon's house with her spikenard.

X

"She is Christ's," I thought that night, "and Christ lives in her." That impression has grown with our intimacy, beloved friend of my soul. We are taught to see Him in the sinner and the outcast, in the sick and in the poor; in all those little ones of the earth to whom if we minister, we minister to Him. But less is said about recognizing Him in a friend. This puzzles me. It would be as dreadful, perhaps more dreadful, to crush His love in a friend, as to refuse to listen to Him in a beggar, or to turn away with loathing from Him in some sufferer from a repugnant disease. I know that this is the secret of your love for me, and of your sweet acceptance of my love.

XI

There are things that can be lived but not chronicled, and our friendship is one of them. Who in the world could understand our moments of union? Who in the cloister either? But they are understood in heaven.

XII

People talk of nuns "immured" in the cloister, using the word immured in a tragic sense. I wish that these people, with their vulgar amusements ending in headache or heartache, or with their dreary resignation to dull and stupid labour, could see how joyous and gay you are, who have been "immured" for more than a quarter of a century. The spring of your ardent humanity has not dried up behind the convent walls; I know no one in the world as human as you are, no one who can enter so perfectly into human aspirations, or be moved to such depths by human griefs, no one more sensible to visible beauty. I know no one in the world with such a genius for loving. Very pleasant hast thou been unto me. Thy love for me is wonderful, passing the love of men.

XIII

Before I knew you, the thought that I might be destined for the religious life came to me often in the silence of the night. It walked by my side in those fresh summer mornings in Rome when I first acquired the habit of going daily to the altar of the Lord. It followed me to England, and knelt by my side in churches during chilly winter dawns. Since I knew you, and through you learned in some detail what the religious life demands, it has been a more persistent companion. I am heavily burdened with debt—a very clear obstacle; and I have long passed the age when those who wish to try their vocation in a religious house are heartily welcome—an obstacle that could be overcome. Yet I never lose hope, I never cease to pray that in the afternoon of life I may do what you did when the day was young. I pray for that very earnestly, but I pray even more earnestly for complete resignation, complete abandonment to His designs. Though He slay me, yet will I trust in Him; though He plunge me in darkness, I will cling to my faith in His infinite love.

Jesu have mercy on me, Mary pray for me, and bring me to sit one day in the great white Rose of Paradise.

September 1911
to
May 1913.